# The Sea Road

Margaret Elphinston is the author of three novels: *The Incomer* (1987), *A Sparrow's Flight* (1989) and *Islanders* (1994). She also writes short stories, including the collection *An Apple From a Tree* (1990) and poetry, including one collection, *Outside Eden* (1991). She has published two books on organic gardening. She lives in Glasgow, and teaches in the Department of English Studies at the University of Strathclyde.

# The Sea Road

a novel

## Margaret Elphinstone

## McArthur & Company

Toronto

First Published in Great Britain in 2000 by
Canongate Books Ltd, 14 High Street, Edinburgh EH1 1TE
First Canadian edition published in 2000 by McArthur & Company.

McArthur & Company
322 King Street West, Suite 402
Toronto, ON M5V 1J2

Copyright © Margaret Elphinstone, 2000

The moral right of the author has been asserted

Canadian Cataloguing in Publication Data

Elphinstone, Margaret
  The sea road

ISBN 1-55278-172-0

1. North Atlantic Region — Discovery and exploration — Norse — Fiction. 2. Vikings —
Fiction. I. Title.

PR6055.L63S42 2000            823´.914            C00-931473-3

Typeset by Hewer Text Ltd, Edinburgh
Printed and bound by Transcontinental Printing, Canada

The publisher would like to acknowledge the financial support of the Government of Canada
through the Book Publishing Industry Development Program (BPIDP) for our publishing
activities.

10 9 8 7 6 5 4 3 2 1

*For Agnar and Hlif*

AUTHOR'S NOTE

The characters and events in this novel are chiefly based on the accounts found in *Eirik's Saga, Graenlendinga Saga* and *Eyrbyggja Saga.*

## Principal Characters
(in order of appearance)


*Agnar*, son of Asleif; a monk from Iceland.

*Gudrid*, daughter of Thorbjorn, wife of 1) Thorstein Eiriksson 2) Thorfinn Karlsefni

*Thorbjorn Vifilsson*, chieftain of Laugarbrekka in Iceland, then of Stokkanes in Greenland. Father of Gudrid.

*Eirik Raudi* (Eirik the Red), from Norway, a settler in Iceland, then of Brattahlid in Greenland

*Orm*, husband of Halldis and foster-father of Gudrid. Farmer at Arnarstapi in Iceland

*Halldis*, wife of Orm and foster-mother of Gudrid, at Arnarstapi in Iceland

*Bjorn Asbrandsson*, farmer at Breidavik in Iceland. Lover of Thurid of Frodriver

*Thurid*, married to 1) Thorbjorn the Stout of Frodriver 2) Thorodd. Mother of Kjartan, lives at Frodriver in Iceland

*Thorodd*, second husband of Thurid

*Kjartan Thoroddsson*, son of Thurid. Latterly chieftain at Frodriver

*Thangbrand* the Missionary. Brings Chirstianity to Iceland

*Einar Thorgeirsson*, a merchant in Iceland

*Snorri Thorbrandsson*, enemy of Thorbjorn, settler at Dyrnes in Greenland. Friend of Karlsefni

*Herjolf*, son of Bard. Settler at Herjolfsnes in Greenland. Father of Bjarni

*Bjarni Herjolfsson*, settler at Herjolfsnes in Greenland

*Thorbjorg*, a witch at Herjolfsnes in Greenland

*Thjodhild*, wife of Eirik Raudi, mother of Leif, Thorvald and Thorstein. Lives at Brattahlid

*Leif*, son of Eirik and Thjodhild

*Thorvald*, son of Eirik and Thjodhild

*Thorstein*, son of Eirik and Thjodhild

*Freydis*, daughter of Eirik by a thrall. Marries Thorvard of Gardar in Greenland

*Tyrker*, a German thrall belonging to Leif

*Thorir*, a merchant from Norway, shipwrecked in Greenland

*Thorstein the Black*, farmer at Lysufjord in the Western Settlement in Greenland

*Grimhild*, wife of Thorstein the Black, at Lysufjord in the Western Settlement in Greenland

*Thorfinn*, named Karlsefni. A merchant from Iceland, husband of Gudrid. Latterly chieftain at Glaumbaer in Iceland

*Thorbrand*, son of Snorri Thorbrandsson

*Thorhall the Hunter*, Eirik's man, lent to Karlsefni as guide to Vinland

*Helgi*, tenant farmer at Sandnes (owned by Thorstein Eiriksson) in the Western Settlement in Greenland

*Sigrid*, wife of Helgi at Sandnes in the Western Settlement in Greenland

*Helga*, a smith's wife, she accompanies him on the expedition to Vinland

*Snorri*, son of Thorfinn Karlsefni and Gudrid. Latterly chieftain at Glaumbaer in Iceland

*Gunnar*, a shipbuilder on the expedition to Vinland

*Thorbjorn*, second son of Gudrid and Thorfinn Karlsefni

*Gudleif*, son of Gudlaug, a seafaring merchant from Iceland

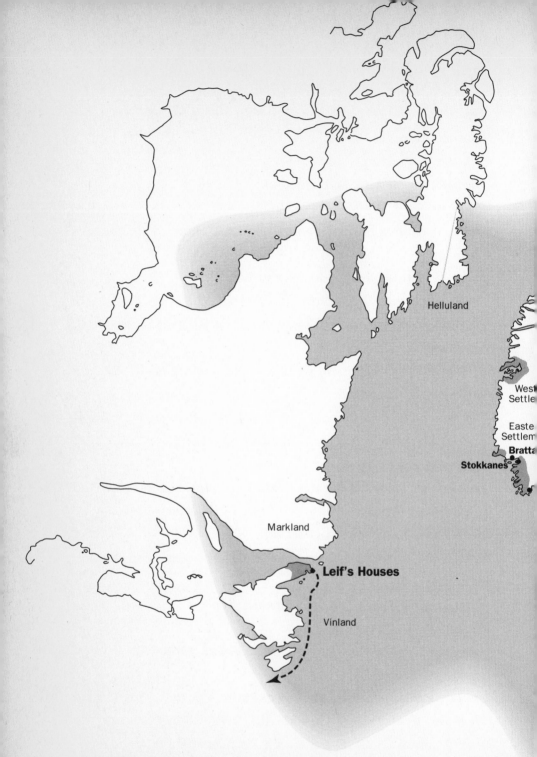

Helluland

West
Settle

Easte
Settlem

**Bratta**

**Stokkanes**

Markland

**Leif's Houses**

Vinland

*ATLANTIC*

*OCEAN*

and

Glaumbaer

Snaefelsnes
Thingvellur

Iceland

Skalholt

# PRAEFATIO

# March 1069, at Skalholt, Iceland

Agnar Asleifarsson writes this preface, so that in time to come the script may be interpreted with integrity and truth.

I wrote her story down in obedience to a command from Cardinal Hildebrand in Rome. When she arrived there first he received her, and later he sent for me. These were his words:

'A woman has arrived here on pilgrimage from your country. No, not from Reims, from Iceland. She brought a letter for me from our brother Isleif Gizursson, the bishop at Skalholt in Iceland. By the way, Isleif had heard that you had come to Rome, and he wishes to be remembered to you. His letter tells a very strange story. This woman, apparently, is one of those who have gone beyond the confines of the mortal world, in the body. She has dwelt for over a year in the lands outside the material world. She has talked with demons and with the ghosts of the dead. The kind of thing, you may say at first, that makes a useful fable for the vulgar. But Isleif thinks there is more in it than that. You know that our brother Adelbert is writing a treatise on the Four Last Things, and we need to collect as much evidence as possible to prepare a statement of doctrine. It's an area where heresy is rampant, and within the next year or two I intend to counteract these errors with a decree from the Lateran, authorised by the Holy Father himself. I'm taking you into my confidence here, Agnar. I know you won't repeat this.

'I'm acting on my faith in Isleif. I learned to trust him when he was in Toul. He could have become a cardinal if he hadn't chosen to return to Iceland. I've met the woman myself. She impressed me. Her manner is alert, and she has the confidence of a man, without any lack of modesty. That would be less acceptable if she were young, of course. We could not converse. She had enough vulgar Latin to greet me and to deliver Isleif's message. I tried her in German, and she said, with a strong accent, in that language, 'I do not speak German.'

'So, my plan is that you should hear her story, and write it down in Icelandic. When you have made a transcription of her words you can translate them into Latin, and improve her crude account, as no doubt it will be, with your own sound theology.'

That was probably the only compliment I ever had from the Cardinal, but I was not as appreciative as I should have been. The whole thing seemed an irritating interruption. It wasn't worth telling Hildebrand that everyone in Iceland tells stories about ghosts and devils, and journeys out of the world. On winter evenings we do very little else. I was a scholar; I was not a purveyor of vulgar tales. It may be useful to a parish priest to have a few fables up his sleeve to frighten ignorant peasants into some sense of their condition. That was not my job. On the contrary, I had been engaged for several years on precisely the opposite task. That was before I left Reims with Pope Leo after the Council in '49 and came to Rome. I had less time for translations after that, as I became more involved in church government. Those were the days of reform, and we were involved in nothing less than a mission to reinstate Rome as the centre of the world, this time upon the basis of a spiritual principality.

But even in this heady atmosphere, I was still working on my translation into Icelandic of the Dialogues of Pope Gregory. I should perhaps mention here that I finished it two years after Gudrid left Rome, and I made a copy myself (I wouldn't have trusted an Italian scribe with an Icelandic text), and then I sent the original to Isleif at Skalholt. I had hoped to finish it sooner, only no sooner had Gudrid left than the Normans were upon us, and there was no time for writing then. But texts have been my real work in life.

The transcription of Gudrid's story proved far more important than I expected. It was an interlude in the most active period of my youth. Now I have been back at Skalholt these fifteen years. Leo IX is dead, and Cardinal Hildebrand bides his time in Rome. Only death is likely to rob him now of the ultimate prize. He has worked towards it for long enough, and I think he will make a memorable Pope. And I think it is not an empty boast to say that I could have worn a Cardinal's hat by now if I had stayed there with him. I chose differently. When Leo died, I made up my mind to return to Iceland. I've never regretted that decision, although my colleagues in Rome tried to persuade me against it. In their eyes, I was committing an utter folly in choosing to go quite out of the world. My argument was that I wanted to help Isleif establish his monastery at Skalholt. That was true: the idea of a monastery in my native land had been in my mind ever since Isleif and I used to discuss it when we were students. Also, I was realising there would never be peace or time for scholarship in Rome. The new Pope Victor finally gave me permission to depart. Hildebrand was angry that His Holiness did not prevent me going, but he has long since been reconciled. I'm useful to him here, in this outpost of Christendom, and we correspond infrequently. It is part of his political genius to make the most of every contact. But I'm no longer so interested in politics; at Skalholt I have devoted my life to translating for my own people.

Possibly Gudrid's story was the beginning of my decision. When she came I had been in Rome two years. I thought of Reims as my home, rather than Iceland, for that's where I'd lived from the age of ten. I was trained at the school there, and my teachers were disciples of the great Gerbert. I think that was important, when I came to transcribe Gudrid's story. As she talked, her words began to take on another meaning for me, besides the one Hildebrand had indicated. I could not tell the Clunyites how I interpreted her narrative; that would have lost me my position in Rome. But at Reims we learned to value knowledge for its own sake, and from that training I learned to trust (I dare to say this here) that the theology would take care of itself. After all, did not God make the whole earth, and all that dwells within it? Hildebrand had instructed me to read Gudrid's tale in terms of Death, Judgement, Hell and Heaven, and so I did. But in my youth I had learned other things as well: particularly the use of the astrolabe, the abacus and the clock. Measurement is in itself a holy mystery, and not, in my opinion, a violation of the infinite.

Also, I was an Icelander, and even though I had not been in Iceland since I was a boy, I knew about sailing directions. I gave the best years of my life to making translations of sacred documents into Icelandic. Now that our monastery and library are well established, I have reverted to the task I once undertook with such reluctance. I find myself writing down the stories that are told here. This makes some people angry. Both bards and common folk say that it is a kind of death, to put into black words on vellum what should be alive, spoken and sung when people are gathered together. My brother monks too have expressed uncertainty, thinking that it may be blasphemous to use the gift of written scholarship for secular purposes. So I say little, but I continue, and what is more, I have a couple of apt pupils, young scholars here at Skalholt. You may think this is a far cry from making and unmaking Popes, but – (if this is heresy, I shall be dead by the time it is read and judged) – I think that what I'm doing now may be the more enduring.

At Reims we were taught to write the best Latin. Translation was an art. I was encouraged there to find a way to write down my own language. When Isleif was in Germany he came to visit me, and we talked for a long time about our work. He inspired me to continue. There was no reason, he said, why our own language should not be written down in Roman letters, if one worked out the principles on which to do it. Nor was there any reason why the great works of our Latin predecessors should not be inscribed in the words we had learned at our own hearths. It was I who had reservations. Meaning, I said, lies in the words themselves. Change the words and the sense is no longer the same. To change a text from one language into another is a kind of lie. I was afraid of distorting the truth, and in retrospect that is not surprising, because we were always dogged by the terror of heresy.

That's why, after I had made the Latin document that Hildebrand wanted, I hid the original transcript. When I am dead, which, God willing, will not be for a good few years yet, it can stay here at Skalholt. Others will decide what to do with it. I am not sure what value it has. It is a woman's tale, and women are good at storytelling. In Latin it became something else; Latin is not a language for women. I don't know that anyone else has done what I tried to do, which is to make into writing the words that a person spoke, at the very moment that she spoke them. Of course I couldn't render them exactly. I'm a fast writer, but no one can write at anything like the speed of speech. She spoke very slowly, to accommodate me, but when she was excited she went faster without noticing, and I had to do the best I could. I was afraid that if I kept interrupting her and asking her to slow down I would lose the story. After each session I had to make a fair copy. I could afford to do that, as the Cardinal supplied all the vellum and ink. It is a laborious way of working, and I am not surprised that no one else I know has attempted it. It would be harder here, as ink flows more sluggishly in a colder climate.

The other distortion that I must admit to is one of natural affection. That is how I describe it, and at this stage of my life I have no need to care that the statement may be controversial. I grew fond of her. I am not referring to godly love, nor even simple charity. It was not common friendship, because she was a woman and I am a man. It certainly wasn't an erotic love – after all, she was nearly forty years older than I was. And yet, I admit now, when all is past, that the worst temptation I encountered in all my adult years was lust. When I was a young man it was often agony to me and it was worst of all during my years in Rome. At the time I attributed it to the heat, which seemed an outward image of the diabolic flame within. Remember that these were the years when celibacy was the central issue of church reform. It was being discussed all round me, all the time. I could have married, of course, but I was ambitious and hoped to make a career for myself in Rome. If I'm to be completely honest – after all, I will be dead when you, whoever you are, read this – I may say that the torment of this particular temptation may have formed some part of my resolve to return to Iceland. I needed to get away from the heat.

I never expected that I would end by marrying. If Gudrid had not told me her story, I think perhaps I would not have done it. By doing so I turned my back on my ambitions for ever. I am now irrevocably a priest of Iceland, I, who stood most staunchly for Leo's monastic reforms. I'm a married man, and the hunger and the loneliness are gone. But in Rome I'm already forgotten.

Perhaps it all goes back to that year. She stayed at the English convent of St Peter, in the Saxon town just north of St Peter's church, across the river from the city of Rome. The nuns were mostly from England, and I think that suited her. It was a tiny foundation. They had no scriptorium, for the place was intended simply as a hospice for pilgrims from the north, but they gave us a cell for our work. It faced south across a small paved cloister, towards the hill, on the top of which one could just see the roof of St Peter's church. We worked with the door open, for decorum, and also because it was a pleasure to let the sun stream in and touch us. Sometimes we used to take the desk into the cloister and work there, with the nuns passing to and fro across the yard, on their way to work or prayer.

At first I used to walk over from the Lateran, crossing the river by ferry at dawn and sunset. Later I stayed with the monks at St Peter's, only a few minutes' walk from the Saxon town. It was a time out of my busy life, when all my involvement with policy and government, and even my precious translation of Pope Gregory's works, paled into the background. I became simply the vehicle for her story, and, as I did so, it became my story too. That's how affection grew up between us.

I visited her several times when I came back to Iceland some years later. She had founded her cell of a few nuns up at Glaumbaer. I used to take them the sacrament. She was always glad to see me, and we would have our evening of talk. Three weeks ago she sent for me when she was dying, and I administered the last rites. One of the last things she said was, 'Agnar, you are an honest man.' Her family had her buried with Karlsefni.

I am not sure that I am an honest man, but in telling her story, I have tried my best to be as honest as possible, because that is how she was with me.

# GUDRID'S STORY

# ONE

# English Convent of St Peter, Rome
# July 5th, 1051

I suggest we work here every morning. The afternoons are getting so hot now I just go to sleep. At home it would be winter, and I would never waste precious daylight resting. When I was young I used to long for a sunlit day, to wake from the nightmare and the dark. Winter and night, it was then, and a sharp fragile summer, brittle in my memory now like ancient leaves.

I see your bent back, tonsured head, black robe. When we were introduced you didn't meet my eyes, and when you speak you mutter so I can't hear what you say. But I know who your father is; I know your family. What do you think about, as the quill scratches its way across the page? Do my words make pictures in your mind? You're a young man and I'm an old woman. Will my words change the world you see?

Before you arrived I was sitting out there in the cloister in the shade, watching the bees over those big pots of herbs in the courtyard. We have thyme at home, of course. I asked what the others were: basil, marjoram, I forget the other, and the tree in the middle is called bay. The bees work all the time and so do the nuns. Only I have nothing to do here but find words for what is over.

My story begins far from Rome, far from this white sun that rises right above the rooftops in the middle of the day. It begins in a place that is all water and shadow, where colours melt and change, a place of space and cleanliness, a long way north of here and lost for ever in the past.

I was born into famine, and weaned on to hunger. My family didn't starve, but there was never quite enough, and the thralls and cattle that lived on our estate were gaunt and silent in the suffering that seemed to me, knowing nothing else, to be simply what this world was. Even now I long for sweet food. Here in Rome we have honey and spices. Everything is cooked in oil, and the meat tastes better for not being boiled. We have olives and green herbs with everything, and wine every day. I eat like a child, because as a child I could not. I was weaned on to sour milk and butter, fish and meat, but never enough, and always, as I remember it, the same muddy colour.

Although when I was born Iceland lay in the grip of hunger, you mustn't think we were poor. I come of good family, and my father inherited the estate at Laugarbrekka when he married my mother, and so he became the chieftain there. My mother's father was Einar of Laugarbrekka. On my father's side too, the story goes that we are descended from a princely house in Ireland. Mind you, I've learned not to be too impressed by claims like that. Everyone had Irish slaves when I was a girl, and it's remarkable how many of those Irish ancestors turn out to be royalty after all. Be that as it may, my grandfather Vifil was Irish, and servant to Aud the Deepminded, and sailed with her from the Hebrides when she first settled in Iceland. He came with her to Hvamm in Breidafjord, and she gave him his freedom and an estate at Vifilsdalur. Do you know it? It's not exactly the best land in the Westfjords. It's a high valley running south from Haukadalur, but there my grandfather had freedom and land of his own, and there he brought up his two sons.

Both my uncle and my father married daughters of Einar of Laugarbrekka, and so they came into a better inheritance, and my father, Thorbjorn, became chieftain in his own right. Unfortunately he had no son to succeed him. It's a pity; Laugarbrekka is a good farm, and it's out of my family now, although our name will be attached to it for ever. I've never been back. It lies to the south of Snaefel – if you look north from our house the ice cap is often lost in mist – but on clear days you can see the white cone of the volcano filling the horizon. So with Snaefel lying like a sleeping giant at our backs, we faced south. Our house was set on a knoll, with a rocky slope below it where I remember scrambling about when I was very small. We had a wide view of the sea on three sides. Sometimes we could see Reykjanes, where Ingolf made the first settlement in my grandfather's time. Close to our shore was a single rock skerry, and almost always the surf broke over it. Laugarbrekka is exposed on all sides to sea and wind, and the weather at Snaefelsnes is the wildest in Iceland. I remember falling asleep in winter to the sound of the wind hammering against our turf roof, the beams juddering under the force of its blows. To this day wild weather comforts me, so long as I'm safe and dry indoors, with those I love. I like to fall asleep to it. Then in spring the terns used to come back, and they'd scream through the light nights like demented ghosts. Although Laugarbrekka is exposed, the farm is good. Our meadows and hayfields stretched down from the steading to the sea, where we had black cliffs rich in birds and eggs. There's a beach, but it's too exposed to make a good harbour, and a flat skerry – I remember it bright with seaweed at low tide – blocks the way in to the sand.

There would have been sons, I suppose, if my mother had lived. Even though there was so little to eat, she always had milk for me, and she let that starve her. I understand that; I would have done the same for Snorri or my Thorbjorn. A woman will die for her children, but not for any other reason if she can help it. It is one of the things that make us different from men. I remember my mother as milk and warmth. I slept with her at night, until the morning when I woke and she was cold and still beside me and didn't move when I cried. Afterwards I would often wake when it was dark and start to cry. When the women couldn't comfort me they used to threaten in whispers to put me out alone in the dark and after that I would be frightened into quiet.

Those early days come back to me like dreams, patches with no threads to sew them together. Our hall at Hellisvellir in Laugarbrekka seemed very long to my eyes. The roof beams were lost in smoke way above my head. The women's room was up a step at the end of the hall. I remember the stone step with the marks of the sea engraved on it in a pale curve. In the women's room were two looms like giant spiders' webs, and the threads made shadows on the wall at night, while the fire still flickered. In the hall there were soft hangings where I could hide away from the fire where the men would sit in the evening. I can remember evenings outdoors when the sun was low in the sky and golden, and the cows used to make their way down from the pasture to be milked. I remember the itch and smell of the hayfield, and the withered flower heads on dry stalks. I can remember the sound of the wind and the dark of winter, and snow flakes falling like silver coins into the mud.

The first outside event that impinged on my world happened when I was four years old, and Eirik Raudi came back, and stayed in our house as my father's guest.

*Red autumn beard, red hair. He tells tales of a land that is empty as the pale skies of autumn. There is space between the storms for a dream. He is a fierce, violent man, but he tells his dreams.*

*He sits on the table in the hall. The meal is over; women and dishes are whisked away. Children and dogs creep in to the fire and are ignored. Men's talk drifts in the smoke around them. The little girl sees pictures in her mind as the red man speaks. He describes a land that is green, but now in Iceland it is autumn, and she cannot imagine green, only red. Red grass, red willow scrub, red bearberries and crowberries. Red hillsides the colour of his beard and hair. Only the sea is green. West over the sea there is a world that is empty and frightening. The man himself frightens her. He is full of anger. She can feel it beneath the honeyed words. The land beyond the sea is desirable, but the man is fierce and hot and red. She creeps closer, grasping at his words. She has heard many stories in her father's hall, but never one like this. In the blue sky he describes she sees a mirror, land and sea, and a figure in the untouched landscape that seems to be herself.*

At first I had Eirik Raudi mixed up in my mind with the volcano. It had always been part of my life, you see – ice and flame, snow and the smell of sulphur – another world from this earthen Italy. I grew up with Snaefel at my back, which your theologians say is the gate of Niflheim. The gates of Hel lead from heaven, the way Lucifer fell, and Laugarbrekka was a kind of precarious heaven, before I was thrown out. So was the land I heard Eirik describing to my father.

'A green land,' he said. 'Empty pastures with grass rich as emeralds, and thick with flowers ready for the sweetest hay, but no man has ever reaped there yet. More head of cattle could graze in one of those meadows than in any dale in Iceland. The winter hunt would bring you treasure kings would buy – white bearskins, fox furs, narwhal and walrus ivory. One cargo of goods from my Green Land would be worth more, weight for weight, than a shipload of spice and silks from beyond Mikligard. I'm talking about wealth you haven't even dreamed of.'

'And has no one else found this Green Land?' asked my father warily. 'They say that devil men and shapeshifters live among the ice floes beyond Gunnbjorn's skerries, and that those lands are the borders of Jotunheim.'

'They say!' scoffed Eirik. 'You must get your news where you get your breeches, off the looms in the women's room. Haven't I just spent three years exploring the Green Land from Gunnbjorn's skerries to the channel that flows north to the Outer Sea? And did I find a trace of a living man? None! Not one!'

'And of the dead?' muttered my father.

'If there are dead they're not our dead, and their ghosts won't haunt us. There are no Norse demons in the Green Land, I swear.'

'Meaning there are others?'

Eirik shrugged. 'Nothing that a man should fear. The land is empty now. We made sure of that. Cowards may turn their backs on riches if they like. I only deal with men.'

Most men were afraid of Eirik. I felt it even then, though I only understood the whole story later. Eirik came to Iceland when my father Thorbjorn was still a boy. They outlawed Eirik from Norway because of some killings. His first farm in Iceland was way up north in the Hornstrands, but when my father met him he was living near Vatnshorn in Haukadalur. That's only ten miles over the hills from Vifilsdalur where my father grew up. Eirik was just the kind of man that young men admire – rash, daring and always ready to fight. He drew Thorbjorn like a magnet, and that never changed, even after all that happened. My father never blamed anything on Eirik. Well, it wasn't long before Eirik was in trouble again, and Thorbjorn supported him every step of the way. When Eirik was banished from Haukadalur he set up his headquarters on one of the islands in Breidafjord, and terrorised his enemies from there.

Thorbjorn was married to my mother by that time, and had moved to Laugarbrekka. You'd think he'd be happy to be out of the feuds, on a good estate the other side of Snaefel, with land and a young wife to keep him at home. Not a bit of it. He seemed to settle for a while, but as soon as Eirik summoned him again he was off, and me less than a year old. I suppose a daughter wasn't of much interest to him. So he went to Oxney, and became embroiled in a quarrel of Eirik's concerning the high seat pillars he had lent – so he said – to Thorgest of Breidabolstead.

If I were a man I'd avoid feud like the fever. Once you're in you never get out again – you're a marked man for life, and life probably won't last that long. But Thorbjorn was lucky that time. It didn't come to more killings. Eirik was banished at a meeting of the Thorsnes Thing, and he left Iceland for three years.

I think Thorbjorn would have gone with him then if he could. My father was a sensible man in some ways, and yet he might easily have traded a fine inheritance and a promising family for outlawry and a voyage beyond the human world with Eirik. He sailed our boat from Laugarbrekka alongside Eirik's trading ship until they were out beyond all the islands and only Snaefel could still be seen behind them. Then Thorbjorn turned unwillingly for home, and nothing more was heard of Eirik for three years. As I've told you, he turned up at Laugarbrekka that winter when I was four, and in a way that marks the beginning of my own history. It's the first event I remember, anyway, the first marker of time. Before that I had no idea that anything could ever change.

# TWO

# July 6th

Often the volcano is visible from a hundred miles away, and sailors use it as a bearing all along the west coasts. When Snaefel itself is out of sight its hat of cloud can still signal where it lies. Underneath its cloak of ice, the mountain moves and melts, and the rocks stir, crushed between fire and snow. Under that smooth cone of white lie the doors of Niflheim, where hel rules.

Above, snow flashes in the newborn sun of spring. The slopes are pied white and mucky brown. The air is sharp and salt, pierced by the whistles of early oyster catchers.

A herd of ponies, dun and grey, pick their way along the path through the lava field between Laugarbrekka and Arnarstapi. Three of them have riders: men in woollen cloaks with hoods thrown back, swords at their belts. Two eagles soar over Snaefel; ponies and men are mouse-like specks below. The eagles rise upward on a spiral of wind, and the long peninsula takes shape below them.

Down in the lava field, the volcano is out of sight, as the path twists between lumps of lava that have dried into the twisted black shapes of giants and trolls. Hooves clink on rock, bridles chink. There is a fourth rider, much smaller than the men. Her cheeks are bright with cold and heat, her hair is a tangle in the wind. She rides like a boy, her skirt caught up over the saddle. She holds the reins in red-cold hands, which she twists in the tawny mane to warm them. She rides the pale mare, whose foal nudges alongside, the one with the lucky star. The little girl wears a brown woollen cloak, just like the men, and a dress and tunic of undyed wool, embroidered with coloured braid at wrist and throat. Her tunic is fastened by two brooches, miniature versions of a grown woman's.

*The herd of ponies come out of the lava into frosty pastures. Snaefel has disappeared behind the hill called Stapafel which looms over Arnarstapi. On the west side of Stapafel sits a great troll woman turned to stone, staring into the sea where the sun sets. One by one the horses cross a frozen stream. When the mare's turn comes the little girl does not flinch. The mare scrambles between frozen banks. Hooves slip on ice. The mare swishes her tail and scrambles back to level pasture, the foal following. The herd moves on.*

I don't think it occurred to my father that I might need a woman to take the place of my mother. His choice of foster parents was governed by other factors. Me being a girl, he must have reckoned I'd need all the loyalty from my own people I could get, if I were to inherit Laugarbrekka. He chose Orm because Orm was a man he knew he could rely on to support me if ever I were left alone. Many women in Iceland have cause to be grateful to a loyal foster father, when they can't count on a man of their own.

I wasn't sad to leave my father's house. I wasn't leaving behind anyone I loved. I remember the first ride to Arnarstapi. It seems strange to me now that the actual journey was only a couple of miles. Out of one life and into another. I was five and a half.

It was a kind fate that made Halldis part of the bargain. She was Orm's wife, and she was the mother I had lost. A kind fate, but in some ways a confusing one. I've heard it said often enough that Halldis was a witch. Of course, Arnarstapi wasn't a Christian household when I first went there. We were all baptised later, when I was about fourteen. Oddly enough, that was Halldis' doing, but I'll tell you about it in its place.

Arnarstapi lay on the eastern boundary of my father's estate. The farm faces east across Breidavik, and on clear days you can see the whole range, white in winter, snow-patched in summer, that stretches down Snaefelsnes, and far away, the ice cap called Langjokull, which years later I was to know when Karlsefni and I used to take the road from Glaumbaer to the Thing – but that comes later. Just below our farm was the bay called Breidavik, and it was from our mooring off the beach at Arnarstapi that we were one day to set sail for the Green

Land. But when I was a little girl I knew nothing of Karlsefni or the voyages I would make.

I grew up in the lee of Stapafel, and the spirits of Snaefel behind it always lurked in the background of my childhood. Sometimes the mountain raged behind us and storms drove across its face; often it was hidden in cloud. I remember clear, short days in winter, and moonlit nights when Stapafel lay like an unearthly black shadow over our lives, and dark evenings when the northern lights flickered over its head. The gods walked up there, and on tempestuous nights we could hear Thor battle with the demons who live in the heart of the mountain. Snaefel is full of lesser spirits too: goblins, elves, trolls, all kinds of unknown things. I've seen them often, but always from the corner of my eye. If you look straight at any of those folk they change shape at once into twisted lava columns, so you're never quite sure of what you've seen. When I was little I was afraid of the mountain, but from early on I dared myself to leave the pastures and go up out of sound of the cattle bells, right into the lava desert that bounded our land. You can't see out once you're in the lava; you're surrounded by odd shapes and blind corners. The lava is cold cinders now, but once it was red and molten. I've seen Hekla throw out red flames and ashes from as far away as Glaum and I know the gods only lend us our land while they choose. Arnarstapi was a gift snatched from Snaefel, and for me it was ten years of childhood snatched from fate. We are never safe.

If I imagine my soul, as I do when I pray, it's shaped like Stapafel. No change of place or religion can alter that. I lived beneath Stapafel from the hour I was born until I was sixteen. I've never seen it since, but that doesn't matter. My soul is in the likeness of a jagged peak with a rock like a man standing on its summit, and snags of rock shaped like trolls along its spine. Screes defend it, although it's not quite inaccessible if you know the way up.

The daily business of our lives lay in Orm's pastures and hayfields. I was taught to herd cattle when my head was no higher than their bellies, and I learned to make butter, skyr, cheese and fermented buttermilk. We kept pigs too, and poultry. Just in front of our house, before you got to the shore, there were a couple of ponds at the top of the cliff, much better than the little tarn at Laugarbrekka. Our ducks stayed all year, and we'd be woken at dawn in winter by them quacking at the door for scraps. They'd be joined on the pond by wild duck and geese, and in spring teal and mallard used to nest in the rushes. We collected the eggs from wild and farm birds alike, and if you do that the wild duck will usually lay twice, just like the seabirds. It was my job to hunt in the rushes for the eggs, wading through green water to my thighs.

We caught mostly guillemots from the cliffs, but also kittiwakes, gulls and puffins. In winter we had one cave that gave off a queer blue light. I never noticed the noise that the sea and the birds make until I got to Eiriksfjord. Everywhere I'd lived before had been within sound of the open sea and the cliffs, and at first the fjord seemed uncannily quiet. Even here, when the gulls fly in up the Tiber and circle over the Saxon town, their cries remind me of home. Sometimes in Rome I catch a whiff of salt in the air, and find myself listening, but of course no waves break against the shores of the Vatican hill.

When I was little I was frightened of the terns, who used to attack anyone who walked through their nesting ground. That may be why the path to Laugarbrekka was not a way I liked to go. My father's house was barely two miles from where I lived, but somehow to my childhood self it might have been twenty. I saw my father most often when he came over to our beach, which was where he kept his boat in winter. Our beach, unlike the one at Laugarbrekka, was sheltered from the west. It was made of grey boulders, with grey and yellow sandy stretches where the boats were hauled up. When the tide was out I could scramble over seaweed covered rocks and gritty sand, the wading birds scurrying away like mice as I came near. I liked going down to the beach in the evening when the men came in from fishing, and watch the baskets being carried ashore, full of cod or mackerel or saithe, depending on the time of year. Occasionally, on a calm evening, Orm took me out to fish with a line, or to set guillemot traps, even though I was a girl. On really calm days we'd row into the beaches under the bird cliffs and come back with a load of driftwood. Once we towed a big treetrunk home behind us. At that time the beaches were still piled with wood, enough for the settlers to build houses and boats as they needed them. But it's all gone now; you're lucky these days to get a bit of kindling. If Orm had had a son, I suppose I'd hardly have been in a boat until we made our voyage. As it was, I could row and steer before I was seven years old, and I knew the coast around Arnarstapi almost as well as any of the boys in the place.

Orm used to take me about the country with him too. I always loved to ride anywhere, and I liked visiting the farms around Breidavik. There were games every year just before Midwinter on our neighbour Bjorn's land under Oxl mountain. There's a volcano on the plain close by – on still winter days we could smell the sulphur at Arnarstapi and see the smoke curling up. It erupted when my grandfather was living at Vifilsdalur. I remember riding along the frozen beach to Bjorn's farm by sledge one year, with the mountains vanishing into the distance as white as salt, and the crisp air smelling of sulphur. People came to the games from all over Snaefelsnes, and stayed for a couple of weeks. The men had ball games and races and, of course, horse fighting, which was still a sacred ritual to us then. The bets were often high, and there'd be fights. One year they caught a slave who'd been bribed to kill Bjorn while the feast was on, and they took him up to the pass over to Eyr and killed him there. We'd had a band of men come over earlier that year to get Bjorn, but they didn't catch him, then or ever. That's how it always was: even in years when things passed off peacefully, the tension of the feuds was always smouldering underneath. As I grew older my main interest at the games was to watch the young men who came to compete. I knew my father would choose my husband from the families on our side in the feuds – Bjorn's family or the Kjallekings preferably. So I silently observed them all while they were around.

Most of our gatherings happened in winter. There was less work to do then, and our summer weather was worse than in the Green Land, I think, although the winters were never as hard. Halldis, who came from Rif on the north of Snaefel, said when she came to Arnarstapi she found peace, and rain. It's true we were fairly out of the feuding, living as remotely as we did, and it's true too that from Rif or Frodriver you can often see the glacier winking in the sun, and behind it a cone of cloud like its shadow, that means on our side it's raining.

As a child I adored the sun. Halldis told me the story of how it was the fate of Sun and Moon to drive their chariots through the sky with the wolves chasing them. My Sun didn't mind wolves. He was handsome and brave and godlike, and while he showed his face our lives at Arnarstapi were transformed. I remember a day – I must have been seven, eight years old – when the sun shone fiercely on the pastures, and there wasn't a breath of wind. I lay on my back, arms and legs spread like a starfish, and felt the heat of the sun go all over me, touching my skin and my closed eyes and my hair. It seemed to reach right through to my bones. I squinted up into blue sky, and felt myself falling and falling, drowning in the splendid brightness and the heat. I was innocent, and yet I knew then what passion was. It's only come to me rarely. Marriage has meant good company, but only passion like that at the very beginning. I love the sun still, even though in this country his favours are cheap, and the magic just a commonplace.

After my first hungry years there was enough to eat at Arnarstapi. We even had grain some winters, which Orm used to fetch from a kinsman of his who had a farm on Reykjanes. I remember grinding the grains in the quern, and then Halldis showed me how to make dough out of the flour, and how to roll out the loaves and bake them on soapstone slabs over the fire. It took a long time, and I can still think of nothing more mouthwatering than the smell of cooking bread. The loaves would bake in black and white blotches, like the rock and snow patches on the glacier. They were flat – we never had this yeast they use in Italy – and we'd cut the round loaves into quarters and smear them with butter. I remember burning my fingers eating them, while butter dripped down my chin and over my fingers, and I used to lick it up afterwards like a cat washing itself on a Roman doorstep. By spring the grain would be long gone, and we'd be eating our butter with fish again as usual. But the loaves were my favourite, and I've never forgotten them.

Late summer was the best time for food. I liked haymaking, and milking in the ring on fine evenings, and the days when we lit a fire outside for dyeing wool or boiling meat. Perhaps because I'd known hunger first of all it satisfied me hugely to see the barrels being filled

22

for winter – layers of meat and fish laid down and preserved in sour whey; barrels of butter and skyr; dried fish and hunks of dried beef and pork and seal meat. Two – or was it just one? – lucky winters we had a whale, and then there was meat hanging to dry everywhere. I liked to see the hay brought in and piled in the barn, and know we could feed enough cattle for the eight months they'd need it, and maybe give extra to a milking cow so we'd even have fresh milk till spring. I suppose those early years have left me with an immense interest in food. I'm a good cook, though I say so myself, and I love to see guests at my table. I love to press food on them and stand over them while they eat as much as they possibly can. My sons used to laugh at me – just as well, perhaps, because luckily they never grew fat. Snorri was always thin, and although Thorbjorn was a chubby baby he soon grew as lean and tough as his brother.

I liked cooking the best of the indoor work. In winter we had to do mostly weaving, and that was all right, but I hated sewing. Halldis wasn't strict; her way wasn't to punish, but to find ways of helping me to like what I must learn. When I was nine she gave me an engraved bone needlecase to hang round my neck, with six needles of different sizes. I liked the case because it was pretty, but I still didn't like sewing. It took me years to discover why I found it harder than other girls. I used to think I was stupid because I could never learn to thread my needle by lamplight, though sometimes I could manage if I went outside into the daylight. Oddly enough it was Freydis who first said, 'But can't you *see*?' during that first winter at Brattahlid, when I was still trying to impress them all. 'Look,' she went on, and shoved a white cloth on to my lap. 'Try that. Can you see the thread now?' I could, too. Isn't it strange that Freydis should realise at once that I couldn't see, whereas Halldis, who loved me, never understood that what I saw with my eyes was different to what she saw with hers? But to this day I've never learned to like sewing. I used to reward my thralls for embroidering my tunics and Karlsefni's shirts, because I gave up trying to do fine work after I married him, and I've never done any since. That's shocking, isn't it, for a wellborn woman like me to be so poor in accomplishments?

Perhaps it was because of my sight that I always preferred to be

23

outdoors. I've always loved the light, and I dread the dark of winter. I remember Arnarstapi in the light: sun on snow; the mountains of Snaefelsnes white against a slate-blue sea; moonlit snow on a winter afternoon, or green and golden summer light, with the land smelling of flowers when the hay is ripening; or the damp grey light that comes with mizzling rain. I remember the paths worn through the grass between buildings. I liked to visit the thralls in their huts, the shepherd and the cowherd families. As a child I was welcome everywhere without ceremony, and I'd always accept food at any house I visited, a bit of dried fish, usually, or a bowl of skyr that I could scrape clean with a shell.

You mustn't think that we were lonely, even though we were distant from the main settlements along the north shore of Snaefelsnes. The next farm along Breidavik was managed by tenants when I was small, but then Bjorn of Breidavik came home to live at Kamb again. I told you about the winter games, but between times too he often used to visit my father, and he'd call on Orm on his way to Laugarbrekka. Sometimes his brother Arnbjorn came too – he had the farm at Hraunhavn further along Breidavik. I liked Bjorn. He was fond of children, I think, and because of Thurid and Kjartan he didn't marry – I'll tell you about that presently – and I enjoyed the attention that he gave me. I often think now of the strange fate he met, and every day I pray for his soul. He must have died long ago, among strangers in the lands outside the world. We might so easily have shared his fate. He left Iceland about the same time as we did, and, although my father never admitted it, I think his own decision was partly influenced by the fact that Bjorn of Breidavik had been driven out of our community.

Once Bjorn and Arnbjorn were back we heard much more about the feuds on the north shore – or perhaps it was just that as I got older I became more aware of these things. You weren't born then, but you must have heard stories. The way I see it now, we were still trying to find a way to live in our new country. We had no king, and so we had to carve out justice for ourselves in a land without laws or precedents. We couldn't just go on as our ancestors did in Norway; everything was different. The phrase that comes back to me, from all the talk I heard at the hearth when I was little, repeated again and again, is, 'Of course, it's his responsibility'. It was a man's responsibility to get justice for his kin when they were alive, and to avenge their deaths when they were killed. That's how I learned about the grown-up world: it was governed by fate, and you had to do your duty, although you knew you had to die for it. My father came from Vifilsdalur, and both he and his father were friends of Styr Thorgrimson of Hraun, and like him they supported Eirik Raudi. That put us against Snorri the Priest and the people from Thorsnes to start off with, and then my father's alliance with his neighbour Bjorn, when he came home from Norway, increased the tension. Yet we all met as neighbours. I can remember Snorri the Priest talking to my father at the fair at Frodriver as if they were the best of friends. But the undercurrent was always there. I think now that Halldis was right when she said only the new God could save us from the fates that trapped us.

When I came home with Karlsefni Iceland had changed, although I was only gone a few years. But those were the years when our land became Christian, and also the time when the Quarter Courts began to work properly. I'm not saying the feuds were over, but the strength was beginning to go out of them. A good thing, naturally, and yet – they don't breed men now of the kind I knew when I was young. Looking back, they seem much larger than this life that we live now. In the stories, of course, they grow more formidable still. I've had a hand in that myself. I'm known in Glaum for my storytelling, and I've made sure my children and grandchildren are well educated in the story of our past. Stories have a life of their own. They grow, as children grow, and perhaps we forget the small thing they once were. But we nurture them just because we respected what was there in the beginning. I'm glad of the world I come from now, although I daresay to you it seems a savage, pagan time.

I could tell you so much about the families living at Snaefelsnes when I was a girl. Those were dangerous years, and the men's talk I heard then was all of fighting and killing. Hardly anyone, after Eirik left, talked of new worlds and wealth, but only of secret plans for revenge. Only the women's talk was the same as always, everywhere –

the farm and the household, summer and winter, a pattern of life that is woven year by year and never changes.

I lived ten years at Arnarstapi. It was a quiet place to grow up, even though those were wild times. Travellers would bring news of feuds and killings, but the real things to me were the farm, and what Halldis taught me. I learned from her everything a good farmer's wife should know. She taught me to treat the land so that it would yield well year after year. I think I was naturally practical, but it was Halldis who made me skilled. Sometimes I've thought of her, when I've used some trick she showed me: when we set up our camp at Hop, for example, or when we were making the wine out of the strange berries. But of course that wasn't all I learned from her. I say men called her witch. All that means, I think, is that there are some who know how to stretch the boundaries of this world a little farther than most people think is possible. I knew even then that witchcraft can be turned to good or evil, like any other power. I was only six when Halldis warned me that I must use what powers I had for good. An evil witch at Holt on the other side of the mountains had been stoned to death, and Halldis used her example to impress her message on me. She succeeded; I was terrified afterwards that I might do wrong. Halldis herself taught me only good: how to see and use the things that lie at the edges of the world we know.

When I tell you about my childhood, I find I don't remember events, just how things were. It wasn't a story then, it simply was. When I think of specific happenings, they're usually things Halldis taught me. Witchcraft, would you say now? I don't know, but for me, they were the important moments. They marked change, whereas in everything else that we did there was no change.

*Twin flames, images of one another, join where oil meets air. A soapstone lamp, and a curl of reddish hair, soft and fine.*

*Gentians, their trumpets drooping, and hearts-ease, smelling of hay-fields. Halldis speaks to the little girl at her side. 'Take one of each flower, with your left hand.'*

*The child reaches out and takes two flowers. 'Now the hair.'*

*She puts the lock of hair between the stems. Halldis gives her a piece of linen cloth. 'Wrap them together.'*

*The child places the white bundle in front of the lamp. 'Say the words over it.'*

*The child obeys, carefully pronouncing the difficult words.*

*'Very well. Now we steep the rest in wine, and we'll tell Thurid to dose the child at night, just before bedtime. Convulsions need a remedy to match their strength.'*

*The little girl nods.*

*'Take the spell, and put it in the safe place.'*

*The child takes the linen cloth, and carries it carefully to a recess in the wall behind the loom. She places it at the back, among the other things.*

Halldis, as well as Orm, took me about with her. She made me feel like a real person when she introduced me to her friends. In my father's house I had always seemed to be just a shadow in the background – a shadow of the wrong sex. Halldis made me feel glad to be myself.

After the hay harvest one year she took me to a farm at Frodriver. It was a day's journey over the hills, and the first time I had been behind Stapafel. We climbed up past the caves where the giants live, right to the glacier itself. Close to, the glacier isn't the smooth white cone you see from out at sea. It's streaked with spines of lava and the snow is dusty with ash. There was cloud over the mountain, where the ice disappeared into a clammy mist that caught us in its breath as we passed. Our ponies trudged through patches of snow, and picked their way among boulders through streams of meltwater. The glacier took a long time to pass. Then we climbed down by a river with many waterfalls, and across the sea to the north I could see land. 'That's Hvamm across Breidafjord,' Halldis told me. 'That's where your grandfather landed with Aud the Deepminded, when Iceland was settled.' I stared at the blue land across the sea: the past, about which I knew all the stories, and yet could never reach.

We looked down on Frodriver as dusk fell, where it lay in a corrie facing the sea to the north. The farm stands on a plain that was saltmarsh when the settlers came. Thorodd drained it, and now it's good land, but I felt shut in there after Arnastapi. The cliffs lower over the plain, and the waterfalls drown the sound of the sea. I remember jumping over drainage ditches lined with kingcups and cotton grass. The farm was where Halldis' friend Thurid lived, who was married to Thorodd and sister of Snorri the Priest. The feuds of my childhood had a lot to do with her.

Thurid was obviously glad to see Halldis. I hung back against my pony's shoulder as they greeted one another. Then Halldis took my hand and brought me forward to the threshold, right in the middle of a group of strangers.

'This is my foster daughter,' she told Thurid proudly. 'This is Gudrid.'

Thurid was so grandly dressed I couldn't take my eyes off her. She was slight and fair, very pretty I suppose, but I saw with a child's eyes, and it seemed to me her face was closed, and she had a tight mouth which I didn't like. She wore a blue linen dress with embroidery round the throat and hem, and a darker blue tunic. Her brooches had animal heads on them, and between them she wore a string of coloured beads. Reds and blues were woven in a pattern I had never seen before, in the scarf over her hair. Beside her my stepmother looked big and austere, a bit too much like a man, in her plain dress and simple bronze brooches. A part of me admired Thurid; I thought for a moment that when I grew up I would like to be like that. Then I felt disloyal and despised myself.

Thurid had a baby, Kjartan, the one whose red curl she had sent so that Halldis could work her spell. We gave him his medicine at once, the first evening we arrived. He didn't look like a child who would have convulsions, but of course I had no experience. He wasn't fat like some babies are, and he crawled about in the rushes by the hearth, moving faster than you'd think possible, and trying to get his hands into everything. I liked him, and I wished he were my little brother. I had never played with a younger child before.

I remember now: I said I'd tell you how it was that our neighbour Bjorn didn't marry. Thurid was already married to Thorbjorn the Stout of Frodriver when Bjorn first set eyes on her. It was hardly the ideal marriage for a woman like Thurid; by all accounts Thorbjorn was a loud, violent man, who used to beat up his own thralls for no other reason than to vent his own rage. He'd been married before and was much older than Thurid. But he was killed in a feud over some stolen horses, and Thurid got the farm out of it, so in the end I suppose it was worth the trouble she went through. Bjorn was already visiting her when her husband was still alive. I think now, from scraps I overheard then and only understand now, that my foster parents hoped, when the news came that Thorbjorn the Stout was dead, that Bjorn would marry Thurid and bring her back to Breidavik. Whether he planned to do that or not, her brother, Snorri the Priest, was too quick for him. That wily man was too quick for most people. When I think about it now, although he took care of his wayward sister, I don't think he ever understood her, or would you say, loved her? I think Thurid was only loved by one man in her life. And Snorri the Priest had every cause to hate Thurid's father; they were only half brother and sister, you see, through their mother.

But you don't want to hear all about that. When Halldis took me to Frodriver, Thurid had been married off, this time to Thorodd, who had grown rich trading with Norway and the islands, and she was living in Frodriver again with her husband. But – I only heard all this years later, from my son Snorri's godfather's sister, whom I used to meet at the Thing once a year, when we were living at Glaum – Bjorn started visiting Thurid again, as soon as she was back in her old home at Frodriver. If one husband hadn't mattered to him, I suppose, why bother about another? Thorodd knew what was going on, and he was as angry as you'd expect a man to be. But he didn't meet Bjorn in fair fight. Bjorn wasn't our Breidavik champion for nothing. No, Thorodd ambushed him just before dawn, he and his friends the Thorissons and a couple of thralls, five of them altogether. Bjorn had been with Thurid and was riding home up Digramull from Frodriver. Bjorn killed the Thorissons, and Thorodd – that proud seagoing trader – fled with his slaves. Bjorn came home so covered in blood they thought he'd had his death blow, but he recovered from his wounds soon enough, and it was after that he was sent into exile. He went first to Norway, and then he travelled far into the east beyond that, fighting in the king's wars. Nine months after the night of the ambush a son was born to Thurid at Frodriver: Kjartan Thoroddsson.

One of the best things that happened for me, when I was a little girl, was Bjorn coming home to Breidavik. I told you about the games, didn't I? I loved that man, Agnar, if a little girl can be said to love a man who's not her father. He had time for me, and yet he had an air about him of a man who'd seen much more of the world than we had – a whiff of something far-off and exotic, of strange places very different from our little peninsula. Only he went nowhere any more, after he got home, just over the mountain to Frodriver, and children were not told anything about that. But I think a part of me knew, all the same. I can't remember anyone telling me who Kjartan really was. I think that's because whoever actually said it was only confirming something that deep down I'd always known. Anyway, I was telling you about my first meeting with him, when Halldis took me on that visit to Frodriver.

Kjartan had a box full of coloured pebbles, shells and driftwood. That evening I played with him by the hearth. I built him towers and he knocked them down, squealing with laughter each time my castles crashed into the ashes. It was easy to listen to the women's talk at the same time. Halldis knew I had sharp ears, but Thurid seemed to assume I was as absorbed as the baby. I was half insulted by that; I wanted her to notice me. But soon I forgot about it and was intent on what they were saying. It frightened me, and being among them all in a warm safe place, there was a perverse pleasure to be got from being afraid.

'No one dare go out after sunset anywhere in the valley,' Thurid was saying. 'If ever a man refused to lie quiet in his grave, it was he. And listen – I had this from Thorgeir the packman – you know he comes every summer now along the coast of Breidafjord – it was he who brought me these beads. Do you like them?'

Halldis glanced at the beads. 'What did Thorgeir say about the hauntings?'

'It began with the oxen they used to haul the body up the valley to the grave. They took him as far from the farms as they could, but as they went the corpse grew heavier and heavier, and at last the beasts could pull no more, and they had to bury him where they were, in the middle of the lava field. They raised a great cairn over him to hold him down. But it did no good, and nor did the spells that were used to bind him to the earth. That same night the oxen were possessed, and harried over the precipices where their broken bodies were discovered the next morning. Thorgeir talked to the shepherd, who said it's as much as a man's life is worth to be out on the hill. But the shepherd is Arnkel's thrall and has no choice about it. "But Thorgeir," he said, "I'm a marked man now, you see if I'm not."'

'Once a man believes in his own death he's doomed,' observed Halldis. 'Arnkel should let him go away.'

'They hear the ghost at night,' went on Thurid. 'It sits astride the roof and drums on the turf with its heels until the whole house shakes. His widow can't stand it. She lies in her bed with the covers over her ears, and won't budge until it's broad daylight. He'll ride her to death, Thorgeir said. Her husband's black ghost will drive all the reason out of her.'

That night I lay beside Halldis on the sleeping platform, and whispered in her ear. 'Do the dead walk everywhere? Do we have ghosts at home?'

It was a while before she answered me. A turf fell away from the banked-up fire, and I could see the embers through the hole it made, glaring at me like a red eye.

'Wherever the living are,' whispered my foster mother, 'the dead will be there too. No one wants to be cast back into the darkness beyond the world. We grow too attached to our selves to accept that. So the dead stay among us for as long as they can. Where they're loved and respected, perhaps they can settle for a while. Where they've been hated, if they have the spirit for it they'll keep the fight going for as long as possible. Already in Iceland the dead outnumber us, for we're the third generation. They do their best to stay until we banish them.'

'How can we do that?'

'By forgetting. But that's how fate tricks us all. You can't forget on purpose, however hard you try. In fact it's the opposite. Forgetting only happens when you're looking the other way. To forget is the only way to lay a ghost for ever, but when you most need to do that you can't use it. There are other spells, but none is so effective. They last for a while, sometimes for long enough, until no one's left alive who remembers any more.'

'Is my mother a ghost now?'

'Your mother was a good woman who did her best for you.'

'That's not what I asked.'

'It's the only answer I can give you.'

I thought that over, and shivered. I didn't fully understand, but I was sure that I did not want to live among ghosts. 'Halldis?'

She started. 'I thought you were asleep. Settle down, can't you?'

'If a person went to a land that was empty, where no people had ever been before, there wouldn't be any ghosts there, would there?'

'Only the ones you'd be bound to take with you. And now, for goodness sake, child, go to sleep.'

Orm and Halldis had no children of their own. Yet I learned from Halldis charms that will make a woman conceive, and prevent miscarriage and bring a baby safely into the world. I don't know if she had ever tried to use them on herself. I could have asked – I wasn't afraid of her – but I never thought of it, until my own son was born, and by then it was too late to ask Halldis anything. I've often wished I could have had her advice later; sometimes even after we had come back to Glaum I would ask myself what Halldis would have done in such and such a case. I've used her remedies all my life, though now I'm cautious about the spells. She made them innocently; we knew nothing about the new religion then. But I've since been given the knowledge of good and evil, and I've learned to take care.

We went to Frodriver again one summer when they had a big fair by the river. Thorgeir the packman and lots of other traders were there, displaying more fine wares than I had ever seen in my life. There were games as well, and feasting out of doors. Thurid was dressed in red with real gold brooches, and an amber necklace. She didn't even notice me. She was talking to our neighbour Bjorn, who at that time had only just arrived back from Norway.

I found my old friend Kjartan, but he wasn't a baby any more, and he didn't want to play with me. He was fair and chubby, half the height of a man, with a little axe thrust into his belt. He strode about, watching the men.

There was a fight. It was nothing important, only I'd never actually seen a man killed before. Someone split a man's head open with an axe. It looked as easy as cracking a hazelnut, only the inside was not firm and white but wet and red. They hid the corpse in a clump of willows. I didn't want to look, but something drew me. A few men were loitering nearby, talking quietly. Then Kjartan dashed past me and dipped his axe in the dead man's blood. He was gone almost before I realised what I had seen. His eyes were shining as he slipped away, his little axe gleaming with real blood. That was the last I saw of Kjartan until years later I went to the Thing with Karlsefni and met him there. He grew into a strong, sensible man, very like Bjorn, and the farm at Frodriver flourished in his hands. They had a lot of trouble with witchcraft there after we'd gone to the Green Land, but Kjartan put an end to all that. He visited us once or twice at Glaumbaer. Karlsefni liked him.

Although my father was often at Arnarstapi, he never had much to say to me. Often Bjorn of Breidavik would be there too, and he was always urging my father to support him in some action against the Thorsnes men. When it was just my father and Orm they talked about the farm more than feuds. Perhaps there was nothing to say about me. I was well, Halldis was teaching me the things I should know. But I used to long for my father to notice me, and be silently angry when he didn't. I had no idea what he wanted me to be or do, but I would have done anything to get a moment of his attention. Even now, it makes me angry to think of that.

I realise now I must have satisfied him. You probably can't see it now, and indeed you ought not to, but as a young girl I was goodlooking. I knew it too, Halldis made sure of that. It didn't mean anything to me, because my father never looked at me.

Other men did. By the time I was fifteen several men had approached my father to find out what his plans were for my marriage. Of course, a large estate came with me, so it might have seemed like a good bargain, but the rumour was already going around that my father was short of money. His heart had never been in his farm; since Eirik went away west something in my father had gone too. He'd never wanted to settle down, but on the other hand he was never fully involved with the Breidafjord feuds either. He made up for it by entertaining lavishly, and at his feasts he would make gifts to his guests that everyone would talk about for months afterwards. It's a way to achieve fame, I suppose, but not a provident one to take if you're not well-off. Thorbjorn thought he was rich. After all, my grandfather had been a slave, although no one ever mentioned that any more.

Thorbjorn was twice the man his father had been, in terms of wealth, but he wasn't interested in his land, and he made a poor husbandman. That's my opinion now. As a child growing up at Arnarstapi I had Orm's good management as an example right before my eyes. Orm and Halldis were like the man in the story who built his house upon a rock. My father's house was built upon sand, and the sands were running out fast by the time I went back to him.

A house built on a rock. You say the rock is faith, and I say, yes, that's true, but faith in God begins with faith in one's self. Go on, write that down. I can see you hesitate, and now you've made a big blot, holding a full quill hovering over your vellum like that. I'm not speaking blasphemy. Isn't God within us all? I repeat, Orm and Halldis built their house upon a rock, and the rock was in place ready when the news of the new religion first reached us. Faith in oneself, good management, a generosity built not upon show but upon substance. That's what I learned from them.

I was fourteen when Thangbrand the missionary landed at Arnarstapi, and was going up to my father's house, but he stopped at our house first. That was a miracle in itself: if he had gone straight to Laugarbrekka we might have heard no more about it. Thangbrand had already travelled over most of Iceland, and made many converts, some by the sword and some by magic. He didn't need to use either with us. Halldis was already interested. Talk of the new religion had been going around for some time. Halldis and Thurid had discussed it at Frodriver, when we stayed there. Thurid was suspicious then, but my foster mother was interested in the idea.

'This is a land of ghosts, but the gods have other things to do than worry about that,' Halldis said. 'It's all very well for a man at sea to pray to Thor, but here on land we're overrun by demons, and more and more people are being driven off their land by the dead who refuse to lie quiet. This new power may be just the thing we need.'

'It's only politics,' argued Thurid. 'Bjorn told me what's happening in Norway now. The king isn't interested in ghosts. He wants our land.'

'But perhaps this god offers a better fate than the old ones. Perhaps he gives us more choice about our own lives.'

'Halldis!' I had never seen Thurid roused before. I crept a little closer to the hearth. 'I don't know how you dare to talk about choices. How do you know what is listening to us, in the dark?' I shrank back, although I knew she did not mean me. 'Who are you to play around with unseen things?'

'I'd still like to know more about this Christ of Thangbrand's. I'm afraid for Gudrid too. She knows and sees too much already, and I don't know how to protect her.'

I supposed Halldis had no idea I was listening. I shrank further behind the hangings, but she must have heard me move. 'Is that you, Gudrid?' she called. 'Come in by the fire, and show us what you bought at the fair.'

I'd been given a silver piece, and I'd bought a knife that I could hang round my neck on a string. Halldis admired it, but Thurid said, 'You take after your foster mother too much. You're a lovely girl. You should buy yourself pretty things. Didn't you look at the necklaces in Thorgeir's pack?'

I didn't answer. I watched Halldis test my knife with her thumb, and nod approvingly. 'A good choice,' she said, and I was satisfied.

When Thangbrand came to Arnarstapi, Halldis took from him the thing she needed, and found a god that suited her. She would have had us all baptised then and there, but Orm was more cautious. He took Thangbrand to my father first. Thorbjorn had no opinions about gods, but he'd been to the Thing that summer and knew which way the wind was blowing in Iceland. Christianity was becoming politic. Thangbrand had been sent by the King of Norway himself, and was a powerful man to have for an ally.

So, each of us having a reason of our own, we all made our way down to the sandy beach at Arnarstapi, one afternoon around midsummer.

*The sea is green. Loose knots of dulse rock over rippled sand. The onshore breeze catches the small company on the shore. Its touch is sea-cold, like the wet sand underfoot. The man who stands, chest-deep, beyond the small waves, is shuddering, his teeth clenched against the cold.*

*It is the girl's turn. She walks into waves as green as glass. Above, the last snow patches on Stapafel shine in the pale sun. The man in the sea lays his hand against her chest, above her breasts, his other arm against her back.*

*'In the name of the Father, and of the Son, and of the Holy Ghost.'*

*Flung backwards into icy sea, she gasps and chokes. Water roars in her ears. Then she is on her feet again. The sea swells against her chest, and salt water pours from her long hair. The shore is a band of cold light. She struggles towards it. Her shift clings to her body, and she tries to cover herself with her arms. Warm hands reach out and lead her on to dry sand.*

And there I was baptised into the faith. It was a long way from here. But you must have been baptised in Iceland too. Do you want to forget that now? What did you feel, when the Cardinal sent for you, because only you could transcribe the story of an old woman from Iceland, who had gone beyond the boundaries of this world? You know, don't you, that that's why they want to have my story written down? You're not at all like the young men I used to know. They wanted to be famous for their skill in arms, their friendships and their generosity. But I think you're equally ambitious. I expect you'd rather be in Rome now than anywhere else in Christendom. I don't think you like women very much, either. Am I right? Perhaps the monastic life is just right for you. I wouldn't have wanted it myself when I was young. It's different now, of course. I've nothing left to feel passionate about.

It's wrong of me to torment you. You don't answer back, only your ears have gone very red, and you bend over the manuscript as if you were shortsighted, which you're not, and you scratch away with that quill as if your salvation depended on it. Take no notice of my teasing. I'm an old woman, in her dotage, you may think. But I have been young and beautiful, and there were men once who could not take their eyes off me.

But now I'm worn out. I'd said we'd stop in the afternoons, and look, the sun's gone from the courtyard, and soon it'll be dark. The dark comes so suddenly here, it always takes me by surprise. I'm hungry, and so must you be. We've worked far too long, and we mustn't make a habit of it. Stop writing, for goodness sake boy, I'm not saying anything to the purpose, and your hand must be terribly stiff. Stop, I said!

# THREE

# *July 9th*

When I was fifteen I made a spell of my own. I never told anyone. I knew it was a dangerous thing to do, but I honestly believed then that I could make my own life the way I wanted it to be. I had a notion, even though I saw no evidence for it in the lives of those around me, that my fate was in my own hands. Arrogant, you think? Perhaps I was only looking for a way to survive. Certainly I didn't like the idea of men weighing up my attractions, and the attractions of my father's dwindling estate, and wondering whether to bargain with him for me. I wanted something else to happen. Spells concerning oneself tend to rebound. I'd never do anything like that now.

I chose my place carefully. For a moment I thought of the giants' caves behind Stapafel but I rejected that spot with a shudder. I wanted to invoke a benign power, and I was scared of the demons in that wild country. Instead I chose the holy well at Laugarbrekka. It's sacred to Freyja, and I'd always known it; it's just a few yards from my father's house. Women used to come there if they wanted a child. I nearly rejected the place because it's so close to home, and I wanted something more exciting, more my own, but luckily I wasn't arrogant enough to put myself above the other women. If I had been, I think my fate would have been far worse than it was.

*Cold water springs from under the rock and bubbles over black stones. Moss grows in clumps, jewelled with waterdrops. Flowers cluster in the damp: kingcups, buttercups, willow herb. The hollow smells of wet* earth. It is midnight, and the sun has gone behind Snaefel. Grey streaks of cloud are drawn across the sky by ashy fingers. The western sky is pink.

The girl stands by the spring. She is tall, and her hair reaches to her waist. She has it tied back with a red band. She holds herself very straight. She is no longer a child; her face is thinner and more secret. There are moments when she looks how she will be when she is old.

Now that the sun has gone there is a chill over the pastures. Beyond them, the glacier is cold and dull. The girl begins to chant under her breath. A small breeze lifts her hair. She takes a silver piece from the sheath that hangs round her neck. She throws it into the heart of the spring, and it vanishes without a glimmer.

She kneels down with her head close to the water. Pebbles gleam like jewels in the mud below. A fleet of shadows chases over the surface of the spring. She looks up. A flock of terns flies over her, then turns west in a flash of white, and disappears into the dazzle.

She has never been to sea, but she knows terns are unsafe guides, as they do not always make for land. This must be the sign for which she asked. She does not understand it yet, but the spell is made.

I thought things were going to change that autumn. We were used to Thorgeir the trader coming to Arnarstapi at that time of year on his way to Laugarbrekka. This year his son Einar came instead, as Thorgeir wasn't as fit as he used to be. I couldn't remember Einar, although he'd been to Arnarstapi with his father before he went abroad. He didn't remember me either, and if he had, I don't think he would have connected an inquisitive little girl with the young woman I was now.

Anyway, once a man sees a woman in a particular way, she has no past or future in his eyes. Einar had been travelling between Iceland and Norway for quite a few years, spending one winter there and one here – in Iceland, I mean. He was another of those Icelanders who grew rich and successful in a generation. Thorgeir was the son of a slave, and a travelling packman to begin with. His son was a shipowner and seagoing trader. Orm would have invited him to stay with us for his father's sake anyway, but naturally he was interested in the man himself. Success is always interesting to us in Iceland.

I knew the trader had arrived, but Halldis kept me busy outside. As a child, I could run in and out as I pleased. Then I was neither man nor woman, so I could work my way into any hearth, like the animals, and be invisible. Now, if men came to the house, she would keep me at the loom or in the dairy, so that I couldn't even listen to the talk. I can tell you, young man, that it's hard to be young if you're a woman. You have to keep to the rules. A child can break them, and an old woman, if she's like me, will do exactly as she likes, but a young girl is attractive to men and must therefore always be careful. Not that I minded being beautiful. It has its compensations, but it's a kind of prison all the same.

So there was Einar in the hall displaying his wares from Norway to my father, and there was I, out in the field with my stool and bucket, milking the household cow. It was a grey evening just at the turn of the year, when for the first time there's a touch of winter in the wind, and the day is no longer than the night. A mizzle of rain came in from the sea with the dusk, and I could feel the chill of it against my bent back. I pressed my head against the warmth of the cow, while the milk squirted down. It gleamed like ice in the half light. I was excited about seeing the trader's wares. I was still scornful of women like Thurid who cared so much for fine clothes and jewels, but at the same time I admired their courage. Thurid defied the world she lived in. We were starved of colour, but she insisted on it. I realised, as I watched the whiteness frothing in the pail, that I wanted colour. I wanted just to see and feel the colours the trader would have brought. I wanted to buy colours of my own.

That was all I was thinking about as I came back to the house. I passed the door of the hall, and I heard men's voices, but I didn't turn my head. I went straight into the dairy and poured the milk, and took down yesterday's buttermilk. It was my job to make the skyr, but before I could go into the hearth to get the boiled milk, Halldis brought it out to me. As I mixed in the rennet I could hear a murmur of voices from the hall. I remember I was wondering if I would feel different if I wore dyed clothes. I never had. I wondered if the colours that people dress themselves in change the way they think? I'd never had the opportunity to find out.

*The farmer and the trader sit in the hall. The trader has opened his bales and spread out bolts of dyed cloth, wool and linen, trays of amber beads and bronze brooches, coloured necklaces and ornaments of jet and silver, knives in decorated sheaths, charms to hang round the neck, sets of pins and needles in cases of polished horn, enamelled crosses to keep away ghosts and devils. The trader is dressed in a red tunic and green trousers, and the rings on his fingers are gold. His belt and knife scabbard are soft woven leather, and his boots are engraved with spiralling patterns. He is tall and fair, and his eyes are pale blue. He has set his scales up on the table in front of him, and as he talks to the farmer he juggles absentmindedly with the weights.*

*Orm the farmer wears rough woven trousers and a sheepskin tunic. He has left his muddy boots at the door. The bald patch on his head is much whiter than his face, because out of doors he always wears a hood. His hands are engrained with dirt, and his fingernails are black and broken. His dogs lie at his feet.*

*The girl passes the door at the end of the hall on her way to the dairy. Her hair is the colour of willow leaves in autumn, and it hangs loose to her waist. She holds herself very straight, even though she is carrying a milking stool and a bucket. She does not seem to have noticed the men at all.*

*The trader stares, and stops juggling. A weight rolls across the table.*

*'Orm, who's that girl? She's not your daughter, is she?'*

*'What girl?' Orm looks round, but there is no one to be seen, only a faint clinking sound from the dairy. 'Oh, that must be Gudrid, my foster daughter. She's the daughter of Thorbjorn of Laugarbrekka.'*

*Einar picks up the weight, and turns it over in his hand. 'She must be a good match,' he remarked. 'I expect there've been suitors for her hand?'*

*'Naturally. But she won't be easy to get. Gudrid is particular about husbands, and so is her father.'*

*'Is that right?' Einar lays his weights out in a row, in order. 'If I were to propose a marriage contract, would you speak to her father on my behalf?'*

Orm raises his eyebrows, otherwise his face is expressionless. It is impossible to know whether Einar's words have surprised him or not.

'I'd repay you with my support,' urges Einar. 'Thorbjorn must think it's a good match. It's hardly a secret that he's getting through his money. Everyone talks about how much he spends, and the estate can't possibly pay for it all. Now I've got land, and more money than I know what to do with, and so has my father. Thorbjorn could hardly say no. Only the kind of contract that a man like me can offer will save him from complete ruin.'

'I'm not sure that Thorbjorn will see it that way.' Orm pauses, and frowns. 'Maybe you're right. I won't say you're wrong. I'd be your friend in this matter, as in any other, but Thorbjorn is a proud man.'

'He's no more to be proud about than I have. Oh yes,' Einar adds, a shade aggressively. 'You're thinking of my ancestry. Is Thorbjorn's any better? If my grandfather was a slave – well, so was his. And at least in my family we've made the most of our opportunities.'

'You've barely seen the girl.'

'I've seen her, and that's enough. I know what I want, Orm, and I'm not afraid to take it. It's time I was married. If you want to do your foster daughter a good turn, you'll speak to Thorbjorn for me. Wouldn't you like to see her the wife of a wealthy man who'll give her the kind of life a woman wants? You know she'd be better off with me to look after her than with her father.'

'I'll think it over,' is all Orm will say, but clearly he has begun to be interested.

I suppose that what attracted me about Einar was his obvious admiration of me. I remember the meal we had that night. He was sitting beside Orm, and every time I looked at him his eyes were on me. I took care not to look too often, but all through the evening I was self-conscious as I had never been before. As I moved round the table, pouring the milk, I was aware of my own body, and the effect that it might have on him. When I poured his drink into the cup for him, he looked at my hair, so close to his own face, as though he wanted to touch it. I was excited, and my heart beat as if I were doing something dangerous. I don't think I've ever been so demure, before or since.

As it turned out, the danger was not mine, but Orm's. Einar went away the next day, without even having spoken to me. I can't remember now how much Orm told me, but I knew what was going on. I don't think Halldis approved, or perhaps she just knew too much. When I tried to speak to her about the young man who had visited us, she just pursed her lips and turned away.

I thought I might see Einar again a week later, at my father's autumn feast, but he wasn't there. The feast was even more splendid than usual. My father, having no rival in hospitality anywhere near us, had taken to striving to outdo himself, and the results were spectacular, although I found myself disapproving – a throwback to my early days of want, perhaps, or a premonition of hunger still to come. Thorbjorn welcomed me with more warmth than usual. Perhaps my new clothes and amber necklace had something to do with it, or maybe he was beginning to make plans of his own about my future. Certainly when we arrived he seemed pleased with me, and with my foster parents.

My father and Orm were sitting together at the top of the table, their heads close together. Suddenly Thorbjorn leapt to his feet with a great shout. I saw him raise his fist and I thought he was going to hit my foster father. Thorbjorn was a bigger man than Orm, but Orm just stood there stolidly. My foster mother shoved the people on the benches aside, and was up there beside the men. She grabbed my father's arm, and I thought he'd hit her but he just pushed her away. The other guests were shouting to him to calm down, and I was pushing my way through till I was just across the table from them. My father never even looked at me.

'So I'm short of money am I?' my father roared. He put his face close to Orm's and shouted right at him. My foster father just looked dour, in the way I knew so well. 'I'm a poor man, am I, who should be glad to be rescued by the son of a slave? Is that what you're saying? I should be glad to give my daughter to the son of a common packman? You think, do you, that I've fallen as low as that? You dare to offer me this, when you're eating my meat and drinking my ale? You dare, you say, to conspire with servants to dispose of my daughter? And yet I trusted you with her. You've had her all these years, and you dare to repay me with this!'

'I mean well by both her and you,' said Orm, without raising his voice.

My foster mother stood between them, her eyes moving fast from one to the other, as if she were waiting to intercept a blow. For the first time in my life I noticed how much taller she was than Orm, and it occurred to me that they looked slightly ridiculous together. I never saw it, until they were both up there facing my father, fighting for my future.

'You mean well?' sneered my father. 'What right have you to mean anything by us at all? No right but what I gave you, and that you have no longer. You can get out of my house, and take your woman with you. But not my daughter. Oh no, Gudrid stays here, where I can keep an eye on her myself. And I'll have no more of your plots. And don't try spreading any more rumours of my poverty. You've seen my feast, you've seen the gifts I have to give. So don't go round telling folk that I'm poor!'

I think Orm tried to answer him. I remember looking at Halldis, and Halldis looking at me. The table was between us. She tried to move towards me, and I stretched out my hands to her. I couldn't speak, there was too much noise. The men on the benches were shouting, trying to intervene. Some of them got between Orm and Thorbjorn. Steinthor of Eyr was holding my father back, yelling at him to restrain himself. The others pushed Orm and Halldis towards the door. I tried to follow, but Halldis looked at me again and slightly shook her head. Then they were gone.

I hated my father all that winter. It was quite the other way round between us from how it had been. He tried to woo me, and I would have nothing to do with him. Whenever he talked to me I would sit there looking stonily at the hangings against the wall. After dinner he would keep me beside him until bedtime, trying to make me answer him. I never would. Nor did I try to go over to Arnarstapi; I wasn't going to give him the pleasure of stopping me. Although we were far from the main routes along Snaefelsnes we did sometimes have visitors, and on those nights there would be stories and singing, which made my silence less noticeable. I was polite to my father's guests, and I always waited on them respectfully as I'd been taught, but I got a reputation for being cold and aloof. Sometimes there'd be someone there who'd watch me move about the room, just as Einar had done at Arnarstapi, but I don't think any man approached my father. The rumours about the state of Thorbjorn's affairs must have made any possible husband very cautious. I thought it was me they didn't like. I had often been told I was beautiful, but I began to think that something else must be wrong about me.

I thought about Einar quite a lot. I had a daydream that one day he would ride up to my father's door, and demand me for his wife. Of course that wasn't very likely in the middle of winter, but I used to lie in my bed at night and imagine it happening once the snow had melted. Einar would confront Thorbjorn and my father would be quite confounded. I used to go over the scene in my head until it was perfect. At the end Einar would turn to me and tell me to come with him, and I would mount one of the ponies in the herd he had brought, and ride away from Laugarbrekka without a backward look. The next part of the story was more vague, because I had only seen Einar once and didn't know what he would be like. Occasionally the fantasy went on until I was in bed with him, but then I used to get stuck, because that wasn't really where I wanted to be. I just wanted to be rescued from hating my father, and there wasn't any man but Thorbjorn himself who could do that. To give him credit, during that long winter he did try his best.

In the spring my father gave his grandest feast yet. People came the whole length of Snaefelsnes, and from beyond Breidafjord. Factions seemed to be forgotten: the Breidavik men were there, naturally, and Steinthor of Eyr, but so was Snorri the Priest and even one or two of Eirik Raudi's worst enemies, the Thorbrandssons. I had no idea what was in my father's mind until he came to give his speech. The hall was fuller than I'd ever seen it. It was raining hard outside and was stuffy inside, the kind of day that makes you want to sleep, even if you haven't eaten and drunk too much. My head felt heavy, and I longed to close my eyes. But as soon as my father began to speak, I was awake at once. I felt that same excitement I'd known when Einar came to Arnarstapi: a fluttering in the stomach and a dryness in the mouth. I'd half hoped Einar might appear at the feast, risking my father's anger.

But this was a different adventure that was being offered. Einar and his fine clothes and rich goods vanished for ever into the mists of memory.

'I've lived here a long time,' Thorbjorn said. 'I've enjoyed your friendship and support, and I'm happy to say that I've always got on well with most of my neighbours here.' If any faction realised that my father was being ironic, it showed no sign. 'I shall look back on my years at Laugarbrekka and remember that they were good.

'It may not be news to most of you that things haven't gone very well for me financially. I've always kept a generous household. We've lived well here, and our guests have always been given the best of welcomes. It would be a disgrace to me to do things any other way. I'd rather leave the farm, leave Iceland, than live here meanly.

'Twelve years ago my dearest friend invited me to join him in a great undertaking. I turned back very reluctantly, when I saw my friend Eirik Raudi set his sail for the Green Land that he discovered to the west beyond Gunnbjorn's skerries. Every time a ship has come back with news of him, I've felt the old temptation. I'm not an old man yet; I'm younger than Eirik. Why should a great adventure not come just as well to me?

'So there it is. This is my last feast here, and I've invited you all here so that I could tell you that this summer I shall go west in search of the Green Land, and so to all of you farewell.'

He didn't mention me, but I never doubted for one moment that this was my adventure too. Everyone was so astonished that they had nothing to say; certainly no one asked what my father planned to do about me. I expect they gossiped about that feast for years afterwards though. My father sent them all away with rich gifts, which left us with virtually nothing. Thorbjorn didn't care. The grandness of the gesture was worth far more than wealth to him.

# FOUR

# *July 10th*

Don't days like this remind you of Iceland? When I woke this morning and heard the rain on the roof and courtyard, and saw the thin light creeping in, it took me a moment to remember where I was. In Iceland the animals will be out, and the pastures will be green with hay. Do you ever miss those things?

You nodded. You actually nodded. You do understand what I mean. Here we are, two people from one country. It's so far away from here that sometimes it seems like a dream. The way the people here see it, Iceland might just as well be outside the world. It's good to be with a fellow countryman sometimes. Have they told you not to talk to me?

You shouldn't be afraid of me. I'm old enough to be your grandmother. Perhaps you're withdrawn because I talk about the place you came from, and it reminds you of too much. Yes, that's it. I can tell by the way you don't answer me. Was it a hard decision to become a monk? Did they send you away from home when you were very young?

\*    \*    \*    \*    \*

Ten. Yes, that is young. Did you mind? Little boys usually think about becoming warriors, seamen, explorers of strange lands. I never met a child that longed to sit in a cloister bent over a parchment. Where did they send you?

\*    \*    \*    \*    \*

So far away. Were you happy there?

\*    \*    \*    \*    \*

All right, I won't ask any more. It was kind of you to speak to me. I haven't heard Icelandic spoken since I got here, except inside my own head. You've no idea what you gave me, saying a word or two in my own language. I'm grateful. We'd better get on with our work.

I'm putting it off, you see, because the next part is hard to tell. I blame myself even now. Look out of the window now. It's raining still, but those finches are out there again. I think they're building a nest near the wall. This courtyard must be a haven even for the birds. They have enough to fear in the forests, and so do we. Did the journey to Rome frighten you when you first came? It's men that I'm afraid of now, not the weather or the sea. When the men – and I believe that they were men – came to Hop, that's when I was frightened, that was when I knew that our settlement was doomed. I'm not afraid of emptiness. The land here has been inhabited so long that men have forgotten when they first came. It's full of ghosts, but I'm old and I don't mind that. I mind the bandits more. The forests of Europe are so thick. Even at Hop they were not as thick as that. Anyone could hide in the wilderness, and everywhere we stayed along the road they talked of ambush, and murder. Even after all I've been through, I prefer the sea to that.

You're not writing all this down? There's no need, I'm just avoiding the point. Young man, will you look up, just for a moment?

Your eyes are the colour of my son's.

We set sail from Breidavik at the beginning of May.

Everything seemed to augur well. Several of my father's tenants and freedmen chose to come with us, as well as the slaves he picked to remain with us. Three of the tenants brought their families. The slaves were mostly couples. One useful thing my father did teach me is that it's a good idea to allow your dependants to marry and to bring up loyal families. It's not only an insurance for the next generation, it's also that marriage keeps men contented in your service. I wish the same could be said of free men, but I never noticed a warrior being subdued by domestic influences. You must know a bull is safer in with the cows, not tethered away from the herd, but then you haven't had to trouble yourself with livestock.

The best of it, as it seemed to me that blue May morning, was that Orm and Halldis were with us too. As soon as they heard the news that we were going, Halldis came to my father and begged the forgiveness for Orm that Orm would never have asked for himself, and asked that they might join the expedition. 'Gudrid and I haven't been separated until this winter, since she was five years old,' she said. 'You know you'll need a woman to keep her company. You don't want some young maid who'll look out for nothing except a man for herself. You want a mother for her. Think of all those young men there must be by now in the Green Land who need wives. Eirik Raudi had three young sons when he went away. What wives can they have found among the seals and rocks? That's what it's like in a new country. You'll have to watch out for her, and if you're careful, you may marry her very well.' Halldis knew my father; kinship with Eirik Raudi was a bait he wouldn't fail to snap at. Halldis didn't mention, of course, that I wasn't much of a prize since my father had given away what would have been my dowry. The despised Einar was probably ten times as rich as my father now. But she did mention to me privately that I'd probably make a better match in Greenland, where women were scarce. Land was there for the taking; no need to marry into it out there, but a woman to run the estate once you'd got it . . . As Halldis said, I was healthy and knew about good husbandry. 'Management and babies,' she said to me, when we were allowed to meet again. 'That's what men will want out there. They won't despise beauty either, in a wild country. I don't think you need worry too much about that dowry.'

She persuaded my father, and maybe it was she who sowed the first seed of an idea about my future. Maybe he had thought of it already. I shall never know, but Eirik's sons were certainly considered as a possibility in my family before ever I laid eyes on any of them. I wasn't unwilling. I still had the memory of a fierce red man, telling us his dream of a new country, while he stood in our hall blocking off the firelight, so that his shadow multiplied into huge shapes on the wall behind him.

I don't think Orm wanted to go to Greenland. Naturally he was anxious about what would happen to his lands when Laugarbrekka was sold to an unknown buyer. Maybe he thought a journey to the Green Land was the lesser risk. He didn't come for love of me as Halldis did, but I think he came for love of her.

Before I was baptised Thangbrand the missionary explained to us about judgement. Even now I have dreams about the end of the world. I suppose I should think of these things now more than ever – my own death can't be far off – and yet, as I grow old, I come to hope more and more that God is merciful. In Iceland death is a small thing. Men must kill; it's their nature. I think women are more haunted by the deaths that they inflict. For men, there's still the dream of the last battle. They fear no judgement, only hope for the fight that will last until the end of the world. But when I dream of the summons from the grave, the ghosts of my foster parents, whom I loved, rise up and tower over me, always accusing. No battle, no feasting-hall, for them. In the dream the sea water streams away from their bodies, which are gaunt and livid after being dead for so many years. They tell me they have never rested all this time, for they have had no grave; they are outcast, lost in the waters that surround the world. And no one is to blame but I, who let them follow me, just because of my need for them.

So now you know what I must tell. We left under blue skies, with a favourable wind; the land already smelt of spring. The cattle were out in the newly uncovered pastures. We even had a couple of young lambs among the flock we took aboard with us. The ship was crammed: cattle, sheep and poultry amidships, the slaves and their families sheltering among them, or forward in front of the sail. We were aft, with an awning rigged to shelter us, for there was no need at first to have the deck clear. We had water and fodder for ten days, besides food for ourselves. It seemed plenty. In good weather, we would have been there within the week. When we came out of Breidavik there wasn't a cloud over the glacier, and the ice shone in the bright sun.

You've maybe heard about that spring, although it was before you were born. It's legend now. We weren't the only ones to be caught out. You know what they say? The story is that it was the first year any Christian folk set out for the lands beyond the world, and the old gods were angry. They had been banished from Norway, then from Iceland. So they took ship with Eirik, or maybe flew before him, and found a place beyond the boundaries of that world which used to be theirs, but was now called Christian. There in the empty lands they found a place to rest. For all I know they haunt those mountains still.

But when they saw ships with Christians aboard following them to their new sanctuary they were angry. Thor flung his hammer from the glaciers above Gunnbjorn's skerries, and it landed in the sea between Greenland and Iceland, and stirred up a whirlpool. Ice that had lain quiet for hundreds of years broke into huge splinters and began to drift, monsters roused themselves from the deep, and waves the height of Snaefel flung themselves the length of the western sea, until they crashed to their death against the cliffs of Europe.

So they say. I tell you this and I tell you that. What I'm not telling you is what it was like aboard that ship. Poor boy. You're so young; but you too will be judged, as we're all judged. Are you ever afraid? Is there anything that you've done that rises up to haunt you? No, you needn't answer. I've made many terrible voyages. I know what the sea is. Not an enemy, precisely, but stronger than any of us and wholly unreliable. Sometimes its face is like a mirror, and sometimes it is a tormented hell. My first voyage was the worst of all.

*There is only cold and the terrifying water, everything turns to water. Feeling requires something hard, a fact, an edge, but here there is nothing, no difference, only numbness of the spirit and the hands that cannot feel. The dead are thrown into the sea; the living are as cold as the dead. The water hides who is there, who has gone. If there were a tomorrow there would be grieving, but time and feeling are swallowed up; we are crushed in the belly of the sea. We are cast away into the deep, in the midst of the seas. The waters engulf us, even to the soul.*

*The sky turns black where there should be evening, and out of the west a wave comes tall and white-capped as Snaefel, like melted land. The ship rises on the wave, her ropes taut as bowstrings, sounding the note that breaks the vessel. The wave crashes into chaos and roaring water, sheep are swept away like froth, the sail is torn to strips of rag. The wind screams on.*

*The days and the nights are water. Nothing changes. The cattle are lost, the people die. Their names have no meaning any more. There is nothing to do, or think, but to keep still and hold on. The body of Orm is flung overboard; the body of Halldis is thrown after it. There is neither light nor dark, only the thirst of hell. To die is to drink at last, to stay alive is to have no water. There is no change, no mercy. The ship is out of the world now, out of time, and there is no pity here.*

When we reached the open sea the fair wind failed us. We ran into bad storms, and made little headway all that summer. We had hardly any water, and disease broke out among us. It was colder than I can even begin to imagine now. Half our company died. Orm died. Halldis died. The sea grew worse. We suffered terribly from thirst and exposure. I have scars on my hands still, look. Those were open sores. But at last, when we had gone far beyond hope, the sea spat us out. We made landfall at last at Herjolfsnes in the Green Land, right at the beginning of winter.

# FIVE

# July 11th

I'm sorry about yesterday. I'm quite ready to go on now. But I must apologise. I have no right to inflict my feelings on you.

The nights had begun to grow dark, and when we saw the sun again at last we realised we were too far south. We turned north as much as the wind would let us, knowing that the land we sought was nearly as far north as Reykjanes. We had no idea if we were west or east of it; my father was even wondering if we would raise Iceland. But as we went on the sea grew far colder than our seas at home, and soon lumps of ice began to appear in it, small and white at first, and then larger and sometimes turquoise or azure, all drifting south past us as we struggled on against the growing current. An intense chill off the water wrapped us round, and each berg blew its cold breath over us as it passed us, like a sigh from the dead.

The land we finally saw was much grimmer than the one we had left, and we could see nowhere where it was possible to make a settlement. The rising sun twinkled against a huge glacier. Great lumps of ice had broken away from it, and threatened our little ship as we drew closer. The mountains were bare rock and snow, with a whiteness behind them that might have been ice or cloud. All that land gave us, when we risked our ship to reach it, was melt water running under a huge twisted crust of ice, but it was fresh, and it saved our lives. The coast tended north-east; my father said that was wrong: Eirik's sailing directions indicated a coast with many fjords, tending north-west. When we put about to follow the land south-west the crew almost rebelled. Winter was coming on, and they just wanted to go home to Iceland after all that we had gone through.

Uneasily we followed that fierce coast. My father reminded us that the settlements were far up the fjords, invisible from the open sea. We passed what could have been islands or promontories, all sheer rock and ice. Long inlets thrust inland. There was no knowing which we should follow. It grew warmer, and with the end of numbness came something like despair. I have more experience of sailing directions than any other woman in the world, and I have learned one thing: like icebergs, directions never show a fraction of what is there. Yet men have gone far into the unknown relying on these fragile words, that never begin to describe the awful nature of the place itself. It never surprises me that so many ships get lost; on the contrary, I have never ceased to be amazed whenever one actually arrives.

I'll tell you one thing, though. I would rather suffer the whole journey, and risk my life every time, than wait safely at home for news of the man I love. I've never allowed that to happen to me, and yet I admire the women who bear it, year after year.

There was a man called Herjolf, the father of Bjarni who first saw Vinland, who chose to build his farm in Greenland on a ness facing south-east into the open sea. Every other farmer in Greenland sought the shelter of the long fjords, but Herjolf's boldness paid off. Each new ship searching the Greenland coast was likely to sight the settlement at Herjolfsnes, and every seasoned traveller made Herjolf's house his first port of call. Herjolf's object was to trade, but he was willing to save lives too, if that were likely to be profitable. He saved ours.

I'll never forget that first sight of the farm at Herjolfsnes. We had passed the mouth of a long fjord, and ahead lay another steep island, or headland. Then, as we rode the crest of each wave, a patch of green appeared. Each time we rose from the trough we strained our eyes to see it. Slowly the ship closed the land. The pastures became studded with brown dots. Cattle. There was a beach with lumps on it, rocks, or possibly boats. Then something else: a thin coil of grey, almost obliterated by the tails of mist that clung to the breakers on the shore. The cry went up from all of us together. 'Smoke!'

We reached a stony beach, and the ship came down hard and

stopped in the breakers. No one waited for orders. Men, women and the two surviving cows struggled towards the bows in a babble of confusion. I was still aft, staring at the new land. I made out the outline of an oblong turf building under the smoke, green as the pasture around it. And then I saw people coming towards us. My hands were pressed to my mouth, in a kind of horror. It seemed so like home, but this was another world, after all that had happened to us, and I trusted nothing.

But in fact it was real and familiar. We were met by Thorkel, who farmed the land nearest the shore, and he took us to Herjolf, who at once invited my father and all his people to spend the winter there. If the ship had been whole we might have pushed on to Eiriksfjord, now we had found our direction, but the spare sail was barely holding together, and besides, we didn't have enough people to man her. It was at the end of that first voyage I learned to work the steerboard, when there were not enough men to cover the watches. Later, Karlsefni made use of my skill. Thorstein never did. He refused even to believe that a woman could steer a boat; even the thought of it was unlucky for him.

When I came ashore at Herjolfsnes I could hardly walk. The solid land was treacherous and never still. At Herjolf's hall we had fresh water and milk, and dry clothes. But I hadn't even got used to that before I realised that even now nothing was simple. The ghosts, as always, were before us.

The ghost of hunger I knew well. The ghosts of loss and fear had hung behind it from the beginning of my life. As the numbness melted away, beside the fire of seaweed and driftwood in Herjolf's hall, I saw how hunger feasted on the gaunt flesh of Herjolf's folk, and how famine had settled itself in their drawn faces and suffering eyes. As I regained my own strength I felt it too. It ate away my insides, so that there was always pain, sometimes dull and sometimes gnawing, as the ghost slept and ate within me like a monstrous child. The greatest blessing any human being could know is to be assured they will always have food and drink. If you are with me, you can say that to me when I am dying, and it will comfort me. Only then can you be sure it will be true. I hope you will never be hungry, Agnar.

A demon must have possessed that summer. We had fought it at sea; on land they'd struggled too. Much of the flock had died for want of new grass, a hunting expedition had never returned, and no ships came with supplies. That winter we didn't have half enough fish, and very little beef or mutton. We ate mostly seal meat, which men said was best, as it would make us strong like seals against the most dangerous enemies in the Green Land, the sea and the weather. But whatever you eat, there has to be enough of it if it's going to make you strong.

Winter came. Outside the snow rose to the roof, and inside was like a cave, dark and muddy and chill, in spite of the seaweed fires. One thing I remember from that winter is the dirt. There was always grime, seal's grease and smoke and mud, and no hot water. One of the things I like most about living at Glaumbaer is the hot spring. Once a week, before Sunday, we can wash. It's a good charm against evil to wash away what is past. In Greenland that wasn't usually possible. This isn't a clean country either, but that doesn't seem to matter where the sun can drive away evil things.

At Herjolfsnes the ghosts thrived in the dirt and the hunger and the dark. There was a man there who was possessed. He used to scream and beat against the walls, and at night he would rush around the room and pull the furs off the people on the sleeping benches, telling them to rise and defend us all. We had to tie him up in the end.

It sounds to you like a nightmare, perhaps, but the people never despaired. Even then I could see enough to realise how much of that was owing to Herjolf himself, and his son Bjarni. In Iceland people still mock at Bjarni Herjolfsson, because he was the first to sight Vinland, and he didn't even bother to land. I can understand it. Bjarni is a man of one thought at a time, and his goal on that voyage was to find his father. You know how it happened, don't you? How Herjolf went off that summer with Eirik, when Bjarni was in Norway, and when Bjarni got home his father had gone, leaving a message to follow him to Greenland? So Bjarni did. My father said he had no imagination. But my father was jealous, of course, because he himself had failed to go with Eirik that first time, and he paid for it in prestige all his life. It counted in Greenland to be able to say you were one of the first settlers. Bjarni had a rich cargo to bring to his father; he'd have been a fool to risk it exploring new lands, with autumn coming on. He did the right thing, Karlsefni always said so. Karlsefni always said, too, that if Bjarni had taken the first land, there might be a Vinland settlement to this day. I'm not saying all the blame lies with Eirik's family. Karlsefni played a part in it too. But Karlsefni had no reason to be jealous, and he was able to admit that in some ways Bjarni would have been the better man.

Anyway, I spent a winter on the edge of death with Bjarni Herjolfsson to guide us, and I found that I could trust him. He was a pagan, like his father, but faith seemed to come to him by nature.

There had been a Christian at Herjolfsnes, a Celtic freedman from the Hebrides. This man had gone to Eiriksfjord for the winter, as Eirik's wife Thjodhild had asked for him. Herjolf said Thjodhild wanted him to talk to her about the new religion. My father was relieved. It had occurred to him that his own baptism might be a distinct drawback in Greenland. Eirik had not been the kind of man to appreciate new gods.

'He still isn't,' said Herjolf, when Thorbjorn asked him about it. 'But Thjodhild wants to hear about them all the time. It's not a happy situation. But you'll see for yourself. I think it would be safer if we didn't discuss the matter here.'

My father might well consider changing his religion if it were expedient, but I wanted to make it clear that I wouldn't. Not because I was deeply religious, I'm afraid, but because I despised my father, and that made me behave like a prig. 'I hope to find Christians at Eiriksfjord,' I said. 'I'm glad you're sympathetic to them here.'

Herjolf ignored me, but Bjarni looked at me thoughtfully. When the others had gone to haul up my father's ship to her winter berth, he called me over to him, and showed me an inscription burnt into the headboard above his bed. 'Can you read that?'

'No.'

'Then I'll recite it to you:

I beseech my Master
To steer my journeys.
May the Lord of heaven
Hold his hand over me.

'That's what it says, as far as I remember. I'm not one of your Christians, but I respect the maker of that. He carved it for me before he went to Brattahlid. I wouldn't be surprised if Thjodhild were convinced by what he says. But you'll see.'

I got Bjarni to say the words until I knew them, and I've used them as a charm ever since. The best charms are just words. They're easy to carry about, and on the whole you don't lose them. I felt that Bjarni was my friend after that. I liked Herjolf too. He was a tolerant man, and a good master. He was under a great strain that winter, accepting that the fate of the whole settlement was his responsibility. He was convinced that the land was possessed by an evil spirit, and at Midwinter he sent for a woman in Thorkel's household, who was known for her skill in witchcraft.

When the witch Thorbjorg came, I'll admit that at first she made an impression on me. She certainly took to me. I think she wanted me to be like her. She was quite different from Halldis in that she liked to make a show of things, and I think she enjoyed the performance of what she did even more than she cared about the substance. But I couldn't dismiss her. I wanted to, because I'd given my loyalty to a different faith, but I recognised what she was doing, and something in me responded to it. I performed my part just as well as she performed hers, and I was awed by the vision that she had.

I don't want to describe anything to do with witchcraft here. It doesn't belong in this sunlit cloister. The woman herself must be dead long since, and it all happened in another country. If I think about it I see things too much from her point of view, and I don't want to.

*I, Thorbjorg, am summoned to Herjolf's hall at Midwinter in the year of the worst famine, and this is what I see.*

*I sit in the High Seat at Herjolf's table. I see the men who have been lost on hunting trips, the men who never returned from the fishing, the* women who died after giving all their food to their children. I see the babies who never lived to know their own names. I see strangers too, soaked with seawater, a larger company than the living guests among us. For the first time in this new country the dead outnumber the living. The time of innocence is already past.

Living and dead crowd around the board, their white skin stretched against their bones. The eyes of the living glitter with hunger, but the eyes of the dead are empty. I see a young girl with a pale face and sores on her hands. Two ghosts hover over her as she sits close to the high seat, her eyes fixed on my face. When the meal, such as it is, is over, I prepare the sacred things. I watch her face as I do so, and I see that she knows very well what I am about.

I ask for a woman to help me by singing the spell, because I know that she is the only person there who may be able to do so. But she does not come forward. Instead she lowers her eyes, and twists her hands together. I wait for someone else to speak to her. As I expect, Herjolf repeats my request. 'Is there anyone here who can sing the spell? Say now, because our lives this winter may depend on it.'

Slowly she answers him. 'I'm not a witch, but in Iceland my foster mother Halldis taught me to sing the spell you mean.'

'Then come.' I sense Herjolf's uneasiness, and when she answers I know why.

'I told you I was a Christian. I can't take part in this.'

She says this, and yet she brings no new gods with her into Herjolf's hall. We had a Christian here before, and his god did not acknowledge me. Unlike him, this girl knows exactly what I am. I wait for Herjolf to settle the matter.

'Gudrid, you're our guest here. We've shared with you all that we have, when you know that our own survival hangs in the balance. What more could we do for you? Perhaps you can save us all. I don't see how you can possibly refuse.'

She is silent for a moment, twisting her fingers together. 'You're right,' she says at last. 'I can't refuse.'

I guess her power before I hear her sing, but once I hear her I feel it in every bone in my body. The note hums through the circle we have made, and before my eyes I see the sacred images grow, a tree of plenty springing from dry twigs. I see spring blossom out of winter, while hunger and disease flee into perpetual darkness. I see our settlement grow and flourish until the passing generations vanish into mist. And I see a young woman passing through our Green Land on a terrible journey beyond the boundaries of the living world. I see a ship sail east until it raises the shore of Iceland just as the sun sets, and the woman, no longer young, stands at the helm. And her power is so much greater than mine will ever be, that I know I have come on this long journey only to prepare her way.

# SIX

# *July 12th*

I hated Thorbjorg. She compromised me, using me as she did, and it affected the whole of my life afterwards. I was young, remember; I didn't realise how serious it was. I thought she was an old fool, and I hated her because she pretended to be what my foster mother had been. Remember too, I'd only just lost Halldis. Nothing was said about that. My father didn't talk to me, and no one at Herjolfsnes had known her or Orm. Death in Greenland is too commonplace to make a fuss about. Sometimes I wonder if I have ever got over that voyage, those deaths. They were my fault, you see. Halldis came for love of me, and Orm came because he loved her. It's been dangerous for people, loving me.

I was bewitched, I know that now. That's a strong word, and I see you flinch. Don't be afraid of me, Agnar. There's nothing to fear now. Karlsefni broke the spell over forty years ago, and that's why I still thank God for him every day. Every day I thank God for him. He took me out of hell, but I'm running ahead of my story. Where was I . . . ? Oh yes, the witch at Herjolfsnes. I hated her, Agnar, I hated her.

\*    \*    \*    \*    \*

Sorry, what did you say? Was I dreaming? I am sorry. Yes, all that winter she pursued me. That's what it felt like. She actually lived at the far side of the settlement from Herjolf's hall. But after the spell was cast, she kept coming back to see me. I didn't realise then what she'd done to me. She never mentioned it. Maybe she was gloating; I just thought she was a nuisance. No, not that – but I despised her, and showed it as much as I dared. It was a confusing time for me, Agnar. I was so young, and had just been shocked out of childhood by that cruel journey. I craved to be ordinary, and that's what I have never been able to be. There were girls my age at Herjolfsnes. I tried so hard to be one of them. I learned to look at men sideways and giggle about them afterwards. We used to sit in the byre, where it was warm from the kye. There was a girl called Inghild, who was a sort of leader among them. She used to sit up on the bull's back, where he was penned in among his cows, daring him, I suppose. He was so wedged in he couldn't move, and the cattle were all exhausted from hunger. If they hadn't been held up by one another they'd not have had the strength in their legs to stand. That bull used to roll its eyes and snort when Inghild climbed on to her perch, but he never budged. The rest of us used to sit up on the wooden partitions in the dark. I can smell the place now. The roof was only just above our heads by springtime, the floor of muck had risen so far. It was the only place to go that was warm, where there were no grown-ups, and no men. When I smell a byre in winter, it always takes me back to that time.

We talked about sex. I knew all about it, of course, from Halldis. But she used to tell me facts. I never, ever, saw Halldis giggle. I wonder if she ever did when she was young? The only time I joked about sex – it was the only chance I ever got – was in that byre. It's strange, when you think about it. We were always hungry, cold, and dirty, crouched there in the dark, and yet there was still this secret excitement among us. So much more exciting than the event, as it turned out. It was as if we expected to be rescued. Not in the way you might think: for a man like you, the life I've described might seem like something to be rescued from. But those girls in Greenland knew nothing else, and expected nothing else. Winter is always winter. No, I'm talking about another kind of rescue: it was as if we hoped that marriage to some dull youth would rescue us from ourselves. The only man I felt could do that was Bjarni Herjolfsson, but he was already married, and I'm sure he never looked at me. But already I was less innocent than the rest of them. Some had more experience of sex than me, but none had my burden of guilt. Did I honestly believe that some man might rescue me from that? I half knew already that I'd been bewitched.

Thorbjorg used to seek me out. For weeks the snow was too thick, and when she didn't come I tried to forget about her. But as soon as they'd made a path I saw her picking her way down the hillside. Wearing her old cloak she looked to me like a great black crow, with the white snow behind her. My only refuge was the byre, but for the first time in weeks the sun shone, and the wind was still. I could feel the smell of indoors, hall and byre, all over me, and I wanted the clean air to take it away. There was no way to go but the path the men had dug. So she found me, and I took refuge in being sulky. I wouldn't talk to her, but she talked at me. If Halldis had been there she'd have sent her off quick enough. But I was a guest in Herjolf's house, and Herjolf was afraid of the witch because his people were hungry and she had the power. I had to stay there, like a fly in a web, and let her talk.

That night I dreamed she came flying at me and swallowed me up, and then I was her, the wings of my old cloak beating through the snow-filled night.

Other people knew it, too. Herjolf himself began to treat me with a kind of deference that frightened me. I didn't want to be set apart. And on one of our last evenings crushed in the byre Inghild asked me to tell fortunes. 'Me?' I said, 'I can't do that. I don't know how.' 'Oh yes you do,' she said. 'We all saw you. You sang the song for Thorbjorg. You're a witch, Gudrid. Don't pretend you're not. Isn't she?' God help me, they all said yes, and they weren't laughing either.

The snow was melting at last, and at night I lay in my bed listening to the rush of water. My father was anxious to get to Eirik's settlement, and though Herjolf was polite, he was just as anxious to have us gone. A hungry winter means a hungrier spring, and Herjolf had staked everything on an early hunting trip. Every day both men would scan the ice, and though they said nothing to each other, I knew exactly what was passing through their minds. I was just as anxious as my father to get out, and one day, when the sky was a clear pale blue, and the north wind had died down to a breeze like a cut from a small knife, I decided to speak to him. I told him about the witch, and my dream, and the guilt that pursued me.

'I don't want to take it with me,' I said to him. 'I want to be ordinary.'

He looked thoughtful. 'You're a pretty girl, Gudrid,' he said. It was the first time in my life he'd ever mentioned my looks, and unfortunately it was too late for me to care. 'It's time you were married. That'll put an end to all this nonsense. We must get you a good man.'

I stood in front of him so that he couldn't walk on. 'You won't do that,' I told him, 'if they think I'm a witch. You mustn't let that idea travel to Eiriksfjord with us.'

'If you want to leave it behind you, you need to put it out of your head.'

'It's more than that. Listen, father, we're Christians, aren't we?'

He paused. 'I'm not sure we want to make so much of that, with Eirik. We'll see how the land lies.'

'No, but listen. If we make it clear to Eirik's household that we're Christians, they can't possibly think I've had anything to do with witchcraft. Men like Christian wives; you saw that in Iceland. Christianity makes women safe and dutiful. You don't have to tell Eirik Raudi you're an enemy of Thor. Just tell him that as a Christian, you disapproved of the witchcraft at Herjolfsnes, and it's the same for everyone in your household.'

'You think that'll help?'

'It would make me feel better.'

'You'd put this witchcraft idea out of your head, then?'

'I would.'

'And if I can arrange a good marriage for you in Eiriksfjord, you'd like that?'

'Of course I would.'

'Very well then, but you must leave me to do what's politic.'

'But you'll tell them we're Christians?'

'Yes, I'll do that.'

It was the most satisfactory conversation I'd ever had with my father, and indeed, it did turn out to be a turning point between us. We'd been among strangers all winter, and that maybe had something to do with it.

I think my father was as relieved as I was to leave Herjolfsnes. We weren't ungrateful. Herjolf had saved our lives when his own community was at risk. Not, of course, that we were destitute. My father gave him good gifts when they parted, but gold isn't much use when you're starving. Anyway, Herjolf lived to enjoy his wealth, and he deserved all the good luck that came to him.

The gift that Bjarni gave me I used for the first time before we ever left the bay at Herjolfsnes. It worked, too. Our ship had been repaired, and we had plenty of provisions, and we were sailing within sight of an inhabited – more or less – coast, with men of Herjolf's to guide us. Bjarni had originally suggested coming with us himself, but Herjolf said, 'Better not.' I saw him meet Bjarni's eyes. Father and son looked at each other for a moment, then Bjarni said, 'Very well. Better not.' I was sorry. The voyage seemed simple, but it was still early in the year, with the pack ice only just breaking up in the fjords. We followed a lead between islands while the ice mountains of Greenland shone to the north of us. After a while the land fell away, so we stood out to sea, still heading north-west. There was nothing green about the land, and yet this voyage was far from chaos. The orderly spirit of Bjarni Herjolfsson, who had ignored those unknown lands and made, after all the storms, a perfect landfall at the place his father had described to him, seemed to watch over us. I said my charm, and the white mountains glinted in the sun, and the swell rocked us kindly as we slowly raised new islands, and slowly, slowly, came even with them and passed them by.

Eventually we raised the mountain we'd been looking for, a long way inland, marking the hidden entrance to Eiriksfjord. Landlocked now, we passed the island where Eirik wintered when he was exploring this new country, and saw the remains of his camp above the shore. There was still no sign of the way into Eiriksfjord, but we had our sailing directions, and kept to the east of the mountain, threading our way through the ice, and, at the last moment, it seemed, a new channel of water opened up in front of us. And then we were sailing with the ghost of a breeze between the sides of a fjord, the like of which I'd never seen before. The water between the ice was charcoal grey, with barely a ripple. A great grey mountain rose on our right, and grew closer, and on the far side of it we passed a narrow fjord that ended in a steep glacier. Blue icebergs towered over us, threatening to bar the way, and then suddenly we were in clear water. The eastern side of the fjord was still sheer and forbidding, but to the west lay a low line of grey-green hills, with a sharp range of snow mountains behind them. We drew into the shore, and saw a place where the hill was green and smooth between the rocks. There was a stony beach below, and soon we saw that the shapes on it were not boulders or seals but boats. On the slope above, the regular green knolls resolved themselves into turf-roofed buildings, and smoke rose from the roof of the nearest. Cattle and sheep grazed on a hillside already starred with dandelions, the first spring flowers, and as we stood into the western shore there came a smell of growing grass that brought tears to my eyes, because it smelt of home.

I'm tired now, Agnar. It's a long time since I let myself remember so much. Have the rest of the day to yourself. Go for a ride in the hills. It's not natural for a young man to be indoors all day. Go on, off with you. I want to be alone now, but you'll find me here tomorrow.

# SEVEN

# July 14th

*July at Brattahlid. Gudrid Thorbjarnardottir sits at the door of Eirik
Raudi's house with Eirik's daughter Freydis. They are scraping sheepskins
to soften them, but neither is working very hard. White clouds sail slowly
over the fjord, and the sun shines between them. The fjord is ice-blue, and
small waves lick at a stray berg that is stranded offshore. Below the
mountain called Burfjell on the opposite shore, a line of newly calved
icebergs seems to block the way to the sea, but here at Brattahlid it is high
summer. The doors of the long byre are thrown open, and the winter dung
is piled outside ready for spreading. Hay is ripening in the fields, and
around the house hens scrape the trodden soil. The angelica that grows
near the door is level with the house roof, and its flowers are entangled
with the lines of fish hanging up to dry. On the beach below the house
swarms of flies hover over drying seaweed, and two men are patching the
hull of an upturned boat.*

*Gudrid Thorbjarnardottir is happy. Eirik's house is built in a safe
place, sheltered from behind by an outcrop of rock, and its walls are
strongly built of turf and stone. His pastures are good; he has twenty-
seven cows and nearly fifty sheep, with this year's lambs. Every day his
men come in with boatloads of salmon or cod, and yesterday his sons
came home with a cargo of caribou, seal and whalemeat from the
northern hunt. There is going to be plenty to eat here, and hunger and
bad dreams seem far away.*

*Gudrid is a beautiful young woman, and she is new here. There are not
enough women in this land, and Eirik Raudi has three sons. He needs
grandsons, because in this place he intends to found a dynasty, rulers of the*

Green Land, and of the lands further west where there is untold wealth for men who have the courage to take it. Eirik has had twelve years to make his mark here. The Green Land will be his and his sons' for ever. But just now he is on the look-out for suitable young women. His son Leif left for Norway three days before Thorbjorn turned up with his daughter. That was fate at work; if Leif had been at home Eirik would have had Leif and Gudrid married before the summer was out. He could always give her to Thorvald or Thorstein, but his instinct is to wait until next spring, for Leif to come back. Eirik's wife Thjodhild is also waiting for Leif to come back. Although her eldest son laughs at her new faith, he is attached to her, and he will honour his promise to her, to bring a priest back with him from Norway, and the consecrated vessels for a church. Eirik knows nothing of this, but he sees clearly that his younger sons Thorvald and Thorstein admire Gudrid, and there are other men here seeking women. Eirik keeps his eye on Gudrid, and makes her father so very welcome that Thorbjorn is overcome. He had no idea he meant so much to Eirik Raudi, or that Eirik had waited so eagerly all these years for his coming.

As Gudrid sits at Eirik's door, she considers the meaning of the warm welcome that she and her father have been given. The sound of trotting hooves interrupts her train of thought, and a pony appears from the shore path, and breaks into a canter. The rider is Eirik's youngest son Thorstein. Stirrupless, he rides easily, holding the reins in one hand. He doesn't look round, but canters across the top of the beach, and out of sight behind the bank of the stream. Gudrid watches him until he has gone.

Gudrid Thorbjarnardottir is happy, and yet her foster parents died for her sake, and she has not atoned for the death she brought to them. Only one winter has passed since then. The past is terrible, so terrible that she has locked it away in one corner of her mind where for the present it cannot escape. Only sometimes she is aware that there is something she should have done that she has not done, and that by living in this sunlit world as if she were an innocent woman, she is tempting a worse fate. Sometimes she has bad dreams, but when she wakes in the night she sees light at the chimney hole, and the soft breathing of the women of Eirik's household surrounds her. She has only to put out her hand to touch

*Freydis, who sleeps beside her. Freydis is a square, solid girl with her father's build and none of his charm. Apart from a grim insistence on having her own way, she seems harmless enough. There is no evidence that she has bad dreams.*

*Sometimes Gudrid's own good fortune overwhelms her. She is a young girl again now, and that is all. Men are attracted to her. Maybe she will marry one of Eirik's sons. Maybe she will have children, and work with the other women on this farm in the sheltered fjord under the ice mountains, and life will be ordinary. The peril that she fears seems far away in the household of Eirik Raudi. There are other dangers, certainly, but they belong to the waking world. The family quarrel with their neighbours, and with each other, but there have been no killings in the Green Land. They dream of wealth, and seem to feel no guilt. Theirs, at the moment, is a daylight world, and Gudrid is reassured. She would like to belong to it for ever.*

Agnar, would you say that you were happy?

\*     \*     \*     \*     \*

I'm glad you don't think it's wrong to talk to me sometimes. It seems that for both of us happiness is about the past, and about a place. I wasn't always happy at Brattahlid, far from it, just as you've been unhappy sometimes at Reims. But the innocent times exist, just as much as the other. You'll find that when you're old. Sometimes the early days are so near, I wouldn't be surprised to open my eyes in the morning and find myself there, a girl on a summer morning at Brattahlid. She still exists, you know. I don't just mean in mind and memory.

And now I'm thinking too of a boy at the Cathedral school in Reims, who discovered through new learning that the boundaries of the world were greater than he thought. I've never heard any stories from these authors that you mention, but you speak of them as Karlsefni spoke of Bjarni Herjolfsson, or Bjorn the champion of Breidavik. You're an Icelander, and of course you respond to sailing directions. It's in your blood. These men you speak of – this Cicero,

Seneca, and the other one – these are the men who gave you directions for your voyage into an unknown world. Yes, and I understand how you got hurt too, in fact I should say it was inevitable. We're only human, and we need an authority to tell us where the boundaries are. Oh, I understand you had to disobey. How could you not? Another headland, another island, another fjord: promises, always promises of riches yet to come, and if you go a little further the dream may become real. The gifts of this life are boundless, but it's still dangerous to go too far.

\*     \*     \*     \*     \*

Don't ever regret what you have done. I don't believe in advice. No one takes it, and usually they hate you for giving it, but if you were my son I'd tell you what I think. You'd have punished yourself more if you'd turned your back on the way that was opened to you. You'd never have forgiven yourself. I know nothing of your Clunyites; I've always hated feuds, but men must have them. Very well, so these men say that you were wrong to study pagan gods. Your master whom you loved defied his archbishop, and went so far beyond the pale that he turned to the infidel, and actually went to the country of the Saracens to find out about ancient writings and the stars. Karlsefni would have done the same. I know that means nothing to you. Karlsefni isn't in your Church; he has no authority for you. But he knew the call you know, to go on, and on, beyond the limits we've made for ourselves. He knew the importance of the stars, although he never heard the word you use, astronomy. You call it an art. To me, it's the heart of the mystery, the thing that gives meaning to all sailing directions, which we in our ignorance do our best to follow. You wince; you think I blaspheme, and maybe I do. We were punished, as you'll hear, not outwardly, of course; there was no Pope or Cardinal for us. But I think you and I are haunted by the same thing. We've both gone too far. We've seen too many ghosts. Isn't your trouble now, Agnar, not that you have been reprimanded by your Church for pursuing pagan knowledge, but that you know that the world they tell you to stick to is not the

70

whole truth? You've brought something back from the wilds with you, that eats away at your faith. Isn't that it?

\*    \*    \*    \*    \*

I'm sorry, maybe I shouldn't have spoken. How did I get on to that? Oh yes, happiness. I was telling you about our first year at Brattahlid.

I was happy, although surrounded by tensions. The relief was that they weren't mine. Feeling detached, as I did, I began to enjoy the drama. It may seem wicked to you, but I enjoyed the sexual tension too. I'd never been fought over before. It was foolish to think I'd get away unscathed, but I wasn't part of Eirik's family yet, and I thought I was still free.

Eirik welcomed my father as if they had been foster brothers. I hadn't realised they were that close; in fact they weren't. Eirik Raudi seems when you first meet him to be a bluff, simple sort of man, but in fact he's as devious as a salmon. He rules – ruled – his Green Land with a wiliness which would do credit to your Lateran. When I say ruled, I mean it. A few of the settlers were also chieftains in their new territories, but there was nothing like the Thing Quarters that we have in Iceland. When we first went to Greenland, disputes in both settlements were referred to Eirik at Brattahlid. One chief can't be the whole of the law, and Eirik had the sense never to claim to be anything but a chieftain among his peers.

In fact the very first summer I stayed at Brattahlid they had the first meeting of the Greenland Thing. It was carefully arranged that the meeting should not be at Eirik's house, and so the first booths were built about a mile to the south, so as to seem like no man's territory. Who came? Einar of Gardar, of course, with his son Thorkel, who later married Freydis, God help him. She had her eye on him even then, because Gardar is one of the richest farms in Greenland, now that they've drained that marshy plain. Who else? Thorkel of Hvalsey, Ketil, Hrafn, Thorbjorn from Siglufjord, Hafgrim from Vatnaherfdi, and, to my father's embarrassment, Snorri Thorbrandsson and his brother Thorleif, old enemies from the Snaefelsnes feuds. They'd arrived the year before and wintered at Dyrnes. Eirik said nothing about old grievances, and my father had to agree to do the same. Eirik was more interested in colonising his new land now than in pursuing old quarrels. No one came from the Western Settlement, but as it was, I was amazed to see how many neighbours we had, scattered among the apparently empty fjords. But Eirik Raudi always came first among them, not only because he was the first settler, but by sheer force of personality.

I had a child's memory of him, as a great, red man towering over everything in our hall. I was a woman now, but that first impression was never quite superseded. Eirik's family were unruly, to say the least of it, and the other settlers were proud and independent men, but Eirik never failed to dominate them until the day he died. You have to understand that if you're to understand our lives in the Green Land.

In a way it was funny to see how Eirik's status had changed. Although my father had always admired him, most people at home had regarded Eirik as a notorious outlaw. In Snaefelsnes we were glad to see the back of him, for he caused nothing but trouble. After he'd left I mainly heard evil spoken of him. His partisans, you see, apart from Thorbjorn, had gone with him. It was typical of my father to be the only one who was twelve years late. As I say, Eirik welcomed him like the lost sheep returned to the fold.

Eirik in Greenland was the same man as the troublemaker of the Westfjords, but in another role. Here, he didn't defy the law, he embodied it. Lawman and outlaw – they're only two sides of the same coin. Each recognises exactly the same boundaries. No one should be surprised, and yet they always have been, that Eirik the lawless should end up ruling the most peaceful country in all the Norse lands.

He had two allies, and I don't mean his sons. The first one I recognised at once, although I didn't take in the implications. In Greenland we had hardly any fermented drink. Does that help you understand why the promise of wine from Vinland meant so much? I'm sure that's why our gatherings passed off so peacefully, but I don't suppose men would agree with me. So there was Eirik, presiding over a country where there were, as far as I could see, no feuds happening at all. His other ally, of course, was the land. If there were a quarrel, a band of raiders couldn't just gallop over to the next valley. They'd have to make a difficult sea voyage. Besides, they were busy. They had to hunt in the summer, if the community were to stay alive. It was the ghost of winter, really, that kept the peace. Even on the lightest days of summer, one could never forget that grim spirit that stalked among our meadow flowers. Whatever we ate when things were plentiful, we had to save more than as much again for the long months to come. At home the cattle are in the byre eight months, but although it rains more in summer, there's more time to make hay, and the winters are never quite so hard. In Greenland every mouthful more than bare necessity is like a gift straight from God. So Eirik had the land on his side, and that was worth more than the army of King Charles the Great himself.

He was a kind of emperor. Here in Rome, I try to see him as a little chieftain of a far-off land, so poor that Eirik was filled with shame when he couldn't feast his guests in the traditional way. I look at the great church of St John at the Lateran, and in my mind I see a hall whose turf roof might reach to the foot of those arched windows. I look at the corn fields and vineyards that surround this city, and I see a hillside scattered with cattle, an island of green balanced between wastes of sea and ice. In winter the whole settlement at Brattahlid is invisible under the snow. Emperors must fight, and hold their own. In Europe they fight one another, while the poor folk struggle to go on living. In the Green Land, a great man must be more than an emperor. He must be like a peasant, and fight the land itself. I think they will tell stories about Eirik Raudi, when Pope Leo and even your Cardinal Hildebrand have been entirely forgotten.

Don't look round so nervously. You know no one could understand us even if they were listening. You've said a thing or two yourself that might interest the Holy Father. No one will ever know, Agnar, unless you're fool enough to write these bits down.

When I talk to you about Eirik he seems so close. He was so alive that death can't destroy his image. I see him now, standing behind you in the corner there. You stoop over your desk, but he stands upright, and he watches us both keenly. He lived by his judgement of men. I never knew him wrong about that. Even his partiality for his sons – I can't call it love, Eirik did not love – never made him misjudge them. He admired Leif most, I think, and trusted him least. Leif was very like his mother, to look at, anyway.

I didn't meet Leif until a year after we arrived, and yet I was always aware of his presence, his place at Brattahlid and his effect on the family, right from the day I landed. In a way his influence was more potent in his absence.

Eirik's family were overwhelming. They seemed to have been living in public so long that they just ignored the fact. Like emperors. There were often guests at Brattahlid. New settlers were still arriving, and sometimes they'd stay the first winter with Eirik. In summer, traders and hunters would come and go. Men would come down from the Western Settlement, and leave their goods for Iceland at Brattahlid, for they trusted Eirik to act as their agent. Besides all that, there was the community at Eiriksfjord. Eirik had given land to his friends and dependants, and Brattahlid itself was worked by Eirik's thralls and freedmen who lived round about. The hall was the centre of all this activity, and there Eirik's family would carry on with their lives, always shouting and bickering, encouraged if anything by the presence of an audience. When my father and I were with them, that first year, I used to watch them enact their quarrels, almost, it seemed, for our benefit. Sometimes Thjodhild or Freydis would glance our way to see how we were taking it. Eirik would magnificently ignore us, and his sons tried to do the same, but their performance was less convincing.

Eirik's two younger sons, Thorvald and Thorstein, were at home. Leif had left for Norway three days before we arrived. We must have passed his ship, and probably he put into Herjolfsnes just a day or so after we left. Sometimes I think how it might have happened. Perhaps our ship was lying to in a fjord one night, when Leif's trading ship slipped past us in the dawn light. Or perhaps Leif, who was the most daring sailor of them all, had taken a course to the seaward side of all the sheltering islands, while we hugged the coast and took advantage of the sheltered channels. It was still early in the year, remember, with a great risk of ice out at sea. I remember that the wind was south-westerly. It was a fate that made us miss one another. Eirik thought so too, I'm certain. He would have married me to Leif, if things had been different. But there it was; Leif was on his way to Norway, and, three days after his departure, a girl who must have seemed to Eirik both beautiful and eligible turned up on his threshold at Brattahlid.

Halldis had been right. Lack of dowry mattered much less in Greenland. Wealth was children, who would grow up to inherit vast lands, and who could hunt and farm and trade for their parents when they were old. But there was a shortage of coin to buy that wealth – by that I mean women. Too many of the settlers were related and of course there were more men to start with anyway. After twelve years a new generation of young men needed wives. That was one reason why Leif went to Norway. Thorstein was fairly sure his brother would come home with a wife, and so he would have done, no doubt, if he hadn't made a complete mess of the business.

So there was Eirik treating me with special favour, making my father the most honoured of his guests, and there were Thorstein and Thorvald, prowling round the place like a couple of bears on an ice floe, with their eyes always on me. I'm no saint, Agnar, and I hadn't had much of a youth so far. I revelled in it, and without really knowing it, I think I teased them unmercifully, though I hardly said a word.

The women were more complicated. Freydis was younger than me, and couldn't spend half an hour with her stepmother without quarrelling. I was appalled by her rudeness. Halldis would have beaten me if I'd spoken to her like that. Thjodhild just ignored it. Freydis didn't like me; I think she was jealous, though she can hardly have wanted the attentions of her brothers. Or could she? I wouldn't put anything past Freydis. Certainly she resented my presence in her father's house, in her mother's room, in her own bed. There was something else going on, I could tell, and fairly soon Thjodhild told me what it was.

*Thjodhild, the wife of Eirik, stands at the door of the sheiling hut where the sheep are milked in summer. It is evening, close to milking time, and she has told Gudrid and Freydis to meet her here. The ewes in milk are beginning to make their way over the rocky slopes, with an occasional clink of hoof on rock. The evening is calm, and the sun touches the pastures with gold before it drops behind the mountains. Sunlight cannot be treasured up, except as a fading memory, but there are other treasures that endure. These are the best pastures in the Green Land, on the low isthmus between two fjords. Once Eirik promised Thjodhild a land where the cattle would flow with milk, where the hunting would bring a living fit for kings, where men could take what pastures they chose and be free. She had allowed him to lead her here, with their children and their cattle and all that they had. It had been a hard journey, out of the old world and into the new. Sometimes the land is everything that he had promised; sometimes it is so cruel that she wants to drop dead from weariness. But now Thjodhild has heard a different kind of promise, brought to Brattahlid by Herjolf's Celtic thrall, who tells her of one who will bring the dead back to life, and give the weary everlasting rest.*

*The thrall has gone now with Leif, who will take him back to Herjolfsnes on his way to Norway. His departure was a hard loss, for all winter while she stood at her loom in the women's room, Thjodhild had Herjolf's thrall to talk to her. She listened to his stories again and again, until now she has them by heart. She can say them for herself now, but not out loud. Her family will not listen, only the thralls flock eagerly to hear this new story, which offers them a freedom they have never dared to dream of. Thjodhild is Eirik's wife, and she cannot be led by her own slaves. Even if she cared so little for decorum in this world, she is too loyal to Eirik to shame him in that way.*

*Already the new promise threatens him. He grumbles, and says, 'Aren't I enough for you? Has Thor ever let you down? Could our voyage to the Green Land possibly have been easier? Don't you see that a good luck has always been ours, and that you're tempting it to desert us? Are you mad, woman? What else can you possibly want?*

*None of her children believe what she now knows. Only Leif is sympathetic. He laughs at her, and puts his arm round her as his father never does, and says, 'As you wish, mother. You're a canny woman. You have your own way of doing things.'*

*He suspects her of something more devious than a vision, which is unfair. It is Leif who is devious, but he should be the one to understand.*

*Of all her children, it is Leif who has the most visions of his own. Visions of wealth, maybe, but always wealth daringly come by. Leif is looking for something too.*

*Thjodhild takes in the sun on the green slopes as if she must remember it for ever. The precious light. She gazes downhill and sees a girl rapidly making her way up through the pastures, as if the steep hill were no toil to her at all. Thjodhild recognises Gudrid, and quietly walks down to meet her.*

# EIGHT

# *July 17th*

When I first met Thjodhild she reminded me a little of Halldis, and it took me a while to learn how different from her she really was. I was still shaken by my meeting with Thorbjorg. A witch like that should never have been in the Green Land, it seemed to me; her familiars were unclean things to bring into a new world. Thjodhild, Eirik's wife, on the other hand, seemed to be a woman of the daylight, but then it was spring when I met her. She was tall, like Halldis, and her hair had stayed white-fair like a child's. I was sometimes conscious of my Irish blood when I stayed at Brattahlid, because I was growing darker, compared with them anyway, though here in Italy they'd have called me fair. Now it makes no difference; old women are the same the world over.

Things flourished for Thjodhild. She had a way with animals, and I never saw so much milk, or such big, round cheeses, as those at Brattahlid. Her hens laid eggs right into the dark months, and more than half her sheep had twin lambs. The fleeces we took from them that autumn were as thick and greasy as any in Iceland. Most people think that the Green Land is a poor country, but I never saw a farm as well provided as Eirik's until I went to Norway. Thjodhild was one of those people for whom the desert flowers. In summer she used to gather plants, and found more than anyone would dream could grow in such a land. And of course she had borne three outstanding sons, who were strong men now, even by the standards of our country.

I think she would have liked a daughter. Her work obsessed her. I can remember seeing her out late at night, in the long twilight, still raking and turning the hay on the slopes across the stream from the hall. She was up before any of us, before the house thralls even. She would sit all night with a cow about to calf, if the birth was likely to be a hard one. Eirik used to say, 'Don't we have enough slaves? Come to bed, woman! You let these people eat their heads off at my hearth, and then you do their work for them!' But he respected her greatly, and rightly so. It was Eirik who said first that the land was lush and plentiful, but it was Thjodhild who made it so for him. Erik used words to make things into what he wanted them to be, but Thjodhild despised words. She listened to men as if they were children, encouraging, but not too bothered, I always thought, about what they actually meant. In a way I was wrong about that; later I realised that she did listen. If the men she loved spoke about their dreams, she worked like one of the fates to make them happen.

What I liked about Thjodhild was what she made. She made a wilderness into a green paradise, those first years at Brattahlid. Her house was always clean and warm. Whether she were feeding a shipload of settlers worn out by a hard voyage, or pulling out a child's bad tooth, as I saw her do the very day I arrived, she gave the matter the same wholehearted energy, and everything was done right.

To begin with I was afraid that I couldn't work hard enough for her. She only understood weakness in men who were wounded, or women who were pregnant, or in the very old, for whom she had a vast respect. Anyone else could never do enough. I needn't have worried. I think she saw in me all that Freydis was not. No wonder Freydis hated me. I couldn't understand that either, at first. Being so alone in my childhood, I always had a dream about a friend. I don't mean a man, I mean another girl. At Arnarstapi I used to imagine I had such a friend. Sometimes I used to look at my face reflected in the water butt, and imagine that was her. When I was alone I used to talk to her aloud. The only real girl of my own age and rank I ever lived with was Freydis, and she saw me as her supplanter, and did all she could to torment me. It's clearer to me now why she felt like that. She was Eirik's daughter, you see, but her mother was a thrall, and Thjodhild took her home and fostered her as if she were her own. That's typical of Thjodhild. I suppose I might have done the same for one of Karlsefni's bastards; I don't know. If he had any no one told me about it. But Freydis was angry with everyone. Her brothers were men, and legitimate, and so she hated them. In fact she hated men because they were men, and she hated any other woman who had been luckier than her. And yet who could be more privileged than Eirik Raudi's daughter at Brattahlid? She had hair the colour of buttercups, and she used to look at men sidelong, and drop her eyes. She wasn't really pretty, but she had more power over them than I ever did.

I had a talk with Thjodhild one evening, when she met me going up to the sheiling at milking time. I'd never talked alone with her before. She never stopped working to chat, unless there were something to say that mattered, and she came to the point at once.

'Gudrid, you're a Christian, aren't you? Are you baptised?'

I told her about Halldis, and Thangbrand the missionary, and the baptism at Arnarstapi.

'So you are of the faith. What does it mean to you?'

The question embarrassed me. I looked at the ground, and watched a clump of gentians in Thjodhild's shadow, slowly curling up their petals as if it were night. 'I don't know,' I muttered, but I was thinking about Thurid's story of the demon sitting astride the roof beam, banging against the turfs with his heels, so that the whole house shook. Thjodhild's question reminded me that I was afraid of ghosts.

'That won't do. You're a sensible girl, and you've had some hard experiences. Did you keep your faith on the voyage here?'

I saw in my mind's eye two men raising Halldis' body, where it lay shrouded in her wet cloak, and heaving it over the gunwale while the swell rose up to swallow it. 'No,' I said. 'I couldn't think about anything.'

'But if you are a Christian, you don't have to think. Your God is what you know.'

'I know one thing then,' I told her. 'I know that Thangbrand said that when God cast Lucifer out of heaven, he fell into the sea, and he lies there still. He is Jormungand, and he lies beneath the waters that surround this world. The sea is his kingdom, and Christ doesn't rule there. He wasn't on that ship with us.'

Thjodhild grabbed me by the shoulders and made me face her. 'But you're wrong, Gudrid, you're wrong! Herjolf's thrall told me another story. He told that when the disciples were in terror of their lives in the storm, Christ said to them, "Why are you scared? Don't you have any faith?" And he said to the wind and the waves, "Peace; be still!" and the storm died away at once.'

'Well,' I muttered, 'He wasn't on our ship. I don't believe he ever sailed on our seas.'

'But he was on your ship! Thangbrand brought him to you. He should have been in your heart!'

I wrenched myself away from her. 'No!' Suddenly I was crying, and that made me angry. 'No! No! No! I didn't make those things happen! It's not my fault! It's not! It's not!'

I would have run away, but although she was big she was always very quick, and she stopped me. 'Gudrid, wait. I'm not blaming you for what happened. I'm saying that the power of Christ is given into our hands. Into yours and mine. We are women, what can we do? This is a hard land, but if we have faith, we can move the very mountains. He told me so!'

All at once this wholesome woman sickened me. If were a man, I thought, I would have my own power, and I would fight to keep it with all the strength in my body. I'd kill my enemies and wrest a living out of the icefields. I wouldn't get involved with ghosts or spirits, white or black. I wouldn't be weak enough to need to bother. I wanted to hit Thjodhild. Her faith made me sick. 'No,' I said. 'My will isn't as strong as that. It's not my fault.'

'You don't understand, do you?' she said gently. 'We're all weak, God knows. But let me tell you something else. My son Leif has promised to speak to the king in Norway. King Olaf wants to make the whole world Christian. Leif will ask him to send us a priest. We can build our church then, our own church, here in the Green Land. If God has his house here, he can watch over us. He will be our shepherd, and he will guard the weak and the strong.'

Even though I was angry, that thought comforted me, and in spite of what she'd said, once again I warmed towards her. I was lonely, Agnar. I missed my foster mother. I was frightened of being in this world without anyone to guide me. I was afraid of my own strength. Mountains do move, sometimes, and ice falls, and the sea sends up great waves that wash away the land where we lead our fragile lives. I've lain at night in a wooden ship, and heard the ice cracking all round us, and felt the wave it makes when it crashes down into the sea. Shall I tell you the worst thing about being on a ship in a storm? What my real fear is? It's the urge to throw myself over. I see the swell come up to the gunwale, or the waves crash against the bow and drench us; I see great troughs open up under our bows; I see huge seas like moving mountains hurling down on to us; and what I want to do is to give in. I don't want to resist, Agnar, I want to go in. I want to throw myself headlong into the chaos that surrounds our little world.

'I would like a church,' I admitted to Thjodhild, although I was sullen still. 'A church built on a rock, like the house that stood when the storms came.'

She linked her arm in mine, and led me up to the sheiling, where the ewes were gathering. 'It'll be all right, Gudrid, we shall have our church.'

Thjodhild had arranged that all the Christians in Brattahlid should pray together on Sundays. If the weather was good we did this conspicuously at the milking ring, right in the middle of the settlement. Only when it was impossible to be outside did we retreat to the new women's room, which had been built on to the end of the hall that summer. These public meetings put my father in a very awkward position. The very mention of a new god made Eirik flame. 'Take away your milk-and-water gods, your god's for infants!' he used to shout. 'What kind of man do you want, if you fancy a god who hasn't the guts to lift a hand to save himself? Don't tell me stories about flocks of sheep! I want men like wolves! What kind of country do you think this is?'

So Thorbjorn kept his mouth shut, and didn't attend Thjodhild's meetings of thralls and women, where we shared out dried fish and buttermilk, because in the Green Land there is neither bread nor wine. I went, though, but it made me angry. In the end I felt so resentful and confused that I climbed up out of the settlement one day, and made a different kind of spell.

It wasn't just a spiritual confusion, it was my body protesting too. I was young. Like the sap in springtime, when you're young, humours rise in your body, and if you're a young girl, you want a man. It's the same itch the cattle feel; every living creature feels it, and I remember it quite well. At night I'd dream I was making love to a man, and I'd wake up heated and damp, and knowing exactly what I desired. I was angry with Thjodhild for always talking about her Christ, and never noticing that her two sons watched me like hunting wolves. I remember sitting at her Christian love feast, while I imagined the body of Thorstein Eiriksson pressed against my own, and when she passed me the sacrament I wanted to spit it out at her feet. There was a struggling spirit inhabiting me that wanted to be freed, and this woman, who seemed now to want me round her all the time, was weighing me down with stones of faith.

When we were all together harvesting the hay I just couldn't stand it any more, and I ran away up the hill, and looked down on tiny figures raking the hay into round coles. They were like mice against the giant Burfjell across the fjord. I laid out in front of me salt and ice, and tinder and flint to make a flame. The chant I used was one that Halldis taught me long ago. It was a song for harvest, a charm to bring plenty to last through the dark days ahead. I changed the words, though, because the fruition I wanted was for myself. I wanted a promise given to my body, not my soul. I wanted nothing more to do with the things that are not visible. I wanted the love that is of this world. I didn't want to meddle with mountains, or powers beyond my control. It was a fate that took Halldis and Orm, and none of my doing. The strong thing to do is to endure. It's only fear of fate that makes people want to control things for themselves, isn't it?

*Gudrid Thorbjarnardottir stands looking over Brattahlid and across the fjord to the empty mountains. She holds her right hand in front of her, and in the hollow of her upturned palm lies a little lump of salt. In her left hand she holds a taper of straw, and a frail flame burns slowly, flickering a little in the ghost of a breeze. She sings quietly, almost under her breath, but there is a small echo that gives her voice a resonance as if there were another singer who shared her voice. Gudrid at Brattahlid is thinner than the Gudrid of Arnarstapi. Her skin is tanned golden by wind and sun, and her hair is the colour of autumn leaves. Between her eyebrows there is the ghost of a line that will be etched in hard as the years ahead come by.*

*Gudrid Thorbjarnardottir carries her virginity like a burden. Ghosts trouble her. She asks for an anchor to this world. The flame burns out. She puts down the salt and squats down, laying her hands across the rocks at her feet. She asks to belong in the earth that she sees. She asks for the touch of the rock to be what is real to her. She asks to be protected from the things that she cannot see. She asks to be the wife of a strong man who will fight his enemies and provide for his own. She asks for his body to join with her body and make children, who will inherit a new country, rich with the wealth of this world, and free of anything that dwells beyond the boundaries of bodily life.*

*Gudrid Thorbjarnardottir steps out of the circle she has made, and releases the powers that held it. She sends them away with a blessing. She puts away the precious salt in the bag that hangs round her neck, and starts downhill over rocks and clumps of turf, running and jumping as easily as the skinny flocks that graze below. She ought to be helping with the harvest and she isn't. She has escaped Thjodhild, escaped work, escaped being good. She is free as a bird when nesting is over. A great weight has been lifted off her back, and she sees it in her mind, tumbling away in front of her down the hill to the cow pastures, knocking away the human concerns that huddle between the houses. She laughs out loud, and jumps off a big rock into clumps of lady's mantle and daisies. She looks up, about to run on, and sees in front of her Thorstein, Eirik's youngest son, hot from the hay harvest, his hair damp across his forehead, and his shirt hanging loose over his trousers.*

# NINE

# *July 20th*

Anyway, we'd better stop talking and go on with the work. We didn't do as much as we should have yesterday either, but I'm glad you told me more about those ruins on the Palatine hill. Have there been empires since the beginning of the world? It's not surprising; after all, gods and giants have always fought one another over who should rule the world of men. So there were gods in Rome too, before there were emperors? I never knew that before. What were their names?

\*     \*     \*     \*     \*

I don't know what you mean, when you say I must believe one thing and not another. You tell me a story about these Roman gods, and then you say I mustn't believe you. You shouldn't worry so much about whether things are, or aren't. What you should care about is whether they're bad or good. It doesn't matter what you believe, it's where you put your trust.

\*     \*     \*     \*     \*

No, I hadn't thought of Thorstein particularly before that day. I thought about Leif, whom I'd never seen. I suspected that Eirik had spoken to my father about making a match between me and Leif when Leif came home. Eirik treated me with special favour. He liked me to fill his cup for him. I used to take round a jug of buttermilk and pour it for the men as if it were wine. Eirik once said it tasted like wine, when I was the cup-bearer, and his two younger sons grinned across the table at one another.

That day on the mountain I talked seriously to Thorstein Eiriksson for the first time. He didn't say he'd followed me up there, and I didn't say what I'd been doing. He talked about his own concerns, but that's not unusual in a young man.

'It was Bjarni who found the new land,' he told me. 'That's a fate, in itself. He had never even thought of it before! He never even wanted to come so far as the Green Land. He just came back from Norway to Iceland with his cargo as usual, at the end of the summer, and found his father gone. He was given the message from Herjolf to follow him to the new country, and like a dutiful son he went. He's just a lump of a man, not a thought in his head. Would you believe he actually sighted a new country, actually saw the forests and the white beaches, sailed along the coasts, and never even bothered to land! All he could think about was getting home to his daddy!'

'But Thorstein, it was the end of the season, and he had a full cargo already. He needed to find Herjolfsnes before the weather changed.'

'But he had a new world at his feet! If he'd claimed it then, he could be the richest and most powerful of us all!'

'You wouldn't like it if he were.'

'No, but I'd think him more of a man.'

'I like Bjarni.'

'"Like!"' sneered Thorstein. 'That's about it.'

'And I respect him. We had a bad winter – you must know that, it can't have been much better here. We were hungry. People were ill. He was a good leader then, and that's a more difficult thing. It's all very well to find new lands, but hunger and sickness and winter and death will come with you, wherever you go. Would you deal with that better than Bjarni, do you think?'

I wasn't trying to taunt him, but he grabbed me by the arm, and made me face him. 'I'm a better man than Bjarni Herjolfsson, Gudrid, and I'll make you know it!'

I twisted out of his grip indignantly. 'Don't you touch me! I'm only saying that you judge him wrong.' And I couldn't resist adding, 'His crew don't agree with you, you know. They say he's a great sailor, a great navigator. They thought they were lost to direction entirely, but Bjarni worked it out. The winds were against him too, but he found his way back. It's much harder to find one farm than a whole continent, you know.'

Thorstein flushed like a girl. He had a fair skin and blushed easily, to the end of his life. 'It's easy to mock,' he said. 'You know I don't have a ship. It's not fair to throw that in my face.'

'I never did!'

'You do. You laugh at me because I've done nothing yet. How can I? Leif bought Bjarni's ship, and now he's gone to Norway in it. But I'll do more, I promise you. We've talked of it for years, my brothers and I. We haven't had our chance yet, but this place is ours, at the edge of an untouched world. We'll claim that land, I tell you, and the whole world will know it!'

'I'm not laughing at you.'

'We have the sailing directions. Bjarni gave them to my brother. If they'd been ours, we'd have guarded them with our lives, not given them away to anyone for the asking. If we'd had a ship we'd have fitted it out the very next season. Leif wanted to take my father's ship at once. But my father keeps it for the northern hunting, because he says everything we have depends on that, and the first thing is to make sure of our family's position in the Green Land. But the Green Land is nothing to what's out there in the west!'

'How do you know that?'

'Because Bjarni described to Leif what he had found.' Thorstein seized me by the shoulders, as his mother had done two weeks earlier, and looked me in the eyes. 'Gudrid, there's a land lying there for the taking. There are beaches for ships all along the shores. The forests have more timber than men could ever fell. There must be herds of deer roaming inland, and flocks of birds nest on all the islands offshore. There're seals and whales and cod, more fish in the sea than all the nets in the world could ever snare. Compared with the life we might have there, in this land of my father's we're only half alive.'

'And no men have ever reached this land before?'

'There was no sign of any human soul.'

'It sounds more like heaven than earth.'

'I don't care what you call it, it's ours. I'm going there myself, Gudrid. I dream of a ship, you know, night after night. When Leif comes back from Norway, there'll be two ships in my family. One for Leif, one for Thorvald, but one day there'll be one for me. I may be the youngest, but the youngest in the end is usually the luckiest of the three. You'll see, Gudrid. Would you go with a man to a new land? Would you marry a man who had a whole new world to call his own?'

'I might,' I said, not meeting his eyes, 'If it should ever happen.'

He seemed to consider for a moment before he spoke again, but he couldn't help giving himself away, his need was so great. 'Your father still has a ship,' he blurted out.

There is a moral there, Agnar, for all young women who think that their personal beauty is irresistible.

Poor Thorstein, he was belated all his life. Leif snatched away every dream of glory before Thorstein could even come at it. I talked to Thorstein often after that day. You know how it is, once you know someone, you wonder how your first conception of them could have been so false. I had thought at first that Thorvald and Thorstein were more or less interchangeable, two young wolves, but it wasn't so at all. Thorvald died a hero's death, but Thorstein did just as bravely. That's a woman's judgement, I know. Thorvald's death was a grand gesture, Thorstein's demanded that uncomplaining acceptance of a fate that takes away not only life but reputation too. Poor Thorstein! He was never tested against equal odds. But he won one thing which his brothers never got. You know what that was?

\*　　\*　　\*　　\*　　\*

You're not being very astute today, Agnar. Very well, I'll go on now to the following summer. For we spent another winter at Brattahlid, at Eirik's pressing invitation. My father said that we should claim land of our own without more delay, but Eirik put him off, and then said at last that his plan was to give us the land by the river on the opposite side of the fjord from Brattahlid, part of the vast holding he'd originally claimed for himself. The gift was a sign of great favour. Not only was Eirik not one to part easily with land, but also it showed that he wanted my father and his household nearby. I'm sure that Eirik's calculation was that the land would end up in the family anyway, for Thorbjorn had no child but me, and Eirik had settled it that I should be his daughter-in-law, one way or another. I knew what Thorstein wanted, and so I'm sure did his father, but no one spoke. We were all tacitly waiting for Leif.

It was still winter when Thorbjorn and I went to have our first look at our new holding. Thorstein drove us across Eiriksfjord on the big sledge. On the other side we left the track made by previous hoofprints and drove into an untouched white plain. Thorstein said this was a river bed, and flooded every spring, but now it was smooth and blank as the vellum you haven't written on yet, and our sledge made a single track across the pristine snow. Steep white slopes enclosed us, and it was hard to see where a steading could be built. On our way home the sky clouded over, and just as we reached Brattahlid the first flurry of a blizzard flew into our faces. It seemed a bleak prospect to exchange the snug hearth at Brattahlid for those blank slopes, but I told myself that twelve years earlier Brattahlid had been just as empty.

Leif never came home that winter. Eirik went around muttering against the son who would dare to seize the chance of a winter at the court in Norway, when his duty to his father was to return home with all the speed he could, and a full cargo. Thjodhild said nothing, but she used to pray at our meetings for all those at sea, and men in danger, although she never mentioned her own son specifically. I don't suppose, in spite of all her new faith, she wanted to tempt a fate. When you're at the edge of things, grim shadows are likely to get between you and the cross on which you try to fix your heart. Sometimes I think the shadow of the fates can reach even here, to the very tomb of St Peter.

That winter was far better than the last. It had been a good season, and even without the ship from Norway we had plenty, as the hunting parties in the north had been successful, and it had been a good year for hay, and the cattle were fat and healthy. It was a happy time. In the spring Thorbjorn and I prepared to leave. Eirik gave us cattle, as ours had not survived our voyage to Greenland, and a couple of extra thralls. I was a little afraid of how much we were growing in Eirik Raudi's debt. It was not that I was unwilling to do what he wanted, and marry into his family, it was just the weight of obligation, knowing that there was no other possibility open to me now. My father seemed entirely carefree. You know how improvident he could be and if I'd said I was anxious, he wouldn't have known what I was talking about.

By the time we moved to our new land in May it had put on quite a different face. The hillside didn't seem half so steep without snow, and now we could see it was covered with trees: willow, birch, alder and even rowan. Often they were waist high and in the most sheltered places they grew way above our heads. At first it was difficult pushing our way through, and even when we'd hacked out paths I found the growth restricting; I was used to open land where I could walk anywhere. But the wood showed us what turned out to be true, that we had a sheltered, fertile spot for our home, and also that for the first time in our lives we'd never be short of firewood. We could use wood for fencing and building too, and before long everyone was calling the place Stokkanes, and that's been its name ever since.

Thorstein was right about the flood plain. All the flat land turned out to be a huge river bed of white boulders, and a river of grey melt water surged over it, so we had to carry our belongings in by pony overland. Later in the year the river was fordable, meandering like a ribbon through its great bed. We could see the glacier now the snow had gone, white against the hills, with two snow-capped peaks behind it. It funnelled the east wind down to us all year, but that made Stokkanes warmer than other places, as the wind off a glacier isn't as cold as the wind off the sea.

We made camp close to the river mouth, and explored the valley from there, shoving our way through the untrodden forest. We decided to build our steading halfway between the river mouth and the glacier, in a wooded hollow facing south. The trees were tallest there, and when we'd cleared and drained the land we had a sheltered cup of land for our home pastures. Waterfalls poured over the precipices behind us, and between them and the river there was always the sound of fresh water. We never heard the sea, although we could see across the fjord to Brattahlid from the door of our house. Where I was used to waves lapping at the shore, we often had only an expanse of grey silt covered with ripple marks as if there ought to be water.

As soon as we'd chosen our site we diverted part of the stream to run under the house, marked out where the walls of the first building should be, brought in stones off our pastures until we had a good foundation, and before long we had the turf walls going up on top of that. We had to borrow driftwood for the roof from Eirik's store at Brattahlid, as we'd had no chance to collect any from open shores. I'll always remember the day we moved into the house, when I was directing the men – it always seems to have been my fate to have few women about me – where I wanted everything: the store barrels, the loom, the rack of tools, the baskets hanging on the walls, the soapstone pots by the hearth, the furs and blankets on the bed platforms. In two hours I had my house the way I wanted it, and as far as I know everything is still there in its place, just as I arranged it that first day. I didn't miss Halldis when I was busy. She was there, you see, her spirit worked inside me, part of me now, and it has always remained so.

Hay was difficult the first two years, because of the trees, and we were feeding the animals seaweed and bits of trees, but after a season or two the cattle had trampled the trees down and manured the ground for grass. In the end our best grass came from the silt plains across the river, though sometimes we lost it to floods. Our sheep grazing was steeper than at Brattahlid, and we lost some animals on the precipices close to the glacier, and we had trouble from foxes too, and set lots of stone traps, which worked – I was able to make my father a fox fur cloak after the first winter, with a white hareskin hood.

I was happy at Stokkanes. As the seasons passed it kept revealing new treasures to us. In July we discovered that we were living on one of the best salmon rivers in the Green Land, and all season we had nets at the river mouth, our only competitors the sea eagles who used to come down from Burfjell to fish there too. Towards the end of the first summer I discovered, myself, a little hot spring close to the glacier. And when the autumn came the land was in its glory, all red and gold. We had more berries than I'd ever seen, so we had fruit soup every night, besides preserving two barrels of fruit in whey for winter. Our traps and nets were never empty, and even the sun seemed to be caught in our valley long after the first gales had blown winter into the fjord. It was worth it to me to have to keep our boats a mile or two away, and as time went on our side of the fjord became less isolated. Before long there were new steadings right up to the head of the fjord, and I could walk that far easily. It was a hopeful time, when everything was new, and quarrels seemed to be left behind in Iceland. But these are women's things I'm talking about, not the kind of thing you want to know. I was telling you about that first winter.

One day before Michaelmas, our shepherd came in to say a big trading ship had come up the fjord and was moored off Brattahlid. The next day, as we half expected, a messenger came over to us, to bid us to a feast for Leif Eiriksson's homecoming.

Remember I'd never seen Leif Eiriksson before. My father had told me by this time that he and Eirik had talked openly of a marriage, and my imagination was already stirred. I had grown friendly with Thorvald and Thorstein, but Leif had what they did not, a ship of his own and adventure to his credit, and a hold on the imaginations of men. Thorstein had visited us frequently since he'd been back in the south, and Thorvald less often, but I was always elusive with them, playing them off against one another, and being busy in the dairy while they talked to my father. I had been waiting too long for Leif. Without knowing it I had created for myself a dream of something that did not exist, that I now know can never be. In the end I grew to like Leif, and I'm sure I never let him know how his false image had stirred my fantasies. But it might have been better for us all if I'd been encouraged to accept a man as he was, and not put off the reality for an idea that no flesh and blood man could ever be.

So Thorbjorn and I dressed in our best clothes, and crossed the fjord the next day in the teeth of a wind that already smelt of winter. I remember that feast at Brattahlid very well, but oddly enough I have no recollection of my first sight of Leif. I remember him there, certainly, sitting at the top of the table beside his father, a powerful man with a look of his brothers, but more arrogant and fairer than either of them. I see him in my mind's eye so clearly, but not as a stranger. The moment when Leif was a stranger to me is buried for ever. In that first moment of memory, I seem to have known him always.

It was a lavish feast. We didn't eat mutton or beef, but only wild meat: caribou, duck, ptarmigan and seal meat. When we sat down our cups were empty. Then Leif sent a thrall of his, Tyrker, round the table, telling him to pour the drink for all. It seemed a large task for one old man, and I saw Eirik frown. But Leif held up his hand to check his father's protest. 'Let Tyrker do as I say.'

Puzzled, I watched across the table while Tyrker filled Eirik's cup. Then he filled the cup that Thorvald and Thorstein shared, and I saw that the drink was not buttermilk, but red. And then Eirik grinned and said, 'So you brought back good German wine from Norway, in spite of all your travels. You did well!'

'No,' said Leif, in a quiet voice I was to know well, for he could make a whole hall full of men hush, just to hear him speak. 'No, that's not wine from Europe.'

'No?' Eirik stared at him. Of course Eirik knew, which we as yet did not, where Leif had been that summer, and I saw a realisation that I didn't understand dawn in his face. 'Are you saying . . . are you telling me that this is wine from the new country?'

'Taste it!' said Leif. 'Taste it all of you! Haven't we done well to bring you wine from a country you have hardly dreamed of? Take it, and drink it! I bring you wine from beyond the end of the world!'

That was Leif for you. Give him his moment, and he'd make ten times more of it. Some thought him a charlatan, and I've been embarrassed by him often, because I like him, but when he chose we were like butter in his hands. He's dead now; he died in his bed of ripe old age, the only brother who lived long or succeeded in all that he undertook. It's hard to believe he's no longer in this world. That's what happens when you get old; the people you know die off, one by one, and it seems impossible that you can be so alone. I never felt close enough to Leif to love him. I never knew him as I knew the men I married, and yet, when I think of those times now, it's almost hardest of all to believe that Leif has gone. He seemed to carry the future in his hands, all the new possibilities. All gone now. I wish you could have seen him then, just back from that first voyage, at the height of his powers and still young, at his father's feast at Brattahlid.

Four things, then, that changed our lives when Leif came home:

One, he'd done as his mother asked and brought a Christian priest back with him. I'll never know if he did it for her or not. Leif was always pragmatic, and I'm sure it took him no time at all to find out how the land lay at King Olaf's court. The way to the king's heart and favour was through baptism, and I'm sure Leif didn't hesitate for a moment. I don't think his father ever quite forgave him, and the irony is that one thing Leif inherited from Eirik was his unregenerate pagan soul. You look shocked, but it's the truth, Agnar. Leif and Eirik are dead now, and if we are ever to know the end of everyone's story, once they have crossed that boundary, we'll find out one day if I'm right or not. But I'd take odds we don't find Leif Eiriksson singing psalms in heaven. Nor will he be with hel, because, though he was devious and often hurtful, he was generous hearted. He belonged with the old world, even though he defied Eirik so often. Leif didn't storm and shout like Eirik. His anger was white not red, and twice as terrible. The pity of it was he was a son for Eirik to rejoice in, but although Eirik loved his exploits, he couldn't love the man himself. He could never see his own likeness in him, though to the rest of us it was mockingly plain.

So the priest came, and there was division in the Green Land ever after.

The second thing. Leif told us his story the night of his feast at Brattahlid, and we learned why he had been so long. He left Norway early in July, a year earlier, and he set out to do what Bjarni had done, only quite deliberately. He had his ship refitted and provisioned, and when he left Bergen he sailed first to the Hebrides, where he had business that I shall describe to you in a minute, and then due west. Fate favoured him, as it always did with Leif. Even the westerly winds gave way before him. For three weeks they sailed across the open ocean, with no sign of land. Can you think of any other man who could lead a crew so far out of the world, with no certainty at the end of it? But Leif's luck held. He stayed so far south that the stars were visible at night, and they could see the sun nearly every day, the weather stayed so clear.

In three weeks they found Bjarni's country. This is how Leif described it:

'We made our first landfall,' Leif said, 'at that country which Bjarni reached last. It was a grim country. Glaciers covered the mountains, and the exposed coast was bare rock. We anchored and went ashore, but there was nothing growing, not so much as a blade of grass. But at least we landed, which is more than Bjarni did. But there was nothing to stay for in Helluland, as I named it, because most of it was bare rock, and so we put to sea again, and followed the coast south.

'As we sailed south the country changed. The ice-capped mountains disappeared and low-lying green lands replaced them. After a couple of days we came to the longest white beach I'd ever seen. We followed it for miles, and at last we landed, where a promontory like the keel of a ship made a landmark. We went up the beach, and found a low-lying country of forests and swamps. The timber wasn't big, like the trees in the Norwegian forests, but there was plenty of it, as far as the eye could see. Because of the trees I called the place Markland, and we went back to the ships, and sailed on south.

'Then the coast began to bear away westward, but as it did so we sighted a further shore to the south-east, as if we were entering some great fjord. I decided then, as we had a north-easterly wind, to make for the further shore. There was a high island in the middle of the fjord, which we climbed, and saw the whole coast that we'd left to the north, and another long land to the south of us. We sailed on, and landed on a beach that shelved so gently that the ship ran aground way offshore. We waded to land, and found ourselves in a green country, with natural pastures and meadows and the forest behind. The grass was as lush as our own hayfields, and covered with dew. Our hands were wet with dew, and when we tasted it, it was sweet as milk.

'We spent some time exploring the country round about, and found salmon in a river nearby, and signs of deer in the forest. It seemed to me that we could winter there very well, if we spent the rest of the season hunting and fishing for our winter food. So we hauled up the ship, and built ourselves shelters above the beach. After that we were busy getting in food, and building houses that would shelter us in winter conditions. I divided the crew into two, so one lot were always out hunting, and the others building, until the houses were finished.

'I sent the thrall Tyrker with the other party, though they complained that he was useless for hunting. When they came back without him the second day, I was furious with them, and with myself. He's not as young as the rest of us, and maybe shouldn't have been on the voyage at all, but he's been a faithful servant to me since I was a child, and I didn't want to lose him.'

Everyone's eyes turned to the thrall who stood behind Leif where he sat at the table, ready to fill his cup with wine again. The man looked down humbly, but Leif turned and shook him by the shoulder, and told him to look up and accept his due.

'Tell them what you found, Tyrker.'

The German smiled back at him, and began to speak with more assurance than I'd expected. Although he'd lived in a Norse household all his adult life, he'd never lost his heavy accent, and it was hard to follow him. 'I was born in wine country,' he began. 'In the south Rhineland. My father kept a vineyard. Wine was like milk to me, until I came to these god-forsaken lands.'

My father raised his brows to me across the table. But I only glanced at him, and watched Leif closely. It pleased me that the man had such an easy relationship with his favourite slave. 'And then to be taken to the ends of the earth, and have to seek food like a wolf, in a pathless country!' The man shrugged. 'I didn't get far at that. These young men who go hunting, they run and force their way through forests and thickets and scramble up and down cliff faces. It's not for me! I dropped behind, and began to look about me. And I saw what not one of them had stopped to notice. Berries. I never saw berries like those that grow in Leif's new country. All kinds of berries. I tasted cautiously, and spat them out, in case they were poisonous. And then I found grapes.' He looked round at us, savouring his moment. 'Yes, grapes. Not the same as our Rhineland grapes, I grant you that, but the fruits looked the same, big blue berries clustered thick on bushes. The leaves and the stems were different, but the taste seemed so familiar, even though it's thirty years now since I saw fresh grapes. So I filled my hood with berries and brought it back to Leif. Even then these thick Norsemen didn't understand.' He gave his master another gap-toothed grin. 'I had to explain what it meant. But as soon as Leif understood he acted. We had barrels of corn and salt aboard the ship. We tipped them into pits, and I showed the men how to gather the grapes and press them, and then we caulked the barrels as best we could and let the juice ferment. Wine should be more than a year old, and I didn't have everything I needed. We could have done with iron bands, most of all. The next crop of Vinland wine will be better, sirs, I promise you.'

'Vinland!' That was the first time Thorstein had spoken. 'Is that what you call it?'

'Yes,' said Leif. 'That's my new country, a promise pledged with wine. This land here is green, with good pastures, but my land has all the fruits of the earth lying there for the taking!'

Eirik scowled. 'And what was the winter like?'

'Better than here,' said Leif lightly, and, perhaps realising that he had gone too far, he stood up and took the wine jar from his slave, and served his father with his own hands. 'You will lead us, won't you, sir, on our next voyage?'

'Not I,' said Eirik, though the angry flush died out of his cheeks. 'It's not my fate to discover more than this country in which we are now all settled. But you'll go on, boy, you'll go on with it.'

Leif, always tactful when it was just too late, glanced then from his father to his brothers. Thorstein was red and scowling, and Thorvald sipped his wine and gazed at the far wall. 'Oh yes,' Leif said confidently. 'Indeed we shall. All three of us, we'll go on.'

And that brings me to the third thing.

I hadn't realised at first that not all the strangers in the hall were Leif's men.

After Leif had told his story, they toasted a man called Thorir, whom I had taken for one of Leif's own men, and talked of his lucky escape. I asked Thorstein, who had come round to sit with me and my father, what it meant.

'Didn't you realise?' he said. 'No, no, those aren't our people at the end of the table there. My brother Leif picked them up on the southern skerries. They had sailed too close inshore and grounded on a reef. Thorir's a merchant from Norway. He's been here before, and knew the way, but they ran into storms, and were blown into the lee of the islands. Thorir had no choice but to wreck the ship in the best place he could see. But it's all Leif's luck. Our men brought away as much of the cargo as they could, and of course by right of salvage it's all my brother's. He's given half of it back to Thorir as a gift. So he makes his profit, and comes off with a reputation for generosity at the same time. Typical.'

'Does Thorir think him generous?'

'What can Thorir afford to think? My brother saved his life, and instead of losing all he had, he loses half of it.'

Leif's luck. We heard of nothing that autumn but Leif's luck. But I learned to know that luck, Agnar. I learned exactly what it meant. No one ever believed that Leif meant any harm, but all the luck he brought was backhanded. Not to himself, no, no, Leif Eiriksson was born under a favourable star, and that was that. He sailed through life, but anyone who followed him had to struggle in the wake of his passage, and I can tell you it was a rough journey. Thorstein was right; Leif was generous in his way, but what was more important was his great reputation for generosity. That's how he made his profit, and men still loved him while he did it. It was the same when he lent the houses in Vinland to Karlsefni. Generous, of course, but a back-handed gift for us.

It was the same with Thorir. Leif's rescue was astonishing, and whether he did it out of generosity, or because a wrecked merchant ship meant great wealth to any scavenger, I leave you to decide. He sailed in close to a lee shore, but he had all the advantage of knowing where the reefs were. He kept men at the oars to keep his own ship afloat, and cast a line across, and hauled men and cargo across in his boat and Thorir's. Not many men would have taken such a risk, and few but Leif would have got away with it. But Leif's luck brought

Thorir no good, and Brattahlid even less. Those men carried sickness with them. Leif's grand gesture killed fifty people that same winter. Thorir was among the first to sicken and die. He had a rash first, and then he couldn't pass water and swelled up like a puffball. Thjodhild said he grew so hot that butter would have melted on his skin. He didn't die for days, and at the end he grew delirious and fearful, and saw the nine fates themselves hanging over him in his bed, leering and chuckling.

Most of Thorir's crew died, and the sickness spread though the settlement. Thorstein came across on a sledge, and shouted to us. He wouldn't come in, so I talked to him from the threshold. He warned us to stay away that winter, and we did. That was why we saw no more of Eirik's family until spring came.

So it was not until the snows were melting, and the pack ice grinding and shifting in the fjord, that I heard about the fourth thing. Once again, it was Thorstein who came across. My father scolded him for making the journey when the ice was dangerous, but welcomed him in when Thorstein said that the sickness had gone with the winter dark. It hadn't, of course. It was a persistent disease, and has been endemic in Greenland ever since. It was a gift from Leif that changed my own life completely, as you shall hear.

I had hoped that Leif might come himself. He hadn't taken much notice of me, it's true, but when we'd met he'd had his mind on so many other things. He had looked at me once or twice, appreciatively, I'd thought. But Thorstein's news put paid to any daydreaming I'd indulged in through the long winter loneliness.

'Leif had a huge quarrel with my father, just a short time after you were at Brattahlid. That's nothing new; my family always quarrels, but we get over it quickly. If anything happens outside, we support each other to the death.'

'I'm sure you do.'

'Eirik talked to Leif about you,' said Thorstein. 'You know he'd ordered him to take note of you when you came to the feast?'

My father sat up on his bench. 'So Eirik had spoken to him?'

'I don't know what he said,' said Thorstein sullenly. 'When Leif comes home, my father seems to forget that Thorvald and I exist. But whatever plan Eirik had, it came to nothing. I thought you'd better know. My brother Leif made a landing in the Hebrides on his way back from Norway, and seduced a chieftain's daughter there. I don't know what he promised her, but he left her pregnant. She insists she is betrothed to him, and she threatened that her brothers would equip a ship, and bring her here to Greenland, with her child.'

'What of it?' said my father impatiently. 'Every man who ever sailed from home could tell the same story. What does an Irish chieftain matter to us? He could surely take her as a slave, and it wouldn't affect anything?'

'You don't understand my brother Leif.'

'I saw him. I can't believe any man could threaten him.'

'You're right about that. No man could. But this woman, Thorgunna, is a witch, and she cast a fate upon him, that if he wrongs her, the child will be her revenge. The child will come here for certain, she said, even if she did not, and if another woman had taken his mother's place, she, Thorgunna, would know it at once. And she swore that whatever happened to her, no woman Leif married before the boy came, would live through her labour, nor bear a live child.'

Horrified, I crossed myself. 'How could she do that?' I whispered. 'What kind of power has she?'

'Leif seems very sure of her power,' said Thorstein. 'We talked about it. No man could ever make my brother afraid – he's not afraid now – you mustn't think that. But he spoke to me more seriously than he's ever done before, and said that while this thing hung over him, it would be better for him not to marry. He said he wouldn't take a wife until this boy came, and then he could see how things were. But if Thorgunna hopes to trap him, she's gone the wrong way about it. I know Leif. She's threatened his good luck, and he'll never forgive her now. I doubt if he'll ever see her again either.'

'That's a terrible fate for a young man,' said my father. 'And he's of an age to need a wife.'

'He won't lack a woman, if that's what you're worried about,' said Thorstein, with a crack of laughter. 'Not Leif. But he's angry. He wants an heir. So does my father. It doesn't help Leif much, but once

Eirik had stopped storming at Leif, it occurred to him that he had two other sons.'

I was thinking about the woman who had made such a curse, and how she must have gone about it. It must have been a more powerful magic than anything I knew of, just to cover such a great distance, for a start, to say nothing of making such a powerful spell. And of course Halldis had never taught me evil, so I didn't know much about how to do harm. Young as I was, I thought Thorgunna must be a wicked woman. I never met her; I scarcely heard her name spoken again, for it brought no good luck to speak of her at Brattahlid, but now, all these years later, I feel a strange kinship with that woman who must have had so much power, and yet got nothing that she wanted. She must have been desperate, Agnar, don't you think? I suppose she loved him. Why else would she have done all she could to get him to take her to Greenland? No chieftain's daughter in her right mind would want to go out of her own world into a strange man's country, among men who despised her own people and thought of them as slaves. Anyway, her curse came to nothing in the end. She died, I believe, only a few years later, and of course Leif did marry, and Thorkel, who is chieftain at Brattahlid today, was born just nine months after. So Leif's luck held. Leif was a most attractive man, Agnar. I forgot to tell you that, I think. But my good luck was that I was never his woman. He became my brother, and no other man could have treated a sister better. Leif had every notion of what was due to his family. I would choose any time to be his kin rather than his wife, now that I look back on it. As a girl, I saw a handsome man who'd proved himself, beside two youths who'd done nothing. I would have had Leif, if I could, and I realise now that I would have been wrong.

'How does she know,' I asked Thorstein, 'that the child is going to be a boy? If they are indeed betrothed, he should be your father's heir.'

'They're not betrothed,' said Thorstein shortly, 'And the boy, and she told Leif that it is certainly a boy, will never be our heir.'

'May she not curse you all for that?'

'She has nothing of mine,' said Thorstein. 'How can she touch me?'

That was probably true, I thought. She probably had enough of Leif to reach him even in Greenland. A lock of hair, perhaps, a shirt, a ring, who knows? But as for Thorvald and Thorstein, she might not even know that they existed. Her spells could never reach so far. And yet, now I wonder. I thought then that the world was very large. But now here I am in the very centre of it, and when I wake up in the morning sometimes I feel I have only to stretch out my hand to reach across both space and time. It would not surprise me to find Karlsefni lying beside me, and to hear the icy winds of Vinland roaring inland across the winter ice. I have all that within me, every moment, and sometimes it seems nearer to me than what you call the here and now.

'I'll be honest with you,' said Thorstein, and cleared his throat. He didn't look at my father or at me, but plunged on with what he had to say. 'I know what you hoped for, Thorbjorn. I know what you negotiated with my father. I know that Eirik wants Gudrid for a daughter-in-law. While you all thought of Leif, I waited. But Leif won't marry for years now. No woman would risk a curse like that, and no man would wish her to do it.'

'Every woman takes that risk,' said my father unexpectedly, 'And every man who marries expects her to do it.'

Thorstein wasn't listening. 'I would never ask it. I haven't proved myself as Leif has done, but I'm one of Eirik's sons, and I've done nothing to disgrace him, and I'll do much more to enhance his prestige, I promise you. I'm one of the heirs to this Green Land, and unlike my brother I know Gudrid, and I want her for my wife.'

Well, of course it wasn't quite as easy as that. My father took a long time to make up his mind. He suspected that the tale of Thorgunna's curse might be a ruse to manipulate him. But when the ice melted, and we could sail across the fjord again, Thorbjorn had long talks with Eirik, with Thjodhild, with Thorstein, and even with Leif. He never entirely made up his mind that Leif's fears of witchcraft were genuine, but he did make sure that Leif was unattainable as a son-in-law, for whatever reason. Meanwhile, Thorstein haunted our house, until it was time to go north for the hunting. He came back in the autumn, looking thin and tough, with a boatload of bearskins, caribou hides, marten and fox furs, narwhal tusks and walrus ivory, and meat to match it, all of which he brought straight to Stokkanes and laid at my father's feet. My father feasted him well, and listened to his tales of distant places, and the traces of an uncanny people, who had left their stone cairns along the deserted shores of the uninhabited north. I listened too, and watched Thorstein closely as he talked to my father. I thought he'd grown older during the summer. He spoke little of his family, and the dangerous magic of empty lands still hung about him, like an echo of something new and desirable. I noted all this, and thought of what I would say to my father afterwards, whether Thorbjorn were to ask my opinion or not.

# TEN

# July 21st

June. Almost high tide. The sea wells over melting ice that lines the beach. Gudrid has come to know this view as well as the view of the glacier from Arnarstapi. Sometimes Brattahlid is invisible, lost in fog or twilight or rain; sometimes the hills are a thin grey line on the horizon. Sometimes the opposite shore is a purple silhouette. And there are days like today when the land across the fjord seems so close that a thrown stone would reach it. Gudrid sees every fold in the hill, every rock and patch of scrub on the pasture, as the morning light throws long shadows over each outcrop. She can see scattered houses, and the cluster of turf roofs which is Eirik's household, and cattle already grazing between snow patches. She can hear dogs barking, and the shout of a man. Ice lines the shore, but a channel of black water has opened up in the deep water of the fjord, and the way south is clear to the open sea. Below the beach ice has been smashed up to clear a way into the black water.

Leif's ship has been dragged down on rollers over broken ice and pebbles, and launched into a sea sluggish with ice that rolls over and grinds in the breakers. Against the ice the ship seems tiny, frail as a child's toy carved from a scrap of driftwood, with a handful of cast wool for a sail. What it promises seems impossible, against the scale of the distant mountains, and the ocean beyond the fjord. And yet the promise is delivered, year after year. The ship seems fragile, like the dreams of the men who sail her, and yet she makes it. Leif's ship has drawn an invisible line across the world now, from Iceland to Greenland to Norway to the Hebrides to Vinland to Greenland, a fine thread knitting the separate pieces of the world to one another, so that they become one.

*Leif's ship is a Norse knarreskip, a good trading ship, high-sided, clinker built, rising to a carved prow at stem and stern. She survives the ocean by adapting to it. Her lines are sinuous, and her timbers are supple, her joints giving against the weight of the swell. When the wind is fair she sails swiftly and cleanly; when the wind is contrary the square sail is not adaptable, and the ship must go with the weather, or wait for the weather to go by. Even her smallness is a concession to the elements; she can ride the swell neatly, and shaking the water off her can drive on her invisible way.*

*Men's dreams are shaped like this; the ship and the dream have made one another. This is Leif's ship, but Leif stays at home this year, to watch over his father's cattle, and to lead the hunt to the far north. Maybe he has affairs of his own to watch over too. His father is angry with him, about the woman who has bewitched him, and about the priest from Norway who is doing his best to bewitch Leif's mother. Eirik is set about with domestic problems, and Leif is aware that he needs to stay and make sure of his position at home.*

*But Leif is always generous. All winter the household at Brattahlid have discussed the possibilities of Leif's discovery of Vinland. If the settlements in Greenland could meet their needs from Vinland, and Eirik's family had control of that whole country, then Greenland would be theirs for ever. If Vinland has wine and timber for Iceland, to add to the profits of the northern hunt, then Eirik's family will be the richest in the whole world. Everything mortal life has to offer is theirs, but it is vital that they do not quarrel. Leif is always the most generous of men. He has offered to lend his ship and his houses in Vinland – lend, mind, not give – to his brother Thorvald. So Thorvald and his crew sail from Eiriksfjord today. The channel is open and the wind is in their favour.*

*Gudrid sees the ship as a black speck anchored in a murky ice-patched sea. She strains her eyes as the boats go to and fro, loading and unloading. She can't recognise anyone from here, but Thorvald will surely be aboard already, and Thorstein and Leif will be there with the boats, and Eirik will be directing them from the shore. The women will be watching from the settlement, making believe to go about their daily work as if nothing were happening. Even a Christian woman like Thjodhild knows to keep her prayers to herself on a day like this. The launching of a ship is no place for new gods. If Gudrid has prayers for Thorvald she does not say them out loud. She is unsure of her power: all she can offer is a wish, that is not quite a prayer or a spell. He is the only one of Eirik's sons that she has not thought of as a possible husband, but he is to be her brother, and he and Thorstein once watched her hungrily when she could not tell one from another. She wishes him well.*

*The tide turns. Fragments of ice break away from the beach and flow with it. The current begins to drain southward, out of the fjord. The sun is high. On Leif's ship the square sail is slowly hoisted. Gudrid screws up her eyes to see. The ship moves out through the broken ice, and into the black water. The current catches it. The breeze coming down from the glaciers fills the sail. The ship turns south, and gathers way.*

It's so hot today, Agnar, I can't even sit out in the shade of the cloister. At least it's a bit cooler in here. It reminds me of Vinland. It was hot there in the summer too, and the insects were terrible. I can remember throwing myself into the sea – into sea water, can you believe it? – to get away from the heat and the insects. They were even worse than Roman mosquitoes. It hurts to open my eyes, out there; the walls glare at me as I go by. I walk a little way in the evening, but even then as I pass each building it throws out the day's heat at me. Under the trees it's cooler, only the soil is so white and dry. How does anything grow in it? I complain too much, you're thinking. And I must admit the food makes up for it. Peaches and apricots – have you tasted them, Agnar? You have? So life in the monastery isn't so austere? Far from it? Really? Tell me what you have to eat.

\*     \*     \*     \*     \*

And wine too? What kinds of wine do they give you?

\*     \*     \*     \*     \*

Yes, we have Tuscan wines in the guest house here. Are they the best? I'm told the vineyards here in Rome aren't very good. Of course, the first wine I ever drank was from Vinland, where the grapes are different. I don't think it's given me a discriminating palate. These

106

things are so much more important here than they seem to be in Iceland. Would you miss such luxuries, if you went back? You'd miss the sun more? I suppose one might. Today I've been sitting here imagining cool water, white rivers and the clean northern air, and a sky rinsed with rain, not this parched pale blue. But when I'm home again I'll remember that there were days when I was much too hot, and I'll try to recall what that can possibly have been like. I'll tell you one thing about this climate. It stops my bones aching. I suppose they do get the rheumatics here. The old people seem to shrivel up like raisins, but I don't see as many cripples. Do you think that's true?

\*　　\*　　\*　　\*　　\*

Yes, and the young ones are so beautiful. It must be difficult for you, Agnar, seeing these lovely brown-eyed girls in the street, and not being able to go to bed with any of them. Or do you?

\*　　\*　　\*　　\*　　\*

True, it's none of my business. But I watched one yesterday evening, going home with a pot of water. She showed more flesh than a Norse girl would ever dare to do, but she looked young and brown and healthy, and with the pot on her shoulder she moved like a queen. It made me wish for a moment that my own youth had been sunnier. I'm not given to self-pity, but since I came here there have been moments when I've thought that my own girlhood was hard. Do you think it was?

\*　　\*　　\*　　\*　　\*

My dear, I don't want you to be sorry for me! God forbid! I've always been able to look after myself. And then I had Karlsefni. I don't know if I can make you understand what that meant. Can I make you see him in your mind? I don't know. He was all Norse, as much an Icelander as ever a man was, but he had a look one sees here in Rome. Was it his smile? He could be subtle, and not everyone trusted him. He had a way of looking at me that made my skin prickle with desire. Thorvald and Thorstein were lustful and predatory, but Karlsefni was different. He liked women. I don't mean sex, I mean women. Do you understand what I'm saying?

\*     \*     \*     \*     \*

I think you would have liked Karlsefni best of all of them. And Karlsefni would have enjoyed Rome. He would have appreciated what you told me about the wine. I think he might even have liked the heat. He was never lazy, but when there was nothing to do he was happy to do nothing. In the afternoons in Vinland we used to sleep sometimes, just as everyone does here. Leif would never have let his men sleep in the daytime, but Karlsefni did, and he always achieved everything he set out to do.

I wish I could just skip ahead and tell you about those days, but the other part must come first. It's a hard story, Agnar. Maybe it's just as well that blade of sun strikes in at the door there. Maybe it's a good thing I can smell dust and cypress, and hear the flies buzzing against the ceiling. It's a comfort to me to hear soft Italian voices across the cloister yard. Soon we'll smell cooking, when they start to make dinner. Olive oil and onions, that's how it always begins. I'm glad of all these things around me, Agnar, because the place we must now go back to is very terrible to me.

I was married to Thorstein at Lammas, the summer that Thorvald went away. He came to live with my father and me at Stokkanes. You may wonder that we didn't stay at Brattahlid, but there was always a large household there, whereas my father had no child but me, and, if I'd left him, there would have been no woman to look after the house and farm. In fact I'd run the place from the day that we moved there. I don't just mean the women's work; I mean the whole management of the farm. The thralls came to me for orders as soon as it was clear that I knew what I was doing. I wouldn't have been happy if Thorstein and I had gone to live at Brattahlid. Over there, Thjodhild was in charge of the women's work, and I'd have had to deal with Freydis too. In fact at Brattahlid there were too many strong-minded people altogether. Thorbjorn had grown easygoing with age, and I knew how to manage him. Also, I loved the place.

Stokkanes suited Thorstein too. Married to me, he assumed he'd inherit it one day, and so he took an interest in the farm. I think he was glad to be away from his family too. Being the youngest can mean waiting all your life for what may never come, at least, that's how it seemed to be in Eirik's family. Thorstein still dreamed of a long voyage, but meanwhile he was content, I think, to live with us in the winter, and to go hunting up north every summer.

The northern hunt was the key to Thorstein's soul, and it was out of my reach, far from women or the domestic world. I once asked him what it was about the north that drew him, and he thought for a long time, and then he said, 'It's the space.' That was strange, coming from a man who never talked about anything but the hunt, and whose idea of a winter night's entertainment was to swap stories with other men about the incredible hunts that had happened during all the years in Greenland.

He wanted a wife because he wanted an heir and a place of his own. I didn't bring him either, but he was happy in his own way, I think, during the three years we lived at Stokannes. Afterwards it seemed to me that I never really knew him, and even now, it's a struggle to tell you what he was like. We were young, and hot-blooded, and attractive to one another. For a while I was satisfied, and my restless body no longer kept me awake at night. Nothing happened between us that sex could not solve; and it was only later that I understood that there's no security in lust. At the time it seemed that to be in his arms was to be in a safe place, even though in my mind I knew that I was in a whole other world from him, and hundreds of years older than he was. But he was brave and active, and very strong. He used to win all the wrestling matches at Brattahlid. I think he would have beaten Leif, even, because Leif would not fight with him, and I can't think of any other reason why he shouldn't.

I felt closest to him when we worked together on the farm. That was mostly in spring, before he went away, when the flocks were lambing, and the cows had their calves. We were good midwives, between us. I loved him more then, I think, than when we were in bed. In bed he could have been anybody; but when we were in the fields together, in daylight, I could see that it was Thorstein, and I can remember his frowning look, whenever he was busy with some job. He wasn't a talker, but he was practical, and handled the animals well. I've always liked that quality in a man. I can remember when he saved one of our best milking cows by sheer strength. The calf was lying sideways inside her, and he reached in and turned the calf and pulled it out by the forelegs. I've done that myself. It takes some strength, if the cow can't help you. But Thorstein was tough, though he still looked young for his age. His hair never darkened but stayed fair as a child's, and he still had round cheeks like a boy's. I'm told he was one of the best hunters in Greenland, and that means the best in the world.

I never told him about the ghosts that haunted my past. I never talked to him about the things I learned from Halldis. Thorstein, like all hunters, had a respect for unseen things. I never doubted his courage; his companions told me enough of what he'd done, but I grew to know his private fears. I knew, as no one else could know, that he had bad dreams. They were usually about his brother Thorvald. Thorstein loved Thorvald as he did not love Leif. Thorstein knew, I'm sure, that his brother was doomed. Perhaps he knew when they parted they wouldn't meet again. He didn't say so aloud, of course, because he would never have done anything that might help an evil fate to overtake his brother. Only at night he would turn over and over in his sleep, and call his brother's name. I used to hear an echo in his voice, as if something in the bedwall heard and mocked him, or as if his voice came from somewhere far away. He sounded then like a drowning man, and I was afraid. But in the morning Thorstein never seemed to remember anything about his nightmares, and I never reminded him. Only sometimes when we went to bed at night he clung to me with a strength that was not all passion, and made love to me violently, as if by doing that he could stave off the lonely night and what it held.

So when Thorvald's ship came home at the end of the third summer with the news of his death, it did not surprise us at

Stokkanes. The cloud was down, so we hadn't seen the ship return, and it was not until Leif came over to fetch Thorstein that we heard what had happened. This is the gist of the story that Leif told:

Thorvald followed Leif's sailing directions, and came to Leif's houses in Vinland without much difficulty. It sounds so easy to say that – it was only when I made the voyage myself I knew what these simple phrases really mean. They didn't have time for much hunting before winter set in, but they were lucky with the fishing, and so they lived mostly on dried fish that winter. As soon as the ice melted in spring they launched the ship again and sailed west. I realised afterwards they must have sailed a long way into Straumfjord, as Karlsefni did later, and certainly the description I heard from Leif tallies with what we found: a warm, wooded land with long sandy beaches suitable for boats. There was no sign of any people, but far down Straumfjord they found a rough building, a sort of drying shed, as far as I could make out. If we had known what that signified! But we were innocent then; the new lands stretched out invitingly before us.

Thorvald wintered at Leif's houses again, and the next summer he sailed east. The east coast was rough and exposed, and a cold current brought icebergs down from the north, making sailing hazardous in the thick fogs along that shore. But then the land became more welcoming, with long fjords stretching inland between wooded slopes. It was hot summer by then, and I know, I've seen, what Thorvald found so attractive about the place. Apparently he'd said to his crew, 'This is the place. This is where I'm going to build my settlement.'

And so fate met him. It was not woven into the destiny of our people to inhabit that land, you see. An angel with a flaming sword stands at the gate of that country, and though a few of us have passed the threshold, the moment we say aloud that we intend to dwell in the place, the sword descends. To keep us out, they have peopled that world with demons, half-men, creatures out of Jotunheim. And yet even as we sailed away, after the slaughter and the bloodshed, we looked back on those green shores and saw it as it seemed at first, a paradise. But we're shut out.

And that's how it was with Thorvald. When they sailed on that evening they found three skin boats drawn up on the shore. Thorvald ordered his men to hide among the trees and wait. Just as it was getting dark nine savages came out of the forest. They strolled over to the boats, carrying strange baskets on their backs. They must have noticed something amiss, because they stopped suddenly and seemed to sniff the air, and look about. Thorvald gave the signal, and the men in ambush leapt out of the forest. The savages were taken by surprise, and it took no time at all to slaughter eight of them. One was too quick. He fled to his boat, which was so light he had it launched and was away before he could be caught. The stuff in the baskets was honey, and our men brought it home to Greenland. Leif gave us some. I remember the taste now; it was like eating the sun.

As soon as it was light Thorvald climbed up the headland at the mouth of the fjord, and saw what he had failed to make out before: a couple of small clearings along the coast, and little humps which might be huts, or boats. There were no cattle. I don't think Thorvald realised that his plans were hopeless. Once blood is shed the fates smell it, and they come faster than lightning. Back in the camp the men fell asleep in the heat of the day, for they hadn't slept that night, and the lookouts fell asleep too. The heat of the forest in the afternoon can have enchantment in it, as I know. Leif wanted to find the men who slept at their post and take revenge on them for the death of his brother, but I persuaded him not to, even though I didn't yet know Vinland. I'm glad to say he listened to me; after all, he knew something about the effect of spells himself.

Thorvald and his men were wakened by a voice that cried out 'Wake up, Thorvald! Wake up, and flee! Flee for your lives to your ship, and get out as fast as you can!'

They stumbled to their feet, still half asleep, and grabbed their weapons. The skin boats were making for them down the fjord, like a swarm of flies that smells carrion. Thorvald and his men reached the boat. There was no wind. They manned the oars and slowly began to move. The skin boats were blocking the fjord mouth. Thorvald told off men to defend the gunwales with their shields, and the others to keep rowing as hard as they could. The savages came alongside and shot them with arrows, but made no attempt to board the ship. So our men couldn't fight, but could only press on towards the open sea under the storm of arrows. Once they were clear of the fjord the savages turned back.

Thorvald asked if any man were wounded. None were badly hurt, but then Thorvald himself fell to his knees. 'I'm shot in the armpit,' he said. 'No, don't touch me. There's nothing to be done. You can pull it out when I'm dead, but listen to me now.'

They laid him on the deck, and as he'd ordered them, no one tried to staunch the wound or pull the arrow out, which would have ended it. He spoke to them in a whisper, for his lungs were filling with blood. 'Get back to Leif's houses, and get yourselves food for winter. In the spring go home to Brattahlid as fast as you can. As for me, I was right when I said that I had found the place I choose to dwell. Take me back there and bury me. Put a cross there, and tell my mother privately that you did so. And tell my father I died well.'

That was all Leif's story. Thorvald's crew had done just as he ordered, and were all safely back at Brattahlid. 'Did Thorvald leave me no message?' asked Thorstein.

'No message to you or me,' said Leif.

Thorstein stared into the fire. 'He knew he need not,' he said at last. 'I shall follow him, Leif. I shall find the place he chose. I won't leave him alone out there.'

'You won't move him?' asked Leif startled.

Thorstein looked at Leif with strange unfocussed eyes. 'Move him? What do you mean?'

'Our mother wants him brought back here.'

'Against his own wish?'

'The priest told her that a soul is damned if it's not buried in Christian ground.'

'Then are all our ancestors damned?' I asked.

They ignored me. 'I agree it's not practical,' said Leif, 'But that's what she's asking us to do.'

'He didn't ask for it,' said Thorstein. 'In fact he said he wanted to lie out there. But I'll find him.'

'And how do you propose to do that?'

'Leif, you'll give me your ship?' Thorstein laid his hand on his brother's knee, pleading. 'I knew he wouldn't come back. I knew it would end like this. I must be the one to go. You understand that?'

Leif looked at him thoughtfully. 'To find Thorvald, or to find a new land?'

'To find Thorvald's place. It's the same thing.'

Leif shook his head. 'A loyal brother, and a born follower. Fair enough. I won't give you my ship, but I'll lend it. I'll lend you Leif's houses too, to over-winter. What will you do when you get to Thorvald's place?'

'He chose it for a settlement. I'll do his will.'

'And the savages?'

'I won't be taken by surprise.'

'You'll not live in peace until you've destroyed them.'

'Then I shall destroy them. You said a couple of small clearings? That won't be hard.'

'Take care, Thorstein, fates have sharp ears.'

I thought the same, and crossed myself.

'A settlement?' went on Leif. 'It's a long way, you know.'

'You're the one to say that? You built Leif's houses!'

'As a trading post.' Leif was frowning. 'I'm not sure it's a world for men to live in.'

Thorstein turned on him. 'Thorvald meant to live there! The truth is you don't want anyone to have it but yourself.'

'No.' Leif was the only one of that family to be even-tempered, and it was just as well. 'No,' he said patiently. 'What I have I share with my family. But I don't want to lose both my brothers.'

'What did you mean by saying I was a born follower?'

'I meant well,' said Leif, 'Thorstein, don't quarrel with me. I'm lending you my ship and my houses. Isn't that enough for you? If you didn't want them I'd be using them myself. I've every right to do that. Your luck's in your own hands; I'm just saying you should think about it.'

Thorstein turned suddenly to me. 'Gudrid, this farm of your

father's has kept us both well enough. It's my turn now. Will you come with me to a new country?'

'Oh yes,' I said at once, because I realised all at once that this had always been my destiny. 'Of course I will.'

# ELEVEN

# July 24th

Until I met Karlsefni, an evil fate pursued me whenever I put to sea. Why I should be punished more than anyone else for daring to trust myself to wind and water I don't know. I think it must have been written in my fate before I was born that I should be a creature of the land. The cruellest part of my bad luck was that it was never fatal to me, only to those I loved. That was why I was so reluctant to go with Karlsefni at first. It wasn't that I didn't want to be with him, quite the opposite. I was frightened that if we trusted ourselves to the sea, where more than anywhere else one is in the hands of stronger powers, he would be lost to me. I never doubted that he was the best thing for me; I was just terrified that I should be the worst thing for him. But Karlsefni said that his good luck would overcome my bad fate, and that from now on the curse of a hostile sea would be lifted from me. I was afraid his confidence would tempt a vengeful ghost, but he was right. I never suffered at sea again, nor did those I loved, after I was with him. And that wasn't due to any action on my part. I have some skill in unseen things, as you know, but I have my limitations, and the shores of land are one of them. I have no power over the sea, or anything that belongs to it.

But I'm running ahead of my story. Thorstein had Leif's ship thoroughly refitted that winter. It needed a lot of work done on it, after a three-year voyage. That meant we spent a lot of time at Brattahlid. Luckily the ice was thick that year, and soon we had a sledge track as wide as a Roman road running straight from Stokkanes to Eirik's boat shed. I forgot to tell you, by this time Thjodhild had built her church. It was small, just about four paces each way; the turf walls were almost as wide as the space inside. It was aligned so that the altar faced east, because Herjolf's thrall had said that churches in Europe must always be built this way to face Jerusalem. That meant it was the only building in Brattahlid whose door didn't face down the fjord. Instead, you came out and saw the waterfall where the river flowed into the settlement over a little crag. Thjodhild said that was suitable – the water of baptism, of life, is supposed to be at the entrance of every church. When we had our mass we'd leave the door open if the weather was good, to have daylight, and the sound of water would accompany the priest's chant. The church was tucked away behind the byre so Eirik couldn't see it from the house: Thjodhild did her best to be tactful, like all that family, just so long as she got her own way in everything. She tried to keep Leif's Norwegian priest out of Eirik's way too, but as the man had to eat, that was more difficult.

And now she wanted Thorstein to bring back Thorvald's body to be buried in consecrated ground, for the saving of his soul. Eirik said that was nonsense, and his son should lie in peace in the place he himself had chosen. 'What greater honour can any man have,' he demanded, 'than to be able to claim a new country, a land flowing with wine and honey? Isn't Thorvald's grave a greater monument to his deeds than the largest burial mound ever raised? What man needs his wealth buried with him if he lies in his own country where riches lie all around him for the picking?'

'I'm not talking about worldly things,' said Thjodhild. 'He was my son and I want to make sure of his salvation.'

'You won't do anything for him by meddling with his corpse. Be thankful Thorvald had no cause to do other than lie still where he's laid. Aren't there enough ghosts walking this world without you digging more up?'

'They're the ghosts of a heathen country. If you would listen to me there need be no more ghosts in Greenland.'

She kept trying to talk to him about her faith, and always in the end he'd resort to blasphemy, as she saw it. He'd use the name of Christ to swear by, just as we used to do with the old gods. Now men do it all the time, and it's hard to remember the effect it had on me when Eirik first used it as a way of silencing his wife's arguments. He succeeded, because she was afraid he would damn himself if she

*117*

provoked him to go on. In the end she said as little as possible, but she had her church. What's more, she wouldn't sleep with Eirik any more, because he was a heathen. I don't know if he was more angry about her refusal, or that she told other people, so everyone, even the thralls, knew that he couldn't have sex with his own wife. He retaliated by being unfaithful to her at every opportunity, which was easy enough, because none of the thralls would have said no to him.

I suppose they were both grieving for Thorvald in their own ways. Families are like that. You think there is a pattern to the way people behave, that they will do certain things in what is supposed to be a normal way. But I have never got to know any household well, where I didn't find quite soon that they don't keep to the pattern. Everything they do is peculiar, and in fact one is forced to conclude in the end that the pattern doesn't exist. I've never met a family that behaved normally. Have you?

\*　　\*　　\*　　\*　　\*

Yes, it must make you long for what you haven't experienced. My sons are both strong men now, much tougher, you'd think, than a churchman like yourself. We didn't have them fostered, but kept them with us at home. I was happy with my foster parents, as you know, but living in a monastery must be very different. Of course, you've never lived in the same house with a woman since you were ten. Well, naturally it's hard for me to imagine that. Did you wonder about women a lot when you were growing up?

\*　　\*　　\*　　\*　　\*

That's true. Girls are much harder to deal with generally, but as far as I can make out boys of that age never think about anything except sex.

\*　　\*　　\*　　\*　　\*

All right then, hardly ever.

*　　*　　*　　*　　*

Yes, I suppose that's bound to happen. I don't think it's natural. If I were you, Agnar, I would go back to Iceland, where there are souls that need you, and I'd get a farm and get married. I don't suppose you want advice; no one ever does, but perhaps one day you'll remember what I said. Now, where were we?

Oh yes, that wicked voyage. Thorstein and I intended to sail first to the western settlement, which should have taken a few days. It was the part of the journey he knew very well, because he went there every year on his way north. He'd claimed land in the western settlement too, a farm called Sandnes, which he'd put in the charge of tenants.

At the foot of Eiriksfjord we put in at Dyrnes. Snorri Thorbrandsson was still living there, opposite Eirik's island and the old winter camp. We were feasted there the first night. I woke early next morning and followed a path made by fishermen along the shore of the fjord. Black crags towered over me, but I was walking through sweet young grass. I stopped by a stream bordered by celandines and river beauty, and looked down into water clear as air. I looked at the path under my feet, and I thought, 'This path is twelve years old. That's how old we are in this country. And this place, lovely as it is to my eyes, has been here since the nine worlds were made. From the beginning of time it has been like this for the glory of God alone.' Our world is made out of the empty places, Agnar, and we'll never touch anything but the fringes of the unknown. That seems to prove to me that it wasn't made for us.

*　　*　　*　　*　　*

What you say is true, but Eden was a garden with walls built around it. Adam never laid eyes on the vastness of the worlds. He never named what has not been seen and known. That's what your theologians in Rome don't see. They can't look out of the world from here; they don't know how small we are.

We sailed on down Breidafjord, where the ice was still very thick, so we thought we might have to go back and wait longer. But we did find a passage to the open sea, and then Thorstein steered us west by a complicated route sheltered by many low-lying islands. The ice wasn't nearly as bad here. The water was calm and black, and in the distance we could see mountains like dog's teeth, and to our north the ice desert that covers the heart of the Green Land. Thorstein and his men were confident and full of hope, and gradually I began to relax. I'd never said so, but I'd been afraid of going back to sea. For a woman who stays at home among the Greenland fjords it's easy not to remember, whereas at Snaefelsnes you have the reality in front of you all the time. I had no excuse – I, of all people, shouldn't have forgotten. And yet when we first came out west of Greenland the sea was benign: there was nothing but a great openness, the silvery light of the north, and icebergs as white as froth on cream. That's how I remember those seas most often now: the distance and the vast light.

The west coast of Greenland is a different world from Eirik's country. The mountain that marks Thorstein's channel through the islands is made like four trolls standing in a circle, and afterwards I saw that as a warning. We came into a heavy swell and turned north, along the most inhospitable coast I'd ever seen, just ice and bare mountains, as if God had abandoned this place on the fourth day. There was a moon, so when night came we kept on sailing. I lay down under the awning, wrapped in my fur sleeping bag, and slept.

I woke to tempest. We were pitching wildly, and I couldn't feel any rhythm to it. It was so dark I thought I hadn't opened my eyes, but I had. I put out my hands and felt wet fur, but no one was there. The ship bucketed so I couldn't move. Water washed over the planks round me. I lay where I was until a faint light began to show, and, holding on tight, I got to the edge of the awning. I was drenched at once. I couldn't see anything but water. Then I saw the men, and made out Thorstein at the steerboard. I couldn't get to him. It was all I could do to carry on with life, to reach food or drink or the bucket, and I would think about each thing that must be done for hours before I did it. It was like that not just a day, but weeks. I can hardly imagine it now. You survive by inhabiting your body as little as possible, like a bear in winter. Your soul is in abeyance. I barely exchanged a sentence with Thorstein in all that time. He held me in the brief watches when he snatched some rest, but speaking was too difficult.

God knows where we got to. We had two cows with us, and a few sheep. Thorstein had been planning to get enough stock for Vinland from his farm at Sandnes. The beasts died of exposure quite early on, but already there was very little water left for us. If we hadn't had rainwater we would have died too. I would rather die of anything than thirst.

When there were storms it seemed we must founder, and when there was a lull in the weather we did our best to sail on, but as we were lost to direction, and had no way of steering a straight course, I've no idea whether we made headway in any direction at all. At sea nothing is where you think it is, and out in the greyness dwell unimaginable things. Sometimes if you stare hard into the mist you half see them. The worse your sufferings are, the plainer they get. They're like carrion crows waiting for the battle to be over, only it's not just your flesh they're waiting to feast on, it's your soul too. People say that the drowned can't enter heaven. I don't know what you think about that. I think about it every time I pray, and I ask, if that is really so, whether Christ who stilled the storm might find it in his heart to change the order of things. Perhaps he can't; there are things that live in the western seas which he never encountered in Galilee.

I still hate being wet. You know what it's like on a long voyage, when you're wet to your skin, so the wind gets through, and your clothes are heavy and chafe you, and you get sores round your neck and sleeves where the cloth rubs, and when you wrap yourself in your cloak at night you hear the water running down the deck round you, and your clothes squelch every time you try to turn over? I hate it as much as the animals do, and you can see how they suffer.

So the weeks of summer passed, and finally we got a bearing, and headed west, where Thorstein reckoned there must eventually be a coast. He thought we might make a landfall in Vinland, or in Africa, but the cloud came down again, and when we could get a bearing at last we had come far to the north again. When we did finally raise a coast the first thing we saw was icy mountains and glaciers falling to the sea. We came further in, and then one of the crew, who had sailed with Leif, called out, 'That's the Green Land! That's home! We're south of Gunnbjorn's skerries.'

And so we followed the coast round at last to the western settlement. We passed the entrance to Eiriksfjord, and we could have gone home, but Thorstein wouldn't have it. He was thinking of the shame he'd face, coming home without anything to show for it at all. So he forced the men to press on, and so we beat slowly up that wild west coast, with the wind as fickle as the fate that followed us. The weather wasn't done with us yet. We sailed into thick fog, and we could feel the cold of ice to the east of us. Thorstein said this was the most exposed part of the coast, where the ice desert meets the sea. We sailed blind through fog and yeasty sea, but the wind held, and so we kept our direction. Though there was a big swell, it was regular, and I could stand up and stare into the fog, instead of just holding on in the belly of the ship. In two days we reached the entrance to Lysufjord, where Thorstein's farm lay at the very head of the fjord. The wind was dead against us, threatening to blow us out to sea again, but Thorstein knew the currents, so we beat to and fro, pitching nastily while we waited for the tide. So he got us into the fjord, and for a day and a night we did our best to beat up it, only the wind was against us, and the rising seas were tossing the icebergs to and fro. At last we sighted a steading on the north shore, a little patch of green under crags, and there we went ashore.

We made a hard landing on stones. There was a hideous grinding and the ship stopped with a jerk. Our hull was damaged just where the bow bellies out into the body of the ship. For the first time in all our troubles Thorstein was visibly upset. It meant that we were stranded here, halfway down the fjord, with our own farm, promising hot food and water and shelter, only a couple of hours' journey away. It was only a week till winter, and a thin fringe of ice was already forming along the shore.

It wasn't Thorstein's fault. The curse that dogged our ship was mine. He should never have married me. I meant to be the best possible wife to him, and in the end I destroyed him. During those weeks at sea I grew to respect him more than I'd ever done in our lives at Stokkanes. I told you I'd never seen him as he really was. Thorstein came alive, I believe, on those hunting trips up north, and men still tell stories of his adventures there. If he could have had a ship sooner, he would have been as great a sailor as his brothers. As it was, he only knew the coast up to the western settlement and the hunting grounds, and the only long voyage he tried to make was doomed. He was a good captain. He ate and drank no more than his men, and as his wife I got no privileges either, which I think was right. He made them go on, for his pride's sake, and again I think he was right. He had to prove who he was before he went home to his father and brother. He didn't care if it killed him; he wouldn't be shamed.

He never complained or confided in me. Sometimes he would crawl into our wet sleeping bag when we were hove to in the dark, and make love to me, briefly and painfully, squashing me between his weight and the hard planks under the flattened layer of hay. I can't say I got any pleasure out of it, but perhaps it helped him through. I don't know if it occurred to him that our bad luck might be my fault. Of course he knew I'd been aboard an unlucky ship before, but he'd never mentioned it. I know he badly wanted a son. I don't know if that's why we always made love so regularly, or whether his body just needed it. In the daytime he was respectful to me, but he wasn't one for saying how he felt. I think he'd got used to me, and relied on me for small things more than he knew. Once he was accustomed to having a wife, she wasn't really the sort of thing he thought about any more. But I liked him, and I did my best to give him what he wanted. I never meant to do him harm, and now in my prayers I do my best to atone for it every day. Do you think that if a soul is ignorant of the harm they do, it makes them less guilty?

\*      \*      \*      \*      \*

I'm glad you told me the truth, Agnar. I know you'd like to give me a kinder answer, and if you did I wouldn't believe you. You're a good priest. I hope you'll go back to Iceland one day. You'd be of use. But

Thorstein. My poor Thorstein. Let me tell you the end of it, and then you'll know all my guilt.

It wasn't a part of the settlement that Thorstein knew well, and the people living near the coast were poor outlanders. They were friendly to us, and took the crew into their houses. In answer to Thorstein's questions, they said that the head man of the place was a man called Thorstein the Black, but he lived half a day's journey by pony up the fjord. Thorstein sent a couple of men to tell him of our arrival. Meanwhile, he would not leave his ship, as he was worried the poor folk living close by might plunder our belongings in his absence. We had a lot of valuables – at least, they were valuables in Greenland – iron tools for boatbuilding and smithying and carpentry, plenty of weapons, and barrels of whey and oil. So he and I made a tent for ourselves out of sailcloth, and camped on the ship where she lay hauled up on the beach.

We spent three days there. It was the only time we were ever alone together. Our sail sheltered us from wind and rain, and there was a stream of fresh water nearby where we drank and drank. No holy water blessed by saints could have seemed a greater miracle. We washed the salt out of our clothes, and back on the ship we hung them all around us, and made ourselves as comfortable as we could without a fire. Now we had enough to drink we were ravenously hungry. The second morning one of our men killed a seal, and brought us fresh meat that they'd cooked in one of the huts. The first night hard rain blew over us, but at least we had land under our backs. On the third morning it stopped raining, and we managed to light a fire outside and cook our own meat, so we ate hot food for the first time since the spring. I shall never forget eating that hot fresh seal meat, with the fat pouring off it. We went on eating all that day, the juice dripping down our faces, until we just could not swallow any more. Dusk fell early, clear and cold, with a million stars shining down on us. We made each other warm, huddled in our damp cloaks. Thorstein was in good spirits again, in spite of everything. He had saved his ship and his men. We could over-winter in this place, and next year was another season. He had no more to say about good luck than about bad, but he was obviously feeling better. He was never idle for long, even when he was exhausted, and already he'd started cutting a patch for the broken hull, and heating seal oil over the fire to proof it. I remember him standing over the fire, working with that intense concentration he had for every job he did. I watched him, and wished, as I had never properly wished before, that I could give him a son. I never did anything about it. Perhaps I had learned too well from Halldis to simply accept what was given, or withheld. I certainly knew charms enough, and I've used them too, for others, but it wasn't until that day in our tent that I ever thought I owed it to Thorstein to make a child come, and by then it was already too late.

Obviously we couldn't stay in our shelter for long, now the year had turned, but I don't think either of us was impatient for a message. I remember we were both unsteady on our feet after so long at sea, and that made us clumsy in the small shelter we had. If Thorstein had sailed as much as Leif, he would have been used to it, and got his balance back again the first day. It's always worse in a small space, and the first day we hardly went out except to lash down our sail-tent when it needed it. On the fourth morning the ground was white with frost, and ice crackled in the small waves that broke on the beach below us.

The ground was so hard that we heard the thudding of hooves before we saw the horses coming. We looked over the gunwale: there was a herd of ponies, three of them ridden, circling across the meadowland towards us. There was no sign of any of our own men. Thorstein frowned. 'Get back inside,' he said, and took down his bow, and notched an arrow to the string. He didn't aim, but held it just out of sight, inside the gunwale of the ship.

From inside our tent I heard the horses come alongside, and halt. 'Who's there?' cried a voice.

'Two people,' said Thorstein. 'Who asks?'

'I'm Thorstein the Black, the chieftain of this settlement. And you are Thorstein who owns Sandnes. I know that, because you sent me a message. You won't repair your ship in time to reach Sandnes now. I've come to invite you and your wife to spend the winter with me as my guests.'

Thorstein glanced at me, where I crouched under the sailcloth, and raised his brows. I nodded. Thorstein laid down his bow where it could not be seen, and stood up. 'We're glad to accept,' he said. 'But I don't like to leave my ship and cargo undefended here.'

'Your ship will be safe enough, if we lash her down for winter, and build a shelter. You can reach her from my farm if you need to work on her. I can send over a cart tomorrow, if you like, and you can bring your cargo back to my house, and store it there.'

'I'd be grateful,' said Thorstein curtly. I stood up beside him then, and saw Thorstein the Black for the first time. He was a big dark man, with matted black hair and a thick beard. His hood was thrown back, and his leather-patched cloak unfastened, showing a greasy leather tunic underneath. He was fat and unkempt compared to the men at Brattahlid, but he looked powerful for all that, and well-armed, with a sword dangling by his side, and an unsheathed dagger stuck in his belt. I looked him over thoughtfully as I added my thanks to Thorstein's. 'May God bless you for your generosity,' I said to him, and his thick brows snapped together in a frown, but then he laughed at me.

'Which god is that?' he said. 'I've been hearing rumours about that sort of thing. Well, we're of the old faith here. No doubt your god is a better one than mine, but don't bother to tell me about it. You'll stay then until the cart comes tomorrow?'

'Yes,' said Thorstein, 'We'll stay here.'

'I'll be back tomorrow then.' Thorstein the Black made as if to go, and the horses plunged forward. Then he reined in his own pony, and added, 'Don't expect much, mind you. There's only my wife and myself, and I'm not much company. It'll be a dull winter.'

Thorstein smiled for the first time. 'Better dull than dead.'

'You may not think so by springtime.'

And that's how we came to the house of Thorstein the Black. I never guessed for one moment, though I often have hunches about these things, what a friend that man would become. I was repelled by his looks when I first saw him. He was a great, gross man, and he made no concessions to anybody. He smelt, and his house smelt, and whatever fleas we brought with us were soon outnumbered and overcome by the most virulent insects I ever lived amongst in all my life. Everything in that house was greasy from the cooking, because Thorstein the Black liked his meat boiled for hours with the blubber on it, and certainly in those northern parts fat gives you warmth for the long winter. Hunks of meat lay about inside the house, and tubs of fermented buttermilk. Thorstein's wife was big like he was, a great tough woman who made me think of a troll wife. But I was soon ashamed of thinking that. They were kind to us, and shared everything they had. Thorstein the Black and my Thorstein packed away our cargo safely in the barn.

Grimhild, Thorstein's wife, gave us the bed space next to theirs. Grimhild and Thorstein the Black together snored more loudly than the whole crew of our own men all asleep at once. Thorstein and I lay in a dry bed for the first time in months, and had barely settled ourselves when the snoring began. Thorstein had me in his arms, but he stopped what he was doing and listened, astounded. Then he began to laugh. He was never one for jokes, Thorstein; he just got on with things, and let others mess around with words and games. But that snoring set him off laughing, when I'd had no idea that anything ever could. He couldn't control it, and he had to bury his face in my shoulder and pull the covers over his head to keep quiet. I could feel him shaking all over with suppressed giggles, just like a foolish girl.

'Thorstein, stop it!' I whispered, though I was laughing too, it was so infectious. 'Stop it! You'll wake them!'

But he couldn't stop. 'Listen,' he gasped. 'Just listen. Did you ever hear anything like it!'

Poor Thorstein. The fleas in that bed were huge. He'd catch them and crack them between his nails. 'It's worth it,' he said grinning, 'to be dry again.' And as if to celebrate, he took off all his clothes, and made me take off mine, and we lay there skin to skin, just as we used to do at home in Stokkanes. He made love to me without a word, as usual, but when he had done he whispered, 'Things will go better now, Gudrid, won't they?' When I said yes, he believed me, because, although he never talked about it, he respected my knowledge of what to him was quite unknown.

We had hardly been in our new lodging for a week when a man called Gardi, who was the overseer of one of Thorstein the Black's farms, was taken ill. People thought he'd been cursed, as he was a hard man, and unpopular with the thralls. So, thinking it was a spell, no one worried too much. He was dead within a week. But then others began to sicken, and then a message came that two of our own crew were ill. Thorstein borrowed a pony and went to see them at once. Thorstein the Black frowned, and sat at home chewing his fingernails. 'We had sickness here last winter,' he said. 'I hope for the sake of your gods and mine it's not still going about.'

He hoped in vain, and within a week the two men who'd sickened first were dead. By the time the midwinter dark was on us we'd lost more than half our crew, and several of the folk in the settlement had died too. Thorstein and I tried to stay with each of our own men when they lay dying. The sickness was beyond prayers or charms. I had no powers at all, only ordinary compassion, and I didn't have as much of that as my husband, who never led a man to success or glory, but who would sit with the least of them to help them die. He didn't have any hope to offer them, and in fact he hardly said a word; but he stayed with them, and it wasn't long before he fell sick himself.

*The autumn night is bitter cold and bright as day. The moon of Urd, which presages death, has risen full, wrapped in a mist that blurs the stars. The ghosts gather under the rafters. They have been here before: they've already known the struggle, the torment of the body, and the strange emptiness of escape. The ghosts drift along the boundaries of the mortal world because the mist lies over the country beyond and they can't see a way on. So they hover over the farmsteads in the Green Land, waiting.*

*The ghosts are watching over the lands of Thorstein the Black, because every night new souls are added to their number. The sickness sweeps through the settlement, and each time a person dies its soul is torn from its body and drawn into the throng. Some are helped on their way with tears and blessings, a few have the mark of a cross made over them, and all are sent with the protection of charms and offerings. But in the dark space under the rafters all these things fade into the same mist, which drifts clear for a moment to let the new soul in, then thickens.*

*In the house of Thorstein the Black a lamp burns and flickers in its pool of oil. Grimhild, the wife of Thorstein the Black lies on her back in her* tumbled bed. There is no sound in the room but her breathing, loud and rasping. Sometimes it stops for seconds at a time, even for a full minute. Each time the watchers think that the terrible insistent noise has ended, but then the great breaths start again, and the ghosts are thwarted. In the other bed, lying in the shadows away from the lamp, lies Thorstein Eiriksson. His wife is curled on the bed beside him. She holds his dry hand in hers lightly, perhaps unwillingly, as if she would rather let him go. His eyes are closed against the dark. His soul is shut away deep inside his body, hidden in a place of its own. The ghosts stir; the lamp flickers as if someone had breathed on it, then flares upward. A shadowy bulk by the bedhead moves. It is Thorstein the Black reaching out to trim the wick. The shadows on the wall dance crazily, then drop into their place again.

The night stands still. A single moment expands into a frozen desert. Outside the stars hang over the glaciers, and the sea is motionless on the ice-locked shore. The ghosts have been here since time began and beyond it. There is no way out.

Grimhild takes her last dreadful breath and stops. A rat scuttles in the dark place under the bed platforms. Gudrid raises herself on her elbow and peers through the dark at the black bulk that is Thorstein the Black. Thorstein the Black stands up. His limbs are numb and heavy, so he moves slowly. A shadow looms above him on the wall. His voice sounds rusty, as if it had been out of use a long time. 'She's dead, Gudrid. We'll need to lay her out.'

'Do you want me to do that?' Gudrid's voice is cool and young, precious as clean water in that house of dirt and death.

'I'll get what's needed.' Thorstein the Black lights a taper from the lamp, and moves past Gudrid on his way to the door. He leans over her for a moment and presses her shoulder.

Impulsively she touches his hand. A little shadow jumps suddenly on the wall. 'Don't be long, dear friend.' Four hands clasp: two become a single shadow on a stone wall, two feel warm, living flesh, and a moment's comfort.

Thorstein shuts the door, and half the light goes out of the room. Gudrid sits up, her feet on the floor, and stares into the night. Silence stares back from the dark, and she recoils. Now Grimhild's breathing has gone she can hear Thorstein. He breathes like a man who dreams uneasily, in broken rhythms, and stops. He lies curled up as he must have lain unborn. She touches his face, and his skin is dry and burning hot. Now that Thorstein the Black is gone, the lurking shadows fill the room with a dank and alien air. Gudrid smells death, and her skin prickles under her shift.

Thorstein gasps and shudders, and half sits up. 'Gudrid?' He speaks thickly, as if he were drunk.

'Thorstein. I'm here.'

'Gudrid.' He falls back against the bolster, his eyes half closed. Presently he speaks; the words come slow and slurred. 'What is that woman doing?'

Gudrid whips round to where his gaze falls on Grimhild's bed. The corpse of Grimhild is rising up, supporting itself against the carved pillar that heads the bed. Gudrid stops breathing, and presses herself back against Thorstein's bed. Her limbs are like clay, and cannot move. Her eyes are fixed to the dead woman's face.

Grimhild sits up. Her white legs show beneath her shift. She is groping for her shoes with her bare feet. Gudrid tries to scream but her throat is dry and no sound comes. The corpse stands up, huger than it ever was in life. Its shadow looms over Gudrid and Thorstein, and they are plunged into dark. In the blackness Gudrid eyes escape the blank face of the dead and the spell breaks. She screams out loud. The corpse crashes down and lands like a tree across Thorstein where he lies helpless. There is a splintering of wood as a bed plank breaks. Gudrid feels damp cloth against her face, and she hits out hard and screams again.

The light comes back and is gone again, and the voice of Thorstein the Black cries out in terror, and the dead thing is lifted away. The bed shifts and judders along the length of the wall as a weight is flung back on to the platform. Gudrid, her hands pressed to her face, looks out through her fingers. Huge shadows leap and curve. In flickering light a man is fighting with a corpse. He pushes it back, but it struggles up. He hits it a great blow and it staggers. For the third time it tries to rise again, its eyes fixed upon the living man. The man backs up against the wall and stands with his arms outstretched as if his hands were nailed to the wall. The ghost towers up in the middle of the room. When its shadow falls across him, the man is released from the spell and like lightning he grabs an axe from its hook and strikes the dead thing in the breast. It falls like a rock. The shadows drop; there is silence, except for a man's sobbing breaths, and the echo of them from the dying man in the bed.

Only the ghosts watch what happens next. Thorstein Eiriksson lies on his back, his eyes closed, his soul wandering again to hidden places where this world cannot reach. Gudrid is curled in a crumpled heap against the bolster, her face buried in its woollen cover, her hands over her ears. She is crying inside, anguished sobs that threaten to break her in two, but no sound comes. If wishing could make her dead, she would never look up again. Under the rafters the ghosts watch dispassionately. From far away they see a man lift up the body of his wife and lay it on the bed. The body has a great wound from an axe in its chest, but no blood comes. The man fetches a wooden board from where he dropped it by the door, and rolls the body on to it. Then he straightens his wife's limbs and lays her out decently, and ties her in her shroud firmly to the board. He closes her eyes and weighs them down with silver coins, and as he does so he mutters a charm. He covers her face last. He glances into the dark space where Gudrid and Thorstein lie, as if he were looking for help, but nothing stirs. He gets up and props the door open. Using all his strength, he manages to lift the corpse and carry it out into the night.

When the room is empty Gudrid lifts her face. Nothing moves. She sits up and holds her hand in front of her face, and sees it shaking. She looks across at the empty bed where Grimhild lay. Presently she gets up and folds the blanket, and smooths out the covers. When Thorstein the Black comes in she puts more seaweed on the fire and blows it into a flame. She sees him and goes to him, holding out her hands. Thorstein hesitates a minute, then takes her in his arms and holds her to him briefly. 'She was faithful to me, Gudrid,' he says presently.

'I know.'

'She wouldn't choose that I should let her ghost walk.'

'May she lie quiet now.'

'I'll see her buried right. I can't do more.'

'No man could have done more.'

Thorstein the Black pauses, and then he says, 'Gudrid, when I went outside just now, and was coming back from the byre with the board for the body, I saw all the dead – all the people who have died here this winter – lined up at the door, between me and the house, watching me. They

131

stood before me as they were in life, but they wore their shrouds over their clothes, and their hats were made of birch bark.' Gudrid gives a small gasp, but she says nothing, and he goes on. 'I think you should know this. I saw among them my wife Grimhild. And I saw also your husband, Thorstein Eiriksson, standing there among the ghosts. Sorrowfully I met his eyes, and then the throng drew aside, and allowed me to pass into the house.'

The night is motionless. Gudrid watches over Thorstein, and the black hulk which is Thorstein the Black waits by the fire. Not a rat stirs. The dying man's breathing grows raw and jagged. Slowly it takes over the silence. Gudrid touches his hand but does not hold it. The soul of Thorstein Eiriksson is beyond restraint now. It wanders in the unmarked spaces at the edge of the world. He is drawn further as he was drawn in life by the light and the emptiness of the far north. At the edge of the world there are mountains of ice and frozen seas, and a sky so vast that all the souls of the world could never breathe it in. No one has gone so far, not even in his mind. And if one did, all he might hope for, beyond the boundaries of what exists, would be to find nothing.

'Thorstein, my Thorstein,' whispers Gudrid. She does not think that he can hear, she hardly sees his face, but she has an idea her words may reach him. 'You were a good man to me, Thorstein, and now you are free to go.' The tears are running down her cheeks now, and dripping off her chin into his hair. 'I thought my fate was bound up with yours, but yours ends here. I don't know what will happen to me, but I shall miss you, my husband.'

Thorstein's eyes are closed and he does not stir again. Presently the harsh breathing stops, and he is still. Gudrid puts her hands on his chest, and though his skin is warm she feels no life in him at all. All her restraint leaves her. She flings herself across his body and weeps bitterly, and the noise echoes back and forth in the dark space under the rafters. Thorstein the Black steps over the hearth to her and picks her up in his arms, and carries her across to the bench on the other side of the room. He holds her in his arms and rocks her, and Gudrid turns her face into his greasy tunic, her body racked with weeping.

The body of Thorstein Eiriksson lies stretched out on its back, its eyes closed, as if it were asleep. The chest is bared, where Gudrid has undone his shirt to lay her hand against his heart. It is a strong, young body, but white and still as wax.

At last Gudrid's sobs subside, and Thorstein the Black speaks softly to her, doing his best to comfort her. He offers to bring Thorstein's body back to Brattahlid himself, when the spring comes, so that it can be buried in the Christian way in the right place, because he knows that Christians believe in these things. Gudrid is not listening to the words, but his tone and his touch comfort her. She rouses herself at last, and goes over to the bed to lay out her husband's body. She stops, and turns to Thorstein the Black at her side, and puts out her hand to him remorsefully. 'You did this for Grimhild, and I did nothing to help you.'

Thorstein takes her hand. 'You've done all you could. This is a hard fate for both of us, but we do what we can.'

The ghosts watch as the body of Thorstein Eiriksson is prepared for burial. Outside the moon of Urd has sunk, and behind the eastern mountains a faint whiteness gleams over the ice. The night passes, and the cold day breaks.

# TWELVE

# *March 25th*

Thorstein complained of pains in his head and limbs. He was hot to my touch, in fact I could feel the heat of him without even touching him, and his skin was dry as old vellum. It hurt him to breathe, and he couldn't pass water. Soon it hurt him if I even touched him, and the weight of the covers over him was agony to him, and he threw them off, but I had to put them back because we dare not use more fuel to make the room warm. In the morning the water buckets were always frozen over, and yet Thorstein was delirious with the heat of his own body consuming itself. His skin came out in open sores, and it hurt him even to drink water. On the fourth day he went into a coma, and on the fifth day he died. I was alone with Thorstein the Black when my Thorstein died. Thorstein's wife died the same night. I've thought all night about how I would tell you what happened in that night, and I don't think I have any more to say about it.

We had to wait until spring, of course. Thorstein the Black and I lived in that house alone. None of his people visited us. They couldn't. Whenever anyone tried to approach the door their way was barred by the ghosts of all those who'd died that winter. Thorstein's wife Grimhild, and my Thorstein always stood among them, close to the door. You can't bury a body until the ice melts in the Green Land, and until they were buried they would not lie quiet.

Thorstein the Black offered to sail our ship and carry back the bodies of my husband and his men who had died to be buried at the church in Brattahlid. Meanwhile we sewed them into their shrouds and covered them with snow. I had an idea that Thorstein would rest in peace if he had Christian burial in his mother's church at Brattahlid, the same church where we were married. Thorstein never professed Christianity. He refused to be baptised, when his mother tried to persuade him, but he never spoke against it either. He was fond of Thjodhild, however, and I knew that his burial in the churchyard is what she would want.

Meanwhile the ghosts outnumbered us in that house, and at night there was always noise. They murmured together under the rafters, and scratched under the bed platforms. When the storms came the moaning in the rafters swelled to drown the sound of the wind outside. In the morning things were moved about. The baskets that hung on the wall would be turned upside down, and their contents scattered over the floor. The buckets of water would be upset, so that broken ice lay in shards across the floor, and the yoke was flung down on top of them. Chests would be standing open, their contents ransacked as if the woman of the house had come back and was desperately searching for something she had left behind. The ashes by the hearth would be scuffled as if many feet had come tramping through.

I could not sleep in the bed where Thorstein had died. I tried it the first night, with the covers pulled tight over my head, but every time my grip relaxed the bearskin on top would be twitched away, and I would lie exposed to the dark. When Thorstein the Black woke in the morning he found me curled on the bench by the hearth. The second night I didn't try to go to bed, but sat by the fire, feeding it scraps of dried seaweed. There wasn't enough fuel to keep a good fire going all night, but it comforted me to let a little flame burst through. The next day I slept heavily, while a snowstorm raged outside, and when I woke we were snowed in under seven feet of snow, and quite cut off from the rest of the settlement.

That was the day Thorstein and I buried the bodies deeply under the snow where they could lie until the spring came. I cooked him a meal that night. Neither of us had eaten properly for several days, and I think our souls were shaken loose in our own bodies, with all that had happened. To eat hot meat again was like a small coming alive. That night I wrapped myself in my cloak and lay down on the hard bench by the fire. Presently Thorstein spoke to me from his own bed: 'Gudrid, are you not going to your bed?'

'I can't,' I said.

'Why not?'

'Thorstein is not gone.'

'Maybe he wants to say something to you. Maybe you should listen, and then he could lie quiet.'

I shuddered. 'No.'

'Well, you can't sit up all night, night after night. Come here instead, and lie down.'

I sat up. 'What, with my husband's ghost watching over me?'

'I don't mean that. I won't touch you. But if you don't sleep you'll die too, and if I have to spend the winter with only the dead for company, I shall go mad. You'd be doing us all a favour, Gudrid, if you'd come here and lie down.'

To tell you the truth, I was glad to be persuaded. If there had been no ghosts, I wouldn't have made even a token defence of decency, but in that place the dead watched everything, and I was afraid that they would judge. In the end I did creep in under the covers with him, and I was glad of his human warmth.

\*     \*     \*     \*     \*

Why do you want to know that? What difference does it make? We did what was necessary to stay alive, no more. It was dark, the snow lay over us, and the dead surrounded us, and for five long months we survived. Thorstein the Black has been my friend ever since. We know each other as no one else possibly can – he knows me in a way that neither of my husbands ever did. He's my good friend, and we came out of that living grave together, intact in mind and body. I'll never tell what he had to do to lay his wife's ghost when she rose from the dead and confronted him, and he'll never betray me either, if we live for a hundred years. All that winter we were outside the boundaries of this world of yours, and the rules you make just don't apply. Good and bad, light and dark – in this country these things may seem to be as inevitable as living itself, but in the Western

Settlement in winter it was not like that. Some days were dark as night, when the blizzards blew over us, and some nights, with the moon on the snow, were filled with uncanny light. We fed the cattle in the byre, and ourselves, and we slept, and we talked a little, and we played hnefatafl. Thorstein the Black had carved pieces out of caribou antler, and made the board from a barrel top. Through the short days we sat over our game, throwing the dice, moving the pieces, scarcely speaking. At first he always got my king – I'd never been much of a games player – but I grew more expert with practice, and in the end we were evenly matched. He told me he and Grimhild always used to play hnefatafl every day in winter. To save light in the evening we sat in the dark and told each other the stories of our lives up until that time. Thorstein the Black is an honest man. He tells the truth whether men like it or not, and he wrests his living doggedly, year by year, from the land, and he accepts from his fate the best and the worst that it offers him. He never resents the luck he was born to, as some men do. He's suspicious of new ideas – he's not a Christian, even yet – and he'll end true to the faith he was born in, and accept the meagre promise that it offers when he dies.

It bothered him that he could offer no thralls to wait on me, and he kept saying that when the snow lifted he would fetch some of the land workers. I kept on telling him that the lack of servants was the last thing on my mind, and I wanted no one near me who had to be bribed to come close to a woman who brought evil fortune with her. It was no hardship to me to cook for us both; I was just grateful that owing to his good provision and Grimhild's forethought the house was well-filled with dried fish and meat. Of course I never said so, but in a way it was a relief to my over-burdened spirit to clean the place up, which I could never have done if Grimhild had lived. You look as if my callous attitude shocked you, and yet you'd not be shocked at all if I were a man and told you I'd wiped out a whole settlement in blood feud. My husband was dead, I was trapped in a house where the dead outnumbered the living by a score or more: you shouldn't grudge it to me that it satisfied me a little to wash layers of grease from soapstone pots in hot water, for the first time since they were carved. At intervals Thorstein the Black would stand over me, frowning, and say 'You're my guest, you shouldn't have to do such things for me.' In the end I snapped, 'And what would you do if I didn't?', which started him off about the thralls again, and I wished I hadn't opened my mouth.

And yet at other times he was as sensitive as a woman. I wasn't the easiest of companions, I'm sure. Well, I know I'm not, I've never been submissive or quiet as most men like their wives to be. My husband Thorstein and I used to quarrel violently sometimes, because I'd set my will up against his, and I'd go on arguing with him until he had no words left, and then he'd hit me and I'd scream at him so all the household could hear the names I called him. Karlsefni and I didn't quarrel, because Karlsefni was an even-tempered man, and over the years I grew less aggressive, I think, for having nothing to oppose. The few times I did make Karlsefni angry, I was frightened. He never shouted or hit me, but his silent rage was worse. I rarely saw it, and almost never was it directed at me.

Thorstein the Black was not my husband, but we had to live alone together all that winter. He had suffered as much as I had, and he said again and again that I was a comfort to him, but what I remember is the hard time I gave him. I used to wake in the night sobbing, and crying out for Thorstein who was dead. In my dreams I killed Thorstein myself, night after night, and it was always the horror of what I had done that woke me. I wish I could have felt pure grief, and mourned him as he deserved, but this was not mourning, it was nightmare. Thorstein the Black took an axe and laid the walking ghost of his own wife, but he only did so because she threatened Thorstein and me. Perhaps if we had not been there she would never have walked. I remember how I lay in the arms of Thorstein the Black and cried out 'I didn't kill him! I never meant to kill him!', and he held me and said over and over again, 'No, Gudrid, you killed no one. You hurt no one. You aren't to blame.'

One night when he was trying to comfort me he said, 'If Thorstein's ghost were to speak to you, it would only have good words to say. You'll take his body back to Brattahlid in spring, and thanks to you he'll be able to rest in peace. He would want fate to treat you kindly, and indeed I think your own fate will be gentler after this.'

'Why do you think that?' I asked, turning to face him, for the fact was I longed for someone to say that life would not always be quite so hard.

'I'm sure of it, Gudrid. You'll marry again. I expect you'll get out of Greenland; it's not the place for a woman like you. Maybe you'll marry an Icelander. But you will marry, I'm sure, and you'll have a long life together, and your children will be worthy of you, and you'll found a dynasty that will last through generations.'

I gave a laugh that was half a sob. 'You're not a seer, Thorstein. You can't know that.'

'No, I'm just an ignorant farmer. But sometimes a little gift is given even to men like me. A farseeing lady like you may mock me' – I pinched him then – 'but I know what I know.'

It's true, Agnar, he did. If he hadn't, I don't think he would have dared defy an unknown fate, even to comfort me. I think he knew. Here in Rome you'd think Thorstein the Black a savage. You'd see him as dirty, with matted hair and a skin wrinkled and weathered to dark brown like leather, dressed in stained sealskin trousers and boots with the fur left on them, and a thick bearskin jacket that had once been white, and two knives stuck through his belt without a sheath for either of them. You'd watch how he tore his food apart with his fingers instead of using a knife, and you'd recoil because he chewed raw blubber all the time, and smelt of it. You'd think him uncouth, without much to say for himself even in his own language, and you'd look down on him for not having a word of any other. No, just to imagine him in Rome is like trying to bring the two ends of the earth together inside my mind. I can't do it; I can't see where I am now and still see him as I knew him, it's not possible.

He kept his word to me in everything, and I'm glad to think I could do something for him. In the spring we left as soon as the ship was ready and the sea was open, and we had an easy passage back to Eiriksfjord. When we got back to Brattahlid Eirik took me into his family as if I were his own. In fact, in his terms, I was his own. Not all widows are treated like that, but Eirik's clan learned generosity from their chieftain, and when the time came Eirik arranged my marriage as if I'd been his own daughter – but that comes later. The point is that when I explained what Thorstein the Black had done for us, Eirik was ready to do anything that I asked for him. That's how it was that Thorstein got his farm, and was treated from then on as if he were the chieftain's own kinsman.

I was afraid when we got back to Brattahlid, because of the bad news we had to give, but when we landed it seemed that our story wasn't unexpected. It was raining when the people came down to help us beach the ship. Without any waste of words the bodies were carried ashore. In the damp air the smell of death hung over us, and flies gathered quickly where we stood. I can't remember how I broke the news, but I shall remember until I die the faces of Eirik and Thjodhild when they heard it. Neither of them made any complaint. Eirik Raudi stood very still, and stared out to sea. Thjodhild seemed to shrink into herself, and I remember noting the outline of her skull over finely wrinkled skin, but perhaps I had become too used to seeing death in everything. Then I felt a touch on my shoulder, and when I looked up I saw Leif. He looked serious, but not grief-stricken; I know he felt the loss of both his brothers, but he never showed his feelings to anyone, I am sure. He said to me, 'It's been hard on you, Gudrid,' which no one else had done, and then he glanced at his parents. 'Gudrid,' he went on, 'Will you come with me a moment? I've something to tell you.'

Wondering, I walked with him along the sandy path at the beach top, among thistles and silverweed.

'It's been a hard homecoming for you.'

'Hard for you, too,' I said.

'Gudrid, your father . . .'

As soon as he spoke I knew what he was going to say, and I realised too that I ought to have known before. If I hadn't been so self-absorbed, so buried in my own strange fate, I had the power in me to know that Thorbjorn had also met his fate that winter.

'How did it happen?' I asked quickly, and Leif glanced at me sideways through the rain.

'You knew then?'

'I ought to have known,' I said ambiguously.

'He went to stay with Thorkel at Hvalsoy for the seal hunt. We had a fine spell just after Yule. He took a hole in the pack ice, not a mile from the open sea. When he didn't come home at dusk they searched, and his thrall found him where he had slipped into the water and drowned. The body was still afloat. As you're Christians he was brought back here, and Eirik let my mother and I have him buried in the churchyard here at Brattahlid.'

I was silent. I should have wept but no tears came. Perhaps I had none left. A man has to stand for hours at one of those holes in the ice, with his spear ready, until the seal bursts to the surface. He has a second to strike, and if he fails the seal breathes and is gone. All those hours alone on the ice he must stay alert and watch that round dark hole of water. Karlsefni used to say it was like watching the doors of hell, because you could see uncanny beings move and vanish, seals shifting shape and becoming nightmare creatures from the unknown bottom of the ocean. He said the round hole would seem to grow, and to be a tunnel, or a mirror; it would be like staring into the iris of your own eye. A man might go in, he said, not because he slipped on the ice but because his own will drew him down, so he couldn't help himself. Karlsefni never knew my father, but I talked to him about Thorbjorn's death as I talked to him about everything over the years.

I'm not sure I ever knew my father either. Thorbjorn used to complain he never knew his, my grandfather Vifil who had been a slave. I felt I had failed my father by my ignorance of his death, and for a long time I strained to imagine how it happened. I've seen the round holes in the ice, and I've seen the seals butchered and brought home. I've never seen the kill: women don't. The tense hours of waiting are outside my experience. But I'm not sure the manner of Thorbjorn's death was even relevant. His whole mind was strange to me, and always had been. I never saw anything from his point of view, and for a long time I felt that perhaps I ought to have done, though I can't see how that would have saved him.

When Leif told me I said nothing at all. In private he could be surprisingly kind, and he did nothing to press me, but walked with me in silence up to the church where it lay tucked away behind a little hill. When I went and looked at the fresh mound where they had buried my father as soon as the ground was warm enough, I neither wept nor keened, but stood frozen, as if the ice had entered my blood and made me a dead thing in a living body. I felt nothing of my father but a great emptiness inside me, and I saw him neither in heaven nor walking the boundaries of this earth, and I have never had any glimpse of him since.

Of course I inherited everything my father had, as well as Thorstein's farm at Sandnes, and now I was also part of Eirik's family at Brattahlid, so I was able to be generous in giving gifts for the first time in my life. I've enjoyed my wealth most of all for that reason; I inherit my father's pride in giving lavishly. Thorstein the Black had told me that he had no wish to return to the Western Settlement. He had buried Grimhild there, but he said, 'She'll rest more peacefully if I'm not there to bother her.' I think the trouble he'd had with her ghost had shaken him more than I knew, and I was so wrapped up in my own troubles, young as I was then, that I didn't think enough about what it all meant to him. But I got him his farm. I asked Eirik if Thorstein the Black could work my land at Stokkanes, as I was now to live at Brattahlid, and Eirik agreed at once, and Thorstein the Black has lived there ever since. When I left Greenland, I made the place over to him outright. I've not heard of his death, so it's possible he lives there still.

Thorstein Eiriksson was buried next to my father by the church, and his men further away by the wall. So many more lie there now, so many men and women that I knew. Who do I tell this story for, when not one of them can ever hear it? Who else would care? It's a bad thing to outlive your friends, Agnar. You can't imagine it now, can you? No one can, until it happens. Who is there in this world now who knows me? My sons? What's the past to them? A few stories that I told them when they were small, that they half remember. And half of that half they'll make into another story, and tell their children, and maybe a fraction of that will go into yet another story, and be told to their children's children. Many generations, Thorstein the Black said to me. No woman could wish for more, and yet what are these people to me, whom I shall never know? When I was young and had children, I thought the most important thing in life was the future, their future. But now it seems that the most important part of my life is buried in the Green Land, and the future belongs to somebody else. When I die I hope to rest in peace. I think the worst thing would be to stay here as a ghost that nobody remembered.

I'm being a miserable old woman, Agnar. Stop writing, and tell me about something else. Remind me I'm a Christian, if you like, or give me a penance. You can't? Never mind. Tell me more about wine then, about these different vineyards you mentioned, and what makes a good vintage. How did you learn about these things? Do you go round tasting them all? Tell me all about it.

# THIRTEEN

# *July 28th*

Some people believe you can read the threads of fate in the palm of a hand. I don't disbelieve them, but I'm not sure that it's necessary. When I look back on my own life I see very clearly that the threads of my fate haven't been spun together firmly, but have woven their ways separately. Sometimes one, sometimes another, has come out on top at different times. When I came back to Brattahlid as Eirik's daughter-in-law, it seemed there was nothing in life but death. Life didn't seem to offer anything more for me, but the truth was the thread of an unlucky fate had spun itself out. Why I had borne this burden from the beginning of my life I don't know; the fates are beyond reason. But I had borne it, and now it was done. I come now to a new phase of my life, and now I look back and it seems as clear as the spring following the winter. I'm not saying everything now was easy, but the dark had cleared.

It still seems odd to me that the sun goes on shining day after day. It's like living in a hot spring, but it's the contrast I miss; you know what it's like lying in hot water with the snowflakes whirling round your head. There's piquancy in that. I do like the light and dark here – walking in from the white heat into a dim room that smells of earth. I hope heaven, if it pleases God we get there, isn't all brilliance; eternity under those conditions would be exhausting. Perhaps the old way is better, just to survive in shadows and memories; at least one day there's an end to that. I'm a great-grandmother by now, I think. Snorri's daughter was pregnant when I left. I'd like to live long enough for the child to have known me – something to tell his (or her) great-grandchild perhaps? I bought a mass for its soul, living or dead. Perhaps by the end of the year we'll have a letter from Iceland.

Has it occurred to you, Agnar, what a cold place this Christian heaven is? For mortals, I mean. Sometimes I wonder if to be immortal is to be free not from time but from cold. Spirits feel no warmth or cold; some souls are content to lie in their graves while the ground freezes, and others wander over the icefields where no living man would survive one night. Sometimes at sea I've looked out on endless water and the cold sky, and I've thought that were I not earthbound, were I not cold and afraid, this would in fact be heaven. It fits, you see: heaven lies to the north of earth, outside the boundaries of the world of men. To the living it's ghastly in its frozen loneliness, but to the dead, untroubled by winter and night, it's the place of everlasting light, the sun that never sets. But cold, Agnar, and so large you could wander up and down forever, and never see the tracks of another soul, not even those you loved. When I see it like that I think I would rather die.

\*   \*   \*   \*   \*

I'm sure what you say is orthodox, Agnar. It may even be true. But that's not the point.

I knew Karlsefni so well, body and mind, for thirty years, that now he hardly seems separate from myself. We didn't get on very well when we were first married. He was so self contained, I felt I could make no impression on him. He never set himself up. I don't think he thought at all about the effect he had on others. He was shockingly single-minded, at least, it shocked me. He looked after his own, and I was part of his own. He didn't care much about anyone who wasn't.

So what did he seem like before I knew him? It's hard to go back to that, but I'll try. Walk around the cloister a couple of times, Agnar, and let me think.

*Eirik Raudi sits in his hall at Brattahlid. His face is wrinkled now like the surface of a glacier, his body hunched into itself. Only his eyes are dark and alert. On the long hearth in front of him the fire that he first lit here* twenty years ago still smoulders. The hall is full of men, but Eirik Raudi looks only into the fire, and tells nobody his thoughts.

Tonight there are guests at Brattahlid. An Icelandic ship has arrived direct from Norway, loaded with goods from Europe and beyond: grain, salt, wine, iron, linen and spices, luxuries hardly seen before in Greenland. The ship took the bold route due west from Bergen, sighting land once two weeks ago, when the last island in Faroe showed to the north, half sunk below the horizon. Leif took the same route five years ago, and now Leif is talking excitedly to the captain of the new ship, whose name is Thorfinn, nicknamed Karlsefni by the king of Norway himself.

Karlsefni answers Leif quietly but with complete assurance. He is a smaller man than Leif, strong and compact. His curly hair is cut short, and his beard is newly trimmed. His eyes are the grey of fresh water under cloud, and his skin is the same colour as his salt-stained deerskin tunic. After making one of the longest voyages in the world, he looks as neat, after half a day ashore, as a man on his way to mass on Sunday morning. He accepts sour buttermilk to drink as if it were the finest wine at the court of Norway, and while he eats he goes on answering Leif's questions steadily. He seems to know exactly what he is about. He has come to the Green Land to make as much profit as possible.

Three women of Eirik's household sit with the men at the high table. Thjodhild has grown larger, her presence sterner. She says little, but she watches the newcomer, she watches her son Leif, and from time to time she glances at her husband's impassive face. Freydis, Eirik's daughter, came to Brattahlid this morning, as soon as the news came to Gardar that a merchant ship had been sighted on its way to Brattahlid. Her husband Thorkel is not with her; he is irrelevant to Freydis' mercantile ambitions. The third woman is Eirik's daughter-in-law Gudrid, widowed for almost a year. She fulfils her role as daughter of the household with more grace than Freydis ever did, but she and Freydis seem to be as friendly now as sisters should be. Freydis has a man and is mistress of an estate, and Gudrid has lost the advantages of both.

At the lower table the crew of the strange ship tear at fresh seal meat and salmon with teeth and knives, and down their fermented milk as if their stomachs had no limits.

Thorfinn Karlsefni has been a trader for a long time, and his face gives *no clue to his thoughts. His manner is open and friendly, but he has said nothing at all yet about the price of his cargo, or his reasons for coming so far off the main trade routes. He seems absorbed in his conversation with Leif, but occasionally his eyes flicker away and glance down the room. They rest for a moment on Gudrid, and a little later they come back to her again, and twice again.*

He arrived at Brattahlid at the end of the summer, and naturally he was invited to spend the winter with us. Leif liked Karlsefni at once – they knew each other by hearsay – and treated him with the utmost friendliness. Eirik was getting old by now, and quite irascible, but he soon took to Karlsefni. They spoke the same language; they were both shrewd, and they both knew how to use the rules to get exactly what they wanted. It was like watching a game of chess to see them together. Eirik made the first move. He was silent and withdrawn for about a week, until in the end Karlsefni asked him straight out if his presence at Brattahlid offended his host.

'No,' said Eirik. 'Far from it. It's not that. But I'm ashamed that I can't offer you better hospitality. We live in a poor way here; dried fish and seal meat and buttermilk are what get us through the winter. But you've been used to wintering in Norway, and I know I can't offer you the fare you're used to at the Yule feast. It hurts my pride to treat you so shabbily.'

'If that's all, there's no difficulty,' said Karlsefni at once. 'I've a cargo here with wine from the Rhineland, spices from Russia, and this year's grain from the Baltic harvest. What's mine is yours, for as long as I'm your guest here. I'd like to make you a gift of all the food we'll need for the winter feasts.'

Eirik clasped his hand at once. 'You're a man after my own heart,' he told Karlsefni. 'I'll accept your offer, and now we can treat you in the way I'd like to do.'

So at the price of half his cargo, Karlsefni set up his winter trading post at Brattahlid, and made a good profit from all the settlers round Eiriksfjord, getting white bear furs and sealskins and narwhal and walrus ivory from that year's hunt. I'm sure everything went exactly as he'd calculated, and all the time he was building up goodwill for future years. There's more than one ship coming regularly from Norway to Greenland now, in fact one of them belongs to my son, part of his legacy from his father, but Karlsefni was the first. No one else had the imagination to go straight from Norway to the new settlement until he did. Certainly the direct link with Norway changed people's lives in the Green Land. It served us far better than trade through Iceland, for Iceland's needs and goods were much the same as ours, which meant that we paid twice for everything. We couldn't send a ship of our own, you see. We were chronically short of wood, and therefore boats, and those we had were used for the northern hunt, without which we'd starve. We needed all our men for the farms and the hunting, so Karlsefni was on to a good thing, and he knew it.

He never meant to go further than Brattahlid, but two things happened that winter to suggest other possibilities. The first was that it wasn't long before Leif was talking to him about Vinland. Leif had been frustrated in his plans for Vinland for years, for the same reason as we didn't trade directly with Norway ourselves: lack of resources. Karlsefni arrived with the biggest ship that had yet been seen in Greenland, and a full crew, all in good health. Karlsefni husbanded his men, like all his capital, with particular care.

The first snow had fallen before we found out what had put Greenland into Karlsefni's mind. He mentioned that he'd called at Dyrnes on his way to Brattahlid, to visit Snorri Thorbrandsson.

'You know him well?' asked Leif.

'I've known him for years. I saw him and Thorleif set out for here, just before I left for Norway.'

'And you talked about visiting him in Greenland?'

'We saw it as a possibility.'

Soon after that we had a fall of good crisp snow, and Leif and Karlsefni went south to Dyrnes. I stood at the milking ring with Thjodhild and watched them ski away, two dark figures like moving holes cut out of the whiteness of the frozen fjord. They were gone two weeks, and when they came back the talk was all of Vinland. I didn't know, of course, exactly what Snorri and Leif had told Karlsefni, and

Karlsefni himself was quiet as usual, and gave away nothing of his state of mind, at least, not about that.

I mentioned two things. The other matter that led Karlsefni on was, in fact, myself.

As Eirik's daughter, I was a good proposition. I owned Stokkanes, conveniently close to Brattahlid, which Thorstein the Black managed for me, and a big estate at Sandnes. I brought with me kinship with the most powerful chieftain in Greenland. Nothing could do more to enhance Karlsefni's prospects in the West. But I flatter myself – no, I know – it wasn't just that. Karlsefni had no plans to marry when he came. He used to look at me, not hungrily, as Thorvald and Thorstein once did, but speculatively, and never for more than a moment. The day after he got back from Dyrnes he started to talk to me. I was startled. I wasn't working in the women's room, as it happened, because I was cutting some of the new linen cloth into a tunic for myself, and, as the men were all out, I was using one of the big tables in the hall to spread the cloth right out. When Karlsefni came in, I began to gather up my things and leave him the room, but he stopped me.

'No, don't move,' he said. 'You'll spoil the cut if you fold it up now.'

I couldn't help smiling. 'You know all about making clothes?'

'Of course.' He sat down on the bench next to me, and watched as I made a nick in the cloth with my knife, and tore the length carefully.

'I'm glad you brought linen,' I said after a pause. 'I've never worn any before.'

'It won't do much to keep you warm here.'

'It's not meant to. I can wear as much wool as I like underneath it.'

'It would hang better if you didn't have to.'

I said nothing. His last comment seemed faintly immodest, but the men I was used to were much more direct.

'I hear you've lived in the Western Settlement,' he said presently.

'I spent one winter there, and that was the worst of my life. I didn't see much.'

'Yes, I know. I'm sorry. But you've an estate there, so you'll go back one day?'

'I've never seen Sandnes,' I told him. 'Thorstein went there every year. Leif went this summer, and brought back what we needed.'

Karlsefni nodded. 'I might go north myself in the spring. I thought you could tell me something about it.'

I stared at him. 'What can I possibly tell you that Leif can't?'

He grinned at me. 'A lot. Leif has no opinions about linen, for example.'

'And you do?'

'I'm a merchant. I study my goods.'

I didn't know what to make of him. He never talked to me like that when anyone else was there, but after that occasion he seemed to contrive to get me alone, a difficult thing to do in a crowded farmstead in winter. But he had a way of finding out where I was. As soon as he realised I fed the hens first thing in the morning he'd turn up in the byre just as I was bringing the bucket of fish skins from the hearth. We'd have another of those odd conversations, just a few sentences, then he'd smile, raise his hand to me in farewell, and walk off. On the second day of Advent he stopped me as I was about to go into the house. 'Can I talk to you?'

'Why not?'

We went a little way along the path past Thjodhild's church towards the pasture. The snow was firm and easy to walk on, and it was one of those clear days when everything seemed very near: Burfjell across the fjord looked scarcely a stone's throw away, and I could hear the ravens on the crags by Stokkanes.

'I want to make an offer to Eirik,' said Karlsefni abruptly. 'I think he'll accept. I want to know if you will.'

'Me?' I'd have liked him to be more humble, and so I made it difficult for him.

'Yes. If he agreed that I should marry you, would you consent?'

'I'm a widow. I have the right to make my own contracts.'

'I know. But I don't want to offend Eirik.'

'Yes, I can see why that's important to you. But if you want to succeed in this, you'd do as well not to offend me either.'

'I don't want to offend you.' He gripped my arm when I would have turned away. 'Gudrid, this isn't for the reason you think. I had no plans to marry here until I saw you.'

'It must have seemed very convenient when you did.'

'No,' said Karlsefni seriously. 'If I'd thought it was convenient to have a wife I'd have got one long ago. I don't need to marry to get what I want – not in business, I mean. But I want to marry you.'

'Why?'

Karlsefni shrugged. 'I want to sleep with you. Is that what you want me to say? It's true. Don't you think I'd make a good husband?'

The truth was that I did, but I wouldn't give him an answer because he'd made me angry, and I wouldn't let him touch me either. In the days before Yule he gave me presents: an amber necklace, a silver bracelet, ivory needles. When I went across to Stokkanes to see Thorstein the Black he asked to come with me, and while we were alone in the sledge I'd have come close to giving him what he said he'd wanted, only it was too cold, even under the fur rug. I'd missed all that since Thorstein died. I didn't want to make things easy for Karlsefni, but from then on I knew I'd give in, and so no doubt did he.

It was Eirik who put a stop to all this by accepting Karlsefni's proposal on my behalf, and demanding a straight answer from me. One didn't play games with Eirik, and so the betrothal was made. I married Karlsefni on the last day of Yule. This time Eirik made no fuss about a Christian ceremony, as he'd done when I married Thorstein. He couldn't, because Karlsefni had been baptised at the Thing, the year that Christianity was declared law in Iceland. The feast that night was the best ever seen in Greenland, nearly all provided by Karlsefni, of course. For me the two most important guests were Thorstein the Black, because he truly wished me well, and Snorri Thorbrandsson, because he had been my father's enemy and was now my husband's closest friend. He was Snorri's godfather too, but that comes later.

Eirik and Leif were bound to support my marriage to Karlsefni, even if they hadn't liked him. It wasn't just the lack of bread and wine to feed his guests that irked Eirik, but the more basic need for timber. In fact we never brought home any wood from Vinland suitable for shipbuilding, but the forests were there, and when Eirik and Leif looked at Karlsefni, what they saw was the fabulous wealth of

Vinland, their own and still unreachable. Leif had never been back to his trading post in the west. His brothers were dead and his father was old, and he was tied to Greenland. The only other person who had the sailing directions for Vinland was Bjarni Herjolfsson, whom Leif saw as a rival, not a friend. Bjarni went to Norway about the time I married Thorstein, and when he did finally come home, he showed no interest in the empty lands he had once sighted.

So I was the keystone of an alliance that seemed to be ideal for everybody, yet Karlsefni spoke the truth when he told me he didn't need a wife to get what he wanted. I realised in the end that I'd genuinely taken him by surprise. He hadn't thought of himself as a man at all likely to fall in love. I found him much more experienced with women than Thorstein had been, and a good lover because he had a curiosity that Thorstein had quite lacked, which made him endlessly interested in what it was like to be somebody else. Freydis said, when I unwillingly answered some of her questions, that I was a lucky woman, but Karlsefni disconcerted me. After Thorstein I thought him coldhearted, although it turned out I was wrong. We seemed outwardly to get on well, but I somehow felt I couldn't reach him, not until the ghosts at Sandnes. But that comes later. Meanwhile, I felt at a disadvantage and I told him so.

'But you've been married before,' he pointed out, 'which is more than I have.'

'But you've obviously not been alone all your life.'

It was dark and I couldn't see his face. We were whispering, because although we had an inner chamber, the dividing walls didn't reach the roof, and we could only be private if we were quiet.

'What do you want me to tell you?' he asked. 'As it happens, I have always been alone.'

'Not in bed.'

Another pause. 'No, not when I've had the chance. What did you expect?'

'Do you have a woman at home?'

'No. I'm hardly ever there.' He sighed, obviously not wanting this conversation. 'If it comforts you, there's no woman anywhere. I'm never in one place for long. When I've wanted sex I've taken it, and sometimes I've paid and sometimes not. When I didn't, it was usually another man's wife, so it wouldn't be fair for me to talk about it.'

It was his last admission that shocked me, and he guessed it from my silence, and laughed under his breath. 'Seducing unmarried girls is against the law, my love, and can get a man into all kinds of trouble.'

'I see.'

He was serious suddenly. 'You don't. It's the past. I wasn't married then. How could I think of you when I'd never heard of you?'

He was right, Agnar, and I was wrong even to bring up the subject. It was none of my business. It wasn't really the women he'd known that bothered me; it was the lack of knowing between the two of us. I did know about that, you see, because I'd had Thorstein. In his way Karlsefni was as inaccessible as the ice desert that covers the heart of the Green Land. I didn't realise that I seemed just as cold to him. He made me desire him, certainly, and he desired me, but I wanted something else, so even the pleasure he gave me made me resentful of him. Can you understand that?

\*     \*     \*     \*     \*

No, you're wrong; he was being honest, and that was more than most men would be. He had integrity; it's you who judge by the wrong things. It wasn't for nothing that the king gave him the nickname Karlsefni, and a gold ring with it, which Karlsefni always wore on the third finger of his right hand. He *was* outstanding. Everyone called him Karlsefni because they recognised what the king saw in him.

When I look back now it's my own ignorance I see. In fact – I've never really thought this out before – what Karlsefni did for me was to lead me back into the world, off the mountaintops and down among the houses. Three years later, when Karlsefni took me to Norway, I loved it. I came alive at the king's court. I had women my age as friends, and I learned to gossip. I went to feasts and games and markets, I spent money for the first time in my life, and I bought things with it that weren't necessary for our survival. I ate so much that winter that by spring I could pinch the fat around my waist and it was as wide as my wrist. I'd never been plump before. I liked it, and he liked it too, and I bought new wool and linen, and paid other women to make more clothes for me, even though I already had two of everything. It was a long way from Vinland, but I must tell you about Vinland first.

He did love me, Agnar, right from the beginning. He did everything he knew how to do to make me fall in love with him, and in return I was resentful about where he'd learned his skill with women. I've been in the world much longer now, and I say I was much too hard on him.

Anyway, he wanted me to go with him to Vinland, and I said I would, although I'd vowed never to face those western seas again while I lived. Once I'd agreed, I made myself part of it. I wasn't going to have men making plans all round me as if I wasn't there, not if I was to share the fate in store for us. Things started to happen very quickly when Snorri came up from Dyrnes at Candlemas over the ice through Isafjord. I remember one day it was snowing, and they were all sitting in by the hearth, and I left my loom and came and stood by the door listening. They were arguing about whose men to take and whose to leave, as space on the ship was going to be very limited. Karlsefni had reckoned on Snorri bringing his own ship, but it turned out that he'd promised it to his brother Thorleif that year. I waited for the right moment, and spoke out clearly: 'I have a ship lying up at Stokkanes.'

They all swung round in amazement at the interruption. Only Karlsefni didn't move. He was sitting where he could see me anyway, and he just watched me, giving away nothing. Legally, the ship that had been my father's and then Thorstein's was Karlsefni's now, but I thought of it as mine, belonging to my past, not his. It was Leif, not Karlsefni, who answered me. 'So you do,' he said. 'What are you offering, Gudrid?'

'A ship,' I said, 'Upon terms.'

Snorri swore under his breath. Karlsefni looked thoughtful, and Leif said, 'Fair enough. Sit down and tell us.'

I sat by the hearth among them all, as I had not been able to do since I was a little girl. I was aware of my heart beating, but I seemed entirely sure of myself, Karlsefni said. 'That ship was my father's,' I said. 'We brought it from Iceland. It was Thorstein's, and we set out on this journey once before. It was mine, and I brought Thorstein's body home in it to Brattahlid. It's been laid up all summer, and Thorstein the Black has repaired and refitted it for me. It's a fine ship, and it's as good as new.'

'That's true,' said Leif. 'I've seen his work.'

'Karlsefni has his own ship,' I said, 'and of course I'll sail with him. I could lend my father's ship to Snorri Thorbrandsson; I think my father would understand that things have changed. In return I'll take my share of the cargo, and as I'm going on this expedition too, I'll be included in your meetings about it.'

Leif smiled at me, and I realised my own need tallied with his; I represented the interests of his family, as no one else would once he was left behind. 'I think that's fair,' he said. 'What do you say, Karlsefni?'

Karlsefni glanced at him, and looked again at me. 'I think it's admirable,' he said drily, and I was left wondering just what that meant.

The other men were so glad to have a second ship on any terms that no one opposed my presence, or tried to stop me saying what I thought, then or ever. Agnar, I don't know why I was so sure of myself, why I was so firm about it, but it worked, and the fact is, I think we may owe our lives to the stand I took that day. If I'd had no authority among them, if I'd been nothing but Karlsefni's wife, then the day the skraelings came would have been our last, I think. So fate works with us, sometimes, for our own good, not that anyone should put their trust in that.

We decided that Karlsefni would be leader of the expedition, and Snorri would be master of the second ship. Snorri's son Thorbrand sailed with him; he was a fine young man, and I still hate to think about his death. But how could we have known? Both ships were to have at least one man who'd sailed with Leif, although Leif was less willing to part with men or information to Snorri than to Karlsefni, who was, after all, now his brother-in-law. He provided both grudgingly, but insisted that the loan of Leif's houses in Vinland was a personal favour to Karlsefni and me, and the others could only stay there as Karlsefni's invited guests. That caused some ill feeling, but Karlsefni dealt with it as he always did, treating the vagaries of men like the weather, just a problem to be solved, not a thing to show pride about.

As Karlsefni and his Icelandic crew had never been to the Western Settlement either, Eirik also gave us a man who knew that coast well, as he'd often gone hunting with Thorstein. We couldn't have had a more experienced pilot, but I heard of the gift with dismay. He was called Thorhall the Hunter, a big, uncouth man, who used to ferment his own drink from juniper berries. Karlsefni said it was the strongest stuff he'd ever tasted. I was never offered any. Thorhall could make other men drunk if he wanted to; for himself, I was never sure if he was drunk or sober. I could never make out a word he said anyway, and that annoyed him. If I didn't like him, he could scarcely stand me. He was getting old now, and grumbled about being sent with us, but Eirik insisted, and gave him silver coins to appease him. He'd always got on with Thorhall; they used to drink together and abuse the new religion that made lambs out of men, women into lawmen, and death into an orgy of self-pitying guilt. But we'd never have got safely so far out of the world as we did without Thorhall's sailing directions.

You must understand, Agnar, that the plan was to make a trading post in Vinland, not a farm. None of us wanted to settle permanently so far out of the world, at least, not until the trade was coming, and then the place might attract settlers. Leif and Karlsefni wanted to make sure of their own rule in the new country before they encouraged anyone else. So we were to build up Leif's houses into a winter settlement that could be a base for all future expeditions. It lay at the gateway of Vinland, which we assumed went on south until it joined with Africa, round the circle of the world. With the resources of such a country behind us, we could supply Greenland with timber for ships, and if the hunting was as good as in Greenland, we could have furs and ivory for Norway too. Leif was obsessed by the possibilities of making wine, though I sensed that Karlsefni was sceptical. He hadn't tasted the Vinland wine as we had.

So Karlsefni committed himself to Greenland in a way he'd never foreseen when he arrived. I couldn't answer all his questions about my estate at Sandnes, and he was wary of talking to Leif about that; it wouldn't have been tactful to show much interest in the property that had once been Thorstein's. But I know he had plans for it, situated as it was so conveniently on the Vinland route. I didn't like that; in my mind Sandnes was still Thorstein's, and I felt protective of the past when Karlsefni talked about it. Sandnes and Thorstein – that was the core of the matter. But I'm tired. I'll talk about that tomorrow.

# FOURTEEN

# *August 3rd*

The most fickle places are at the edge of the earth, where a way can be impassible one year, and wide open the next. Not only that, but you're not allowed to believe it could ever have been different. My second journey to the Western Settlement was all sun and wind and sparkling light. We left Brattahlid first; the arrangement was that we'd rendezvous with Snorri at the mouth of Lysufjord in three weeks' time. The sea was dark blue, the icebergs gleamed like jewels, and a fresh following wind whipped the crests off the waves and filled our sail. On land the mountains looked as if they'd been scoured, and the precipices cast purple shadows that moved round slowly as the long days passed. Lysufjord was blue and innocent. We passed Thorstein the Black's farm, a snug steading on an open slope that looked as if it had never known a winter since the world began. In a sudden pearl-grey calm we moored off Sandnes, and the smell of spring lapped us round.

My tenant at Sandnes was a man called Helgi, but it was his wife Sigrid who was in charge of things. She seemed glad to see me, especially as when we rode over the farm I could only praise the work that had been done. The cattle were out eating the new grass, and seemed robust already. We rode inland to the sheep pastures, where the bleating of new lambs competed with the rapids of a swollen river lined with withies. Karlsefni rode behind us, taking in everything, while I questioned Sigrid and Helgi; I could tell he was satisfied.

We chose sheep and cattle and a couple of ponies to take with us, and enough food for the rest of our voyage. In the space they were to occupy we'd brought Norwegian goods, which Snorri and the crew had unloaded while we were out. It pleased me to watch Sigrid look into the barrel and the sealskin sacks that were for her use. I've always liked watching people receive my gifts. Sigrid put her hand into the grain sack and ran the golden stuff through her fingers, and Helgi weighed the nuggets of iron in his hands, and smiled. Karlsefni gave them instructions about trading the rest of his goods for furs and ivory, to be stored at the farm until we came back. When Sigrid realised we intended to leave so soon for Vinland she was distressed, and took my hand, patting and stroking it. No one mentioned Thorstein, but these people knew him well, and used to look for his ship every year at just this time.

That night I dreamed that the door of the house was flung open, and my husband Thorstein and Grimhild the wife of Thorstein the Black pushed their way into the hearth, throwing aside Sigrid's spindle and the chessboard to make room for themselves. I screamed, and sat up. There was a crash from the fireside, and Karlsefni was out of bed, grabbing his knife from under the pillow. Something moved across the room towards him. The fire glowed in the draught from the open door, and then a turf was taken off it, and a lamp flickered into life. I saw a huge shadow on the wall, but before I screamed again I realised it was Karlsefni standing by the hearth in his shirt holding the lamp high. The light fell on a white face, and I recognised Helgi. Helgi pointed with his sword to something by the hearth, and Karlsefni lowered the lamp. The big soapstone pot which had held our meat at supper was broken into three pieces.

The second night I had the dream again, and that time the big chest in the corner was thrown open, its lock broken, and winter clothes from it were left smouldering over the smoored fire.

On the third night Karlsefni didn't come to bed but sat by the fire, his drawn sword across his knees, and the lamp burning on the bench beside him. Helgi waited with him. I would have sat up too, but Karlsefni ordered me to sleep, which to my surprise I did, almost as soon as I lay down. Afterwards he told me he'd given me poppy seed, because he had to make sure of the dream.

That night the dream was worst of all. When the door flew open it wasn't just Thorstein and Grimhild who thrust their way in, but everyone who'd died among us that winter. I saw them fall upon the living men, and when I woke up there was nobody beside me. I saw the lamp burning by an empty hearth, and the fire scattered in glowing embers across the room. Sigrid was crying when she came over to my bed to find me. I couldn't move, and it seemed so long before the men came back, and when they did, they were soaked through from the rain. They'd followed the taunts and footsteps through the dark, but it had been as hopeless as following the wind.

Sigrid wept again next morning, and said we needed a priest to sprinkle holy water, but the nearest priest was far away at Brattahlid. 'Nothing like this ever happened here before,' she sobbed. 'It's been a good place. We've been happy here.'

'And shall be,' said Karlsefni. He sat at the hearth all that morning, frowning into the fire, while the rain beat down outside. Then, when we'd had our meal, and the crew and thralls had been sent to work, he called the four of us together. 'Sigrid and Helgi,' he said, 'you were friends of my wife's first husband Thorstein. I want you to listen, and see now that justice is done. Gudrid,' he turned to me, 'the ghost of Thorstein never came here before, although this was his farm. Why do you think he's coming to claim the place now?'

Tears were running down my face; I couldn't help it. 'He was never my enemy,' I said. 'I loved him. I don't want to hurt him now.'

'So what do you want for him?'

'To rest in peace,' I answered, and tried not to sob aloud.

'Very well.' Karlsefni stood up, and led me outside, and the others followed. We all stood facing the house door, and the rain drove against our backs. 'We don't have any spiritual powers,' Karlsefni told us, 'but we all have the authority of our own laws. This is my house, it belongs to the living, and the dead are trespassers here.' He raised his voice, and called into the empty room. 'Thorstein Eirik's son, you no longer have any rights here. I summons you for trespass in the house of the living. Come out!'

Although we'd left the house warm the wind that blew out of it then was as dank as an open grave, and the door banged outward, wrenching its hinges. Sigrid screamed, and clung to Helgi. Helgi drew his sword.

Karlsefni didn't flinch. 'Thorstein Eirik's son, and all those you've brought here with you, listen to your judgement!' He pulled me to him. 'Go on, Gudrid. Judge!'

I don't know if he could see, but I could. I saw Thorstein, with the earth of the grave staining his shroud, his eye sockets empty, and white bones showing through his parched skin. I saw Grimhild beside him, her skin yellow and shrivelled on the bone, and I saw all the dead gathered behind them, between us and the house door, more than I could count.

My legs seemed not to hold me, and I fell back against Karlsefni. He held me against him hard, but he made me face them.

'Gudrid, they've obeyed my summons. They stand to be judged.'

I looked into the dark holes that had been Thorstein's eyes, and they seemed to draw me, so I felt I would fall in and drown. I tried to draw breath but my throat was too tight.

'Judge, Gudrid, judge!'

I made myself stand upright, Karlsefni behind me, and I wrenched my eyes away from the empty eyes of the dead, and I whispered, 'You must go now to the place prepared for you. You must go forever and not come back. And may you rest in peace.' Out of the corner of my eye I saw Sigrid cross herself, and I made a cross too, not on myself, but in front of me, for the ones on the other side. They bowed their heads, resigned, and slowly they began to slip away.

Thorstein was the last. He drifted past so close to me I could have put out my hand and touched him. I knew I must not, and so I let him go.

There was nothing now between us and the house door. I turned and flung my arms around my husband's neck, and sobbed as if my heart were broken. He brought me in out of the rain through to the privacy of our bed place. He held me in his arms and told me again and again that he loved me, until I was calm, and ashamed of the fuss that I was causing. Of course I never said so to him, ever, but while I was still crying I could feel that he was trembling. On ordinary occasions he had no patience at all with women's tears, and he used to walk out of the room at the smallest threat of them. Not that I caused him trouble that way; I'm not given to weeping. But I never forgot what he did for me that day, and I never held anything back from him that I could give, ever after.

*The ghosts gather in the shadow of the mountain, and look down on Sandnes. They see a patch of green pasture, hayfields in squares like blankets spread to dry. They see buildings like spindlewhorls hanging by the threads of paths woven by hooves and footsteps. A strip of shore hems the settlement, and needle-shaped boats are tucked in here and there along its length. The ghosts see how carefully made the place is, how neatly it is threaded together, but how fragile the green material is, spread between the bare rock and the sea. The ghosts look down through the grey rain they can no longer feel. Then they drift inland, and now there is no green, only the eternal, unforgiving ice. In the north the clouds shine like diamonds, illuminated by the reflected gleam of ice.*

    *The ghosts can never go back down among the houses. There is no hearth fire for them. Caught between the love that binds them to life, and the promise of a brilliance that they cannot feel, they vanish into the empty north, lost in the freezing light.*

# FIFTEEN

# *August 7th*

We'd better work hard today to make up for yesterday. But I enjoyed our talk, and surely we're allowed to relax sometimes. The story grows, doesn't it? You've nearly covered that roll of vellum, and soon you'll get to the stick. Can I look while you write?

\*    \*    \*    \*    \*

It's strange to think that any man who can read could look at that and hear my story, just the way I've told it to you.

\*    \*    \*    \*    \*

No, and he wouldn't see me standing here looking over your shoulder either, and he wouldn't smell the cypress and the cooking smells, or see that hen pecking in and out over the kitchen doorstep. Come to think of it, he might be somewhere completely different, in another country even, or another time of year. He might be sitting in a cold scriptorium with woollen mittens on to keep his hands warm, and the snow swirling outside. He might not be able to imagine how we sat here in the courtyard with the sun so high in the sky that the cloister hardly seemed to cast a shadow. He certainly wouldn't be able to share these walnuts with us – have another, take a handful – it must be a strange experience to be a man reading a book. How do you manage without a voice to guide you? How do you know who's talking? Where would you look while you imagine everything? Do you have to look at the writing all the time, just the black and white? How do you see pictures in your mind when you're doing that?

\*　　\*　　\*　　\*　　\*

Yes, I suppose wise men in Italy have gone thoroughly into all these questions.

\*　　\*　　\*　　\*　　\*

What, different colours? Like the pictures on a church wall? Or more like weaving?

\*　　\*　　\*　　\*　　\*

I didn't know that. I never knew a book could be beautiful. Does it take the monks a very long time? Do you know how to do it?

\*　　\*　　\*　　\*　　\*

For the glory of God. Yes, I understand. Agnar, if one were a woman, if one were never able to enter a scriptorium, or stand at the lectern in the Cathedral – is there any way – would it be at all suitable – that one might have a look at one of these books?

\*　　\*　　\*　　\*　　\*

Would you? Would you ask him? I'd be so grateful. Yes, I'd like it very much. It would be something entirely new.

So where were we? I never saw Eirik Raudi again, Agnar. He'd been dead two years when we came home. He was a lawless, dangerous man when I first knew him, but he came into his own. He meant more, in his outpost of the world, than the Holy Roman Emperor means here. He wasn't just an idea, shrouded in majesty and politics. He was a man, and we all knew him. He wasn't good. He was violent, partial and overbearing. Men were attracted to him because he was brave. He seemed to be generous, but the advantage was always on his side in the end. He made a country for men out of the wilderness beyond the end of the world, and I suppose his descendants will live in it now until time ends, and so the world is left a little larger than it was before.

I ought to explain the sailing directions for Vinland. We had to start from the Western Settlement to pick up the prevailing wind down the far coast. From Lysufjord we sailed west until we raised the high mountains of Helluland. Then we kept the new coast in sight to starboard, and followed it south until rock and glacier gave way to forest. The landmark we had to watch for was a sandy beach so long and white that Leif named it Furdustrands. It had a distinctive headland halfway along it shaped like a keel, that we called Keelsnes. From there it was a day's sail to a place where the coast began to fall away to the west. Then we had to look out for a high island to the south-west, so it was important to have good visibility after Keelsnes. Thorvald and his men had camped there for days waiting for the fog to lift. Once we got to the island, which was called Bjarney because Leif's party killed a white bear there, the coast of Vinland was visible to the south on a clear day.

Directions can be so simple, and in clear weather life is that simple too, and yet at any moment the weather may change and snap the taut thread you've dared to hang your life upon. Later men found that in some years it's impossible to get through to Vinland, but we sailed across the strait that now marks the boundary of the inhabited world, and for us the doors to the empty lands stood wide open. And so two wooden ships containing forty-nine men, five women, six cows and a bull, a dozen sheep, six horses and a coop of chickens sailed blithely out of the world we know into the sixth day of creation. Only of course it was not like that; we carried our own past with us like an unburied corpse. We saw everything, just as Leif had described it, and a week after the two ships met at the rendezvous in Lysufjord, we made our first landfall on Bjarney, having sailed all the way without parting company.

The water was deep, and we found the one place where we could bring the ships alongside a flat rock. Bird cliffs towered over us, making our voices echo. There's a wonderful harvest to be had from the Bjarney cliffs every spring, and even more from the eider who nest on top of the island. Karlsefni found the way up, and while they were going up the cliff I climbed over the gunwale into the other ship, to talk to the four women who'd sailed with Bjarni's crew. They were all peasants, respectful to me, but not subservient like thralls. Helga was married to a smith from Snorri's estate at Dyrnes. I liked her; she was young, but she seemed tough and sensible. The swell rocked us gently, and the sealskin fenders squeaked each time they were crushed against the rock. Birds screamed over us, and sometimes their droppings splashed around us. The cliff seemed to be leaning over us as we lay in its shadow. The sea was quiet and black as ink.

'I've been waiting to speak to you,' I said, after we'd chatted for a bit. 'Have you ever delivered a baby?'

Her eyes opened wider and fell to my waist. 'I know what to do,' she said. 'I've seen some born. When will it be?'

'Yule, I think.'

'Yule. Where do you think we'll be by then?'

'At Leif's houses, I hope.'

'I hope so too,' she said, and then, 'Do you suppose anyone was ever born in this country before?'

'I don't know,' I told her, 'But Thorvald died here.'

When Karlsefni's party came down off the island they said that the shores of Vinland were visible to the south, and the land we'd left behind that morning was disappearing into a grey line of cloud, and they could feel the cold breeze coming before the change of weather. After that there was an orderly haste on both ships, and in a few minutes we were hoisting our sails again, this time for Vinland.

We travelled together very well, Karlsefni and I. When I remember those early days I see them as a long journey, never knowing where we might be next. For four years we travelled, and then we settled at Glaum. I've been mistress of a big estate for more than half my life, wife and widow of one of the most respected men in Iceland. I know I've been lucky, but sometimes I've struggled with a dreadful hollowness inside. It doesn't usually last long. It often comes in the autumn, and for a few days I have to fight it. I've never told anybody. The worst is when it strikes after Yule. If it comes then it gets a stronger hold, and I carry it for months.

I'm nervous telling you this. I feel shivery, and if I hold my hand up now I think it trembles – see? Am I talking about possession? A hollowness inside, I said. There are worms that get into men's guts and eat them slowly from within. You can catch them if you eat herbs from land where sheep have grazed. Horrible. But this comes from somewhere else. A kind of soul worm, perhaps. It eats away under my ribs, and I have nothing inside to face the world with, only an emptiness that at all costs I must hide. I know now it'll always go away again, so I can bear it, knowing that when the light comes back the thing will melt away, for a while at least.

I was free of that particular demon in Vinland; indeed I never experienced its hold until we were safe, living at Glaum with everything in life that one could wish for. The Vinland journeys were often frightening, dangerous and uncomfortable, but I was content inside myself. I never felt that I needed more in life than what was happening. I knew some painful things, but not disappointment.

We landed at Leif's houses at dusk: there is dusk there, even in June. The bank of cloud had engulfed Bjarney, so the route we had come by had melted into nothing, but in front of us was solid land. We found the two offshore islands which we were to know so well, and almost at once we saw the cairns Leif's men had built on the ridge behind them. Sure enough the bay was tucked in between the islands and the ridge, shelving so gently that our boats beached a hundred yards or more from the shore. As soon as the ships grounded, warmth wrapped us round, smelling of trees. There were no waves, so it was quiet. We could see soft green shores, and a grey beach. The animals smelt the land and began to push against their wooden partitions; the sheep began bleating, and then the cows mooed, and the bull let out a bellow and kicked wildly against his stall and tried to toss his head. A rope snapped. Someone shouted, 'He's going berserk!', and the ponies in the next stall squealed and tried to rear against their halters. We had no choice but to get the ramps out fast: animals at sea are usually so miserable, cold and hungry, that they give little trouble. Maybe we'd kept ours in too good condition, as the voyage had been easy, but I've never known such a landing. As soon as that bull was out, he flung away the men who held him with one toss of his head, and lumbered off towards the nearest shore. The cows bellowed and tugged, and their droppings splashed into the sea. One of the ponies was plunging and screaming, terrified by the white water he'd stirred up around himself, as if it were a monster trying to drag him down.

By the time we'd got ourselves and the animals ashore, and the lead cow and the ponies hobbled, we were soaked and sweating. The bull had vanished, but he'd come back to his cows soon enough no doubt. The ships, moored in knee-deep water, looked far away and danger-ously small. We were standing on a curved beach facing east. We climbed up the dunes, where marram grass stung my legs – and something else. I looked at the ripening ears in awe. Wild wheat, Leif had said. I'd never seen grain growing in my life before. Now I've seen the fields in Europe I know our wheat in Vinland wasn't the same, but it seemed wealth enough to us. Ears of budding grain brushed my skirt, and I thought of Halldis and the smell of fresh hot loaves, and with that promise of comfort I looked for the first time at Leif's houses.

They were set on a grassy plain, with a river running through marshes behind them. To our right was the low ridge with the cairns outlined on its spine. Trees covered gently sloping land, except in the cleared space before us where the three houses were built in a curve that followed the line of the beach: low green familiar shapes, just like the homes we'd left behind, but alien in their emptiness. I'd never seen a deserted settlement before, for all I'd seen so many new ones spring out of the wilderness. I'd never in my life approached an uninhabited house. I was scared; they seemed so secret and with-drawn. There were no doors. Karlsefni walked round the middle house and I followed him. There were doors, of course, but they faced west, away from the sea. Before the others came I saw him quickly cross himself before he raised the latch. The door swung open on darkness. We hadn't thought of that, and we had neither lamp nor fire with us. Karlsefni stepped in, and I followed. It took a little while to get used to the dark, and then I saw the cold hearth full of ashes from the fire Thorvald's men left burning here five years ago.

Karlsefni found the rope and tried to open the chimney hole, only the boards were nailed shut against the weather. The benches were bare, but the walls were hung with ropes and baskets and tools, just as they'd been left. The cooking-pit was choked with dead embers, and pots were piled on top. I felt in the darkness of the water barrel, but if they'd left it full, the water had evaporated long ago. Five winters had left the place damp and earthy, like being underground, but it wasn't cold. I was the first woman who'd ever entered this house, and I looked again at the cooking pots and thought of the men who'd wintered here. I'd never seen a free man cook a meal in my life, and in the nature of things I never will. But there were the pots, the pit, the flat stones and the hearth, telling me a story that I would never be a part of. Does that seem foolish to you, Agnar? I've never thought of saying all this to anyone before.

The place never felt like that again. We lit the fires and moved in, and within a day it was our own. Karlsefni and I took Leif's own house, the southernmost one next to the river. We had our own room at the river end, and our ship's company were in the hall next to us. Snorri and his folk had the other two houses, which had to serve as workshops as well. We were quite cramped the first winter, so the following spring we built more sheds: one by the shore for boat-building, and two for other work, alongside the storehouse Leif had left. We got the smithy going the first spring, just across the river from our house. We had our smith, and bog iron was available from the marshes round, just as Leif had said, but in spite of all the work that went into it we never got the iron we hoped for. It was one frustration after another, that smithy. Snorri lost his temper with it, and wouldn't have any more to do with it, but Karlsefni still persevered. But that's all later.

Our first winter should have been much better than it was. We had three months of the hunting season left, but although Leif had found caribou not far away, our hunting parties were unlucky. They found old trails, but for some reason the caribou hadn't come as far north that year. We'd missed the birding season, though we were in time for the salmon and the cod. The berries were wonderful, more kinds than I'd ever seen, though we picked mostly squashberries, partridge berries and cloudberries. Half a day's sail down the coast we found blueberries, and they seemed the right colour for the wine that Tyrker had made. Karlsefni said they looked like grapes though he'd never seen fresh ones himself, only dried. We were short of red meat, having no cattle to spare for slaughter, and by the time the seals were coming ashore in the autumn the year was already turning. Karlsefni had a couple of fairly successful days seal hunting in the islands, but when Snorri went along the coast he came back almost empty handed. The first blizzard came early in October, withering the last berries on the stalks, and killing off the last of the dreadful biting insects that plagued us through every Vinland summer. The cold came with it, and never went. Our cattle gave less milk every day. Leif had said that winter wouldn't start until just before Yule, and though we were never as fortunate as that in our three winters in Vinland, certainly the first winter we had was much the worst. But that's fate for you, never generous except when you're not relying on it.

By mid-November the snow was beginning to lie, and I was haunted by the ghosts lurking in our half-filled stores. All of us had known bad winters, but perhaps I had the most reason to dread the want and isolation ahead. I prayed, as we all did, but God seemed far away in this land where no prayer had ever been said before. I was aware of my baby inside me growing strong and active – once he started to move he hardly seemed to rest – and I couldn't bear the thought that he should be born into hunger and grow weak, and know all the fears that I had known. So I climbed to the cairns one day to make a spell. It wasn't far, but it was hard work toiling up there in my pregnant state, carrying a pot of embers from the fire. The ground was hard and white. The autumn blanket of reds and yellows had turned brittle and threadbare, and skeleton branches scratched me as I passed. I scrambled between rocks and juniper and stood on a rocky plateau patched with lichens. Below me smoke rose from our roofs, and I could see Helga and the other women turning the cod that was spread on the beach to dry. There were no men about; good weather was too rare now to waste, and they had all gone hunting. It was a clear day, and Bjarney was visible as a thin line on the horizon.

I made a fire spell, using twigs of bog myrtle and juniper so the smoke smelled sweet, and I conjured warmth and wealth and plenty out of the wintry air. I wasn't sure if I'd been heard. The land seemed so empty, not threatening, because there was nothing there to fear, but not sustaining either. If God created this world, he left it on the sixth day with nothing human in it. I don't think there can be any road to hel or heaven from Vinland, and I wonder sometimes if Thjodhild was right, and Thorvald's body should have been brought home. Perhaps we should have brought Thorbrand back. His death seemed so wrong: a youth wasted. A few years after we'd gone, Freydis left behind the bodies of the men she killed at Leif's houses, and no one will ever avenge them. There are ghosts in Vinland now, I imagine, and none could be more troubled than they have cause to be. But no one died when we were there, and I'd like to think we left the place as empty as we found it. I'm not sure, though. When I made that spell I may have been too careless, because the place seemed innocent, but of course we were changing it all the time.

That same evening we noticed Thorhall the Hunter wasn't around. Each of the hunting parties had assumed he'd gone with one of the others, but when they all came back, blown into the shelter of Leif's houses by the beginnings of the next gale, he wasn't there. For three days we huddled in our houses while the storm flung itself against our walls, and everyone thought Thorhall must have perished. On the third night I dreamed I saw him, lying on a cliff top staring at the sky, his eyes and mouth and nostrils wide open. He was pinching himself and mumbling. Then Karlsefni was there too and he asked Thorhall what he was doing, and Thorhall said, 'Mind your own business. I'm not a child, and I don't need nursing. Leave me alone!'

I woke in the black dark, and heard the wind battering at the house, vibrating in the platform under me. I woke Karlsefni and told him what I'd dreamed. He said it sounded so typical of Thorhall he was inclined to think the augury was true. I shivered, and he asked me why. 'If Thorhall's safe,' he said, 'that's good news. I don't fancy telling Eirik that I've lost the man, and what's more he's useful to us. You should be glad.'

'I don't like being used.'

'Used?'

'Even in my own bed,' I could hear hysteria in my voice, and I made myself whisper. 'Inside my own head. Even if I want to shut it out. Can't I even have my dreams to myself?'

He took me in his arms and comforted me, and I could feel my baby inside me kicking against his hard stomach. I wasn't frightened so much as angry, and while I did feel safe in Karlsefni's arms, I knew at the same time that he couldn't protect me from what he could never see. My dreams were my own problem, wherever they came from. He loved me, and that's a powerful charm against evil, in its way, but the trouble was he caught my suspicion off me, and I should never have woken him.

The next morning the wind was blowing itself out, and the sun hung like a silver coin in a washed-out sky. The hills were white, and the wind that was left had a wolfish bite. I was just coming back from the midden when I saw Thorhall striding down from the ridge. Reluctantly I went to meet him. He looked wild, his eyes red-rimmed and his fleece jacket stiff with frost. It seemed to me he couldn't have survived that storm in the shape of a man, and something alien still hung about him, a predatory smell, a whiff of wolf or bear perhaps, or some Vinland creature we knew nothing of. He came right up to me and I met his eyes.

'So you make spells, not prayers, Gudrid, and I lie out in the wilderness,' he said to me. 'It's a good thing some of us dare to do what's needed.'

'I don't know what you mean.'

'Say what you like, or dream what you don't like,' he said. 'Will you believe me if I tell you there's a whale sixty feet long washed up in the storm, good fresh meat lying just two beaches along from here?'

I clasped my hands together over my swollen stomach. 'There is? Truly?'

'You should know,' he said, and walked on past me without another word.

Karlsefni listened to Thorhall's news with uncomplicated relief. We all set out at once, the two ponies loaded with ropes and knives and saws, and everyone carrying empty baskets on their backs. We walked along a grey beach, between the high water mark and the forest, shoved through scrub, and there on the second beach was a massive grey whale, just as Thorhall had described.

There was no smell. I walked round to its eye, which was quite small and human looking in that vast body, and saw it still had the sheen of life on it. When the men began to climb up the body the tail gave a feeble jerk, and when they made the first cut, the creature flailed so hard that one man was flung off into the sand. Karlsefni climbed up behind the great head, drew his sword, and plunged it down the blowhole. Dark blood spurted over him, and dribbled down the body. The creature twitched once and was still. Gradually I saw its eye glaze over. Karlsefni wiped his sword and sheathed it, and slid down off the body beside me. Thorhall strolled over to him.

'So what d'you say now, you Christians?' he said. 'Hasn't old Redbeard turned out to be a bit more use than your Christ? Aren't you glad there's one man in your company who still makes poems in praise of Thor?'

'You'd better keep quiet about that,' was all Karlsefni said.

'Quiet about the truth? Why should I do that?'

'Because you know as well as I do that if the men think this is devil's work they'll not touch it. Winter's nearly on us, and if we don't get this meat home and dried, we're done for. Is that sense enough for you?'

'And what about you, Karlsefni? Aren't you afraid of the devil? What kind of creature do you think this whale is?'

Karlsefni glanced at the whale, where the men were already stripping off the blubber, and for a moment I saw doubt in his face, but when he turned back to Thorhall there was no sign of it. 'I think it's meat,' he said, and strode away.

That night we slept hard after our long day's work. Before we got up in the morning I asked Karlsefni what he'd been thinking when he looked at the whale like that. He was lying curled up with his back to me, and it was a minute before he answered. 'Nothing,' he said eventually, 'only I thought I knew every whale in the sea, but I never saw one like this.'

'How's it different?'

'They're all different. But this one – did you see under its head? Grey on the left side, white on the right. And its fin was too far back. It isn't any kind I've heard of.'

'The meat's the same as any other.'

'That's true. It's the way it came I'm thinking of. What's a monster, Gudrid? It can be an animal, I suppose, and it can be a ghost, and maybe there are stranger matings in the sea than anyone knows anything about.'

'Not so strange,' I remarked. 'What's a man, if it comes to that? Don't we come in the middle too, between the animals and the ghosts? Perhaps a monster is only something we fear because we know too much about what it's made of.'

'A dream, you mean?'

'A winter's meat isn't made of dreams.' I pulled his shoulder and made him turn on his back and look at me. 'We're quite far south, and they say there are all sorts of beasts in Africa. And it was his namesake and yours that Thorhall prayed to, your own god who's protected you all your life. It's not like you to be confused, Karlsefni.'

'No.' He twisted a lock of my hair round his finger, not looking at me. 'But this country didn't belong to the old gods, and Christendom ends at Thjodhild's church. You know I don't rely on anything but my own judgement, and that's what I've always done. In my opinion Thorhall is a dangerous man.'

'He found the whale. We needed food.'

'And how did it come there? No, don't answer, I don't want to know. But keep away from him now, Gudrid, please.'

I remembered Thorhall in my dream, and I was frightened. I had no way of shutting him out from there, and that meant he had found his way into the intimate centre of our lives. Karlsefni wasn't the man to stand for that; he was more jealous even than most men of his married privacy, of mind as well as body. I thought of my fire spell, and I wondered where Thorhall had been at the moment that I made it, and whether I should have been more careful to exclude evil things. I hadn't bothered with the whole ritual that Halldis made me use at home, because I thought in Vinland we were safe from ghosts. I thought of my unborn baby, and I wanted passionately never to have Thorhall's eye on me again.

Karlsefni must have been watching my face, because he pulled my head down on to his shoulder, and held me. 'It's not your fault,' he repeated. 'It's not your fault. And thank God we've got the meat. If it came by evil means it's nothing to do with you, and we certainly can't reject it. But keep away from Thorhall. Don't do anything that could bring him near you. We have enough food now. You don't need to take any risks now. Do you?'

'No.'

'Then will you do that?'

'Yes.'

'Fine. Don't worry, I can manage the rest.'

He did manage that winter very well. Now that the ghost of hunger was banished everyone relaxed, and as the sea froze over, our little settlement settled down to its indoor life. The winter was more severe than Leif had led us to expect, with few clear days, just one blizzard after another. But even at Yule there was quite a lot of daylight, and we had good fires. The smell of woodsmoke always makes me think of Vinland. The first things we made in our new workshops were a couple of sledges, and every fine day we'd bring in wood. We never had to use seaweed or dung for fuel in Vinland, and we could have our fires as big as we liked. My son Snorri was born on the last night of Yule, and he first opened his eyes on firelight, and in the days that followed, while his soul still seemed new and strange in his little body, he used to turn his head and watch the fire with that unfocussed blue gaze that new babies always have. Sometimes he does the same now. He's chieftain at Glaum in his father's place, his own sons are as tall as he is, and you'd think there was nothing vague about him anywhere – he seems to see things so very clearly – but sometimes I look across the hearth to him, and I see him withdraw into some other world, staring into the flames, as if the human world around him were only a shadow flickering across the edges of his sight, and I think of where he came from, and the strange places that were home to him, and I wonder what he still remembers.

Having no priest, we baptised him ourselves, and Snorri Thor-brandsson was his godfather. I was relieved when it was done. It would be a terrible thing to be a soul without a name wandering for ever in those deserted lands, and coming into the world is the most dangerous journey of all. It's a cruel thing to have a God who's indifferent to it, only offering the protection of his name when the worst is over.

Even after Snorri was safely baptised I hated Thorhall to come near us. He knew it, and somehow he was always with us. Although his place was in the north house, furthest away from ours, he frequently seemed to have a reason to come and sit at our hearth. He was welcomed by the company because he was a poet, and used to entertain us in the evenings with epigrams about us all, and all the things that happened in our new settlement. But he was quarrelsome too, and he never left the business about the whale alone. He was always making poems and jibes against Christianity, and mocking the men who'd turned their backs on Thor. Around Candlemas we had an outbreak of dysentery. Thank God it didn't get into my milk and the baby was all right, but more than half the men were ill, and Thorhall seized the opportunity to raise doubts about the whalemeat, out of sheer mischief, I suppose, since he'd been the one who found it in the first place. A lot of them refused to touch it after that. Maybe it wasn't just superstition: it puts you off a food anyway if you start to associate it too much with vomit. But things came to a head when some of Snorri's men raided the storehouse one night, took the rest of the meat, and flung it into the sea.

That was one of the times I saw Karlsefni in a rage. He forced Snorri's people to say who'd done it, and when the men were dragged out of the house to face him I think they thought when they saw his face that he'd kill them then and there. Only one dared speak, and he was defiant, insisting that they'd thrown away the devil's meat to save us all. He was still talking when Karlsefni strode up to him and smashed his fist into the man's face. The man dropped like a slaughtered ox and writhed in the snow, gasping. Blood poured from his broken nose, but no one dared move. Karlsefni kicked him in the back where he lay, and would have done so again if Snorri hadn't got between them, grabbing my husband's arm, shouting: 'He's my man! Don't touch him!'

I thought they'd fight each other, but slowly Karlsefni lowered his free arm, and he and Snorri stood, almost chest to chest, staring into each other's eyes. Then Karlsefni said breathlessly, but in his ordinary voice, 'Your man. So what will you do if he's killed us all?'

'He was afraid.'

'He may well be.'

'They say that meat was devil's work.'

The man on the ground rolled over, and struggled groggily to his hands and knees. The snow around him was pink with blood. 'So you cast out devils,' said Karlsefni to him softly. 'You've given us our Lenten fast with a vengeance. So what about Easter? Any plans for our resurrection?'

The men around looked baffled, as well they might. 'Don't I make myself clear?' went on Karlsefni. 'Very well, do you understand this? It's February. We don't know when spring will come. May, perhaps June. Now that you've thrown away most of our food, we have barely enough for a month. So what are you going to do about that?'

Snorri said, 'It's no use blaming anyone for what's done. We'll just have to hunt for what we can.'

'Out there?' Karlsefni swept his arm out and everyone looked out obediently into the white world that surrounded us, and in the sudden silence we could hear the wind moaning across the pack ice.

'We'll have to ration ourselves,' said Snorri doggedly.

'True. And maybe we'll have to die.'

'Thorfinn,' Snorri was one of the few people who sometimes used Karlsefni's name. 'This won't do. Let the men go in. You and I need to talk.'

'Talk!'

But Karlsefni did go with him. They went into our house, and nobody followed. I took Snorri and went to Helga's hearth. I felt shaken, and I had learned to trust in her matter-of-fact strength when Snorri was born. She gave me hot buttermilk, and we talked, lowering our voices so the others couldn't hear. I'd never said anything to anyone about Karlsefni; that would have been disloyal, but I found myself telling her about Thorhall.

'So where's Thorhall now?' she said. 'He wasn't there this morning, was he? Is it his doing, do you think?'

I shook my head. 'But why should he? He says Thor gave us the meat. Surely he'll be furious?'

'I'm not sure.' Helga looked away from me into the fire. 'He says it's the women here who've caused the trouble.'

'How?'

'Oh, a lot of them think so. If there are to be women, they say, it should be women for all – slaves. Men shouldn't bring their wives, they say, and carry on as if they were at home while other men have nothing. It's the worst of all worlds, Thorhall says, and a lot of the others agree with him. Oh, they'll hardly say so to your husband – look what he did today – but my man's a smith, not a chieftain, and they don't hesitate to get at him. He told Snorri he wouldn't come without me, you see, and Snorri gave in because he needed his skills.'

'I didn't know that.' I said slowly.

'No, you don't know a lot of things. But you're not an ordinary man's wife.'

'But the women here had nothing to do with the meat.'

'You don't think so? Some people think you have more powers than you say, Gudrid.'

That scared me. 'What do you mean?'

'Do you think we'll starve now?'

'No.' I shook my head firmly. 'No, it may be hard, but I'm sure we won't. It's not our fate.'

'You see? How do you know that?'

I couldn't answer her, but I think I insisted because I had Snorri, and I would defy any power that existed to protect him. There's no witchcraft about that; it's just what any mother would do. But more than ever I wanted nothing to do with Thorhall. He was back the evening after the whalemeat went, and though he must have heard what had happened, he never referred to it, and all the want we suffered for the rest of the winter just seemed to make him more cheerful, and more aggressive.

So there was no magic in the luck that brought us a brief spell of fine weather, so that the men were able to drag the boats across the ice, and harpoon two seals in open water. It wasn't magic that brought a wakeful bear snuffling round our middens, where it could be trapped and killed with a spear. It wasn't magic that made men risk their lives fishing off the edge of the ice in a freezing sea that grudgingly yielded a few dogfish. It certainly wasn't magic that made us kill our pitifully skinny sheep, who should have given us the next year's lambs. Long before Easter the winter closed in again, and we endured it until June. And then the spring came with a rush, and the pent up anger of all the hungry months erupted with it.

# SIXTEEN

# *September 12th*

I did appreciate the things you sent, my dear. The wine is so good – smooth and rich, the best I've yet tasted. Did it come from your monastery vineyards? It was kind of you, and I enjoyed the grapes too, they were much bigger and juicier than I'd expected. Were they really grapes, I wonder, those fruits we picked in Vinland? If they were, then hundreds of years of cultivation must have changed the ones in Italy out of all recognition. How long have people eaten grapes and drunk wine in this country, Agnar?

\*  \*  \*  \*  \*

Since the flood, you think? And what about before that? Were there grapes in Eden? You can't answer that, can you? Rome is so old I'm not at home in it. So old and so cultivated; the past weighs it down. When I was ill I thought at first I didn't want to die here. I watched the sun move across the wall in my cell, showing up the cracks in the plaster, and lighting up clouds of dust that the shadows never show us. Dust from the past, dust of people, maybe, or whatever they once made here that's fallen and forgotten. I lay in my bed, feeling too weak to raise my hand or turn my head, and I watched the dust. It floated and floated in the heat and never seemed to settle. Why do we stir up the past, Agnar? Why not let it lie? The sun moved across the wall, I lay under my sheet and I felt as dry and light as vellum, after all these months of heat and stickiness. When the sun left, the night swept in like velvet and wrapped me softly round, and I thought then I wouldn't be afraid to go quietly onwards into the dark. I thought of my love, as if I were young again and close to him, and it seemed that I might stretch out my hand into the sweet night and his hand would be there, waiting for mine. He was there, I could tell, in his body, just as he was a long time ago when we were young. I remembered how his weight pressed down on me, and how he moved inside me, as if it were his body not his soul that was waiting for me now. I thought then that perhaps there had been times, when we were together, when body and soul were truly one, and that it would somehow be in the image of our mortal love that my soul would find his. Age is only the husk that grows around us, Agnar; I am still myself inside this shell, and when I die I think I shall be just as he remembered me.

When I knew he was there it didn't matter any more that I was a long way from home. I thought about what it must be like for him, and wondered how he found his way into this place which is so unlike anything he ever knew. Did the throng of alien ghosts trouble him? Was he afraid to come so far, when his own resting place is half the world away? I don't think he was frightened; perhaps the thread that binds me to him is short and straight, and he didn't have to make the long journey that we make in life to get from there to here. We once meant to find a new country, he and I, and maybe we did, in our own way. I don't think it was as new as we thought, though. Perhaps there were more before us, and more after, than we could ever have dreamed of.

Anyway, Agnar, I'm tougher than I look, and I didn't die this time. Don't look so solemn, my dear. Your gifts pleased me very much. I don't think I'm fated to die in this place. It's getting cooler every day, thank God, and even though the air is so old and tired and dry, I can smell the freshness of autumn in it. Are you worried that when my mind should have been on the last things it was the spirit of a mortal man that comforted me?

\*     \*     \*     \*     \*

You're right, and more sensible than I'd given you credit for. What are sacraments for, if not to do for us what our own minds can't do? Yes, the priest did come, and committed me to the mercy of a God whom I still can't apprehend. I think he'll have mercy on me even for that. I have more hope now that he is merciful enough to give us a heaven inhabited by the people we loved, because that's the nearest to divine love most of us are going to get.

\*     \*     \*     \*     \*

I know. No marriage nor giving in marriage. Just as well, because after all I had two husbands, and have had more than one mass sung for each of them, so heaven is where they both should be. No, no, I'm not worrying about the logic of it. But I've had to make some journeys on my own, and some with a man who loved me, and though I'm quite able to take care of myself, I have to admit, having experienced both, I prefer to travel with someone I love. Yes, even on the last journey of all. Go on, then, cross yourself. I can still shock you, then, even though you should know me quite well by now.

\*     \*     \*     \*     \*

That's true too, but it's a long time ago. Grief passes, and one heals so well in the end that one almost feels guilty about it. I can't remember grief now. The worst pain I can recollect is toothache. Sadness comes and goes, sometimes it's in your head and sometimes it isn't, but toothache just stays there with a vengeance, and there's no melancholy satisfaction in indulging in it either. I lost my first adult tooth when I was pregnant with Snorri – a tooth for every child they say – and then I was lucky for a long time. The year Karlsefni died my back teeth began to rot, and one by one they fell out. It was agony. Losing him was agony too, but I remember the toothache better. It made me want to die. I could think about life without Karlsefni, when it came down to it, but not without my teeth. Losing my teeth felt more like the end of me. But I have some still, as you see, and that's an achievement at my age, and what's more they don't bother me any more, and I don't cry for the dead any more either.

\*     \*     \*     \*     \*

I know, I know. We have to go on with the story. What else are we here for, after all? But I'm tired today, Agnar. Couldn't we have a cup of your wine, and sit out in the shade? There are ripe figs on the tree out there, and bunches of little green grapes on the vine that grows over the cloister roof, and the leaves are just beginning to go yellow. We don't have much time, Agnar, and we can't afford to waste it all writing things down. Think about where we are now! You want me to talk about Karlsefni. He would think us mad to bury ourselves in shadows. He wouldn't dream of wasting his days telling you a story about his life. He'd be thinking about the present. He'd have talked to me about you, about Rome, about the significance of this strange new world we're living in. He seemed a quiet man in public, but he was usually very self-possessed; he didn't give much away. He was always observant. Even at the very end, when his body let him down at last, he was still wanting to know, still trying to find out. Even when he couldn't leave his own hearth, he still wanted the news, he still insisted on speaking to every passing stranger.

Maybe you don't know – you were so young when you left – and of course you're a Southerner anyway – but Karlsefni made the chieftain of Glaumbaer one of the most important men in Iceland. Snorri has inherited what his father made, and he holds it well. But though Karlsefni was of good family himself, he had to make his own place in the world. He bought Glaum when we got back from Norway. He paid a good price for it, but Vinland had made us rich, and Karlsefni never minded spending money on what he'd set his heart on. He never left Iceland again, which you may think strange for a man who spent the first half of his life travelling nearly all the time. He'd found what he wanted, you see.

It was easier by then to avoid being involved in feuds. Karlsefni managed it, anyway. Apart from one outlaw, whose name I can't tell you, to whom he secretly gave food and shelter when he was hiding on the island called Drangey at the mouth of our bay, Karlsefni avoided taking sides. We went to the Thing every year – at least, Karlsefni always went, and once the boys were big enough I went with him – and Karlsefni gained a reputation for being impartial. Cold-hearted, some said. But men often appealed to him to arbitrate in quarrels, and in fact a substantial part of our income came from fees he earned that way. We needed the money. Our house was always open; Karlsefni was always mindful of his prestige, and I liked to give good feasts and gifts to our guests, though I was far more provident than my father. Karlsefni and I were both good managers, and our farm became one of the best in Iceland. Glaum is a wide flat valley between two lines of hills, with the river winding through it, and so we had plenty of room to expand. Over the years we bought up several small holdings along the length of the valley, until now it's all ours.

He liked beautiful things, especially metalwork: there was a smith he knew in Norway from whom he'd order goods nearly every year – jewelled cups, platters, brooches, amulets, that sort of thing. If he hadn't been a chieftain he might have been a smith himself, though God knows trying to get ore out of that bog iron in Vinland was enough to put anyone off for life. He liked to give me jewels and dyed cloth, and it pleased him when I did him credit. Any longings I'd had for fine things as a child were amply fulfilled, and yet human nature is perverse. Sometimes I'd think of Halldis, in her undyed tunic, driving the cattle in from our muddy fields, or harvesting yarrow or thyme from the fields and hanging it up in bunches over the hearth at Arnarstapi, and I'd feel trapped, as if I'd been dressed up as someone else who wasn't me. I'd want to get out and run into the empty hills. Sometimes during those years I thought too of Thorstein, and our farm at Stokkanes, and the days we'd spent clearing the scrub, or driving ponies loaded with dung and seaweed, and spreading muck across next year's hayfields. I'd think about the times we waited up at night, just the two of us, for a cow about to calf, or winter evenings when we went out to the byre in a blizzard to fill the hayracks, or days when we forced our way through drifts digging sheep out of last night's snow. Sometimes I could hardly remember what Thorstein looked like, and then I would dream of him again and see his face, never older, of course, but unlined as it had been when I saw him last, freckled like a boy's, his hair still fair and thick, falling over his forehead.

Don't get me wrong; Karlsefni and I were farmers too, like

everyone else, and neither of us was afraid of a hard day's work. But we had more thralls at Glaum than anyone had in the Green Land, or than my father had ever owned at Laugarbrekka, and quite a lot of our land was worked by tenants. It was never just us. I told you once that Eirik's family lived their lives at Brattahlid with the world looking on, because they were at the centre of things and never alone. It was like that for us at Glaum. Karlsefni never understood why I sometimes felt withdrawn from it all. We talked about Vinland occasionally, but as far as he was concerned that was the past, and therefore over. The thread that tied our early lives to Glaum was spun out of gold, in his view. He liked to be rich, and he made sure that he was. He liked to play an influential part in men's affairs, and he made sure that he did. In some ways he was much simpler in his wants than me. There were times when I wasn't happy, and when that happened he always knew. He never understood, and he hated fuss. I never let him see me cry after we got back to Glaum, except when I lost a child, which happened twice after Thorbjorn was born. He was always as kind then as he was able to be, because he knew that these things affect women unduly. I didn't inflict my vague discontents upon him, and as the years passed I didn't bother about them so much myself any more. Don't get me wrong, Agnar, I'm not complaining. It's just that being ill these last weeks, I've had a lot of time to think about these things.

When I thought I would die here I admitted to myself for the first time how much I wanted to make this pilgrimage. This is my last adventure, you see, my last journey into the unknown. It was the first time I'd put to sea for nearly thirty years. I used to hate and fear the sea, but it's the only road out of Iceland, and I'd been shut into my little world for too long. I always wanted to travel again, but Karlsefni was content. He'd seen all that he needed to of Europe before I ever met him, and he had no reason to go back. He had sons who were making their own way in the world. Snorri and Thorbjorn each went to the court in Norway, and Thorbjorn has gone far beyond. It's young men who go out into the world, not their mothers; that's how Karlsefni would have seen it. I loved him, Agnar. We were very happy together.

I told you when you and I met that after this winter I'd go home to Glaum, and so I will. I won't go back to our house though. Snorri has a wife and grown children, and they don't need me there any more. No, I'll make a place for myself as much like this nunnery here as I can. I shall have my little cell, just as I do here, and the nuns will create their own little world, just as they do here, and it will be a haven and a sanctuary for those who need it, just as it is here. I'm not going to die in Rome. There is something more for me to do in Iceland, quite apart from my family.

Are you still writing all this down? It's not the story I'm supposed to be telling you. I don't know, I just can't be bothered any more to get to the point. But you need me to, I realise that, and for your sake I'll make more effort tomorrow. Come a little earlier, before the sun gets to my brain. Otherwise I won't be any use to you; I just won't be able to convince myself that this work of ours matters any more.

# SEVENTEEN

# *September 13th*

Vinland. Leif promised us a land that flowed with wine, but I had to come here, to the heart of the old world, to find that, and, what's more, to acquire a taste for it. Vinland. Snorri's son died there. Thorbrand. A young man in his teens. He died in a scuffle that should never have taken place. I hope to God neither of my children will die before I do. Snorri was as hard a man as any of them, and when the skraelings were gone he raised the body of his son and carried it into his hut without a word. But I saw his face, and I knew him well enough to read what was not written there. Vinland. My own Snorri was born there, and I looked after him alone. There were times when I longed for a family; that's what a baby, and its mother, need most of all. When we went back to the world we came from he was three years old, very active and talking fluently. In Vinland he still fell asleep at my breast, and when his father came to bed he used to lift the baby out of the place that was his, and lay him in his basket and tuck the blanket round him. I'm the only person who ever saw Karlsefni do anything as tenderly as that.

Vinland. Do you know how important a ship is, Agnar? You don't, because you've not been in Vinland. Norway is the place where ships are made. Of course you know that. A ship in Vinland is as little as a needle, and without it there is no following the thin thread back again across the world. When spring came the first year in Vinland, my baby was five months old, and you could see he was taking a firmer hold on life, as babies do when they start to eat solid food, and so I was beginning to dare to realise just how much I loved him. We were very short of food. When the ice melted Karlsefni went straight back to Bjarney to collect eider ducks and eggs. Before he came back . . . But wait. I must tell you about the quarrel first.

It was the first day that the sun had a bit of warmth in it. The land was still snow-dappled, with patches of flattened yellow grass. It was the light that drew me out. I took a sheepskin and sat on the bench on the south side of the house, blinking like a bear just woken from its winter sleep. It was so light I felt almost drunk with it, unfocussed, and not able to see very far. The yard was quiet, but I could hear voices from the beach, where the men had gone to haul the ships down from their winter shelter. Otherwise there was only the rushing of the unfrozen stream, swollen with meltwater, flowing at my feet. I was glad to be alone, and rejoicing in forgotten warmth. I was feeding my baby, and I could feel the heat of the sun on my breast. I pulled back my shawl so I could get more of it, and I leaned back and shut my eyes. I could see the red blood in my eyelids against the sun, and I could feel my baby suckling, and everything else seemed dreamlike and far away. The sound of water wove itself into my thoughts, dissolving them into incoherence, like the moment when you realise you are falling into sleep.

*The fates look down at Leif's houses, and they find the people they have been waiting for all winter. As the fates spin, a triangle is woven, a tight thread binding the three who unsuspectingly move into their appointed places. Gudrid is there first, leaning back on the bench in the sunny spot at the south side of the house. Her eyes are shut, and her face is turned up to the sun. She is suckling her baby, and her tunic is unfastened and pulled away from her breasts, and underneath it her dress is undone to her waist. She pushes her shawl off her shoulders so she can feel the warmth of the sun on her skin. After the long winter it feels like a benediction. She spreads herself out to the sun, stretching out her legs and her free arm like a starfish, and she smiles as the heat touches her body, which has been cramped in the dark for a whole winter.*

*Thorhall the Hunter arrives next. He has come down from the cairns on the hill. He has been up there for some time, and he has been watching the men on the beach slowly hauling Karlsefni's ship down to the tideline.*

188

*Every man is needed for the job, and Thorhall is the only one who has not been there. He has had matters of his own to consider. He reaches the smithy, and follows the line of the stream round to the house doors. But he stops suddenly on the bank, just to the south of Karlsefni's house, arrested by the unexpected sight of Karlsefni's wife. Gudrid is alone, apart from her infant, lying in the sun's embrace as if she were in the arms of her lover, as unaware and vulnerable as he is ever likely to find her. Thorhall stands rigid, his gaze fixed upon her, like a wolf that has sighted its prey, and only waits for the rest of the pack in order to be ready for the kill.*

*Thorfinn Karlsefni has seen his ship safely moored, and is on his way to the storehouse because he needs a coil of rope that he remembers putting there when the ship was laid up last autumn. His mind is entirely on rigging, when he reaches the top of the little hill by the smithy, and sees Thorhall the Hunter below him, poised as if he were about to strike. Puzzled and wary, Karlsefni looks the same way as Thorhall, and sees his wife, lying as he has only seen her do when he has made love to her at length, without letting her touch him back. It is not a thing he has often done, because the very notion of it was new to her when she married him, and she seldom lets it happen. It has been among his rarest and most private pleasures, being all the more piquant for having being entirely unshared and unguessed at by any other man.*

There came the sick thud of a blow and a shriek. I jumped up and the baby screamed. I couldn't see; there were two men fighting just across the stream, but my eyes were all sunspotted. Then I heard Karlsefni: 'I'll kill you! I'll kill you!' Footsteps came from the yard and stampeded past me. The baby wailed furiously, then gradually I could see. Karlsefni was locked against Thorhall, with both hands round his throat. I saw Thorhall raise a knife to strike over Karlsefni's shoulder, and I think I screamed a warning. Karlsefni twisted away just in time and seized Thorhall's knife arm by the wrist. I watched the knife move in an arc as Thorhall forced his own arm down and Karlsefni strained against it. Karlsefni still had his other hand round Thorhall's throat, but you can't strangle a man one-handed, and Thorhall was trying to shake him off, but Karlsefni held on, like a dog at a bull. Then Thorhall wrenched his knife hand round, and at the same moment Snorri came past me and leapt the stream, and grabbed Thorhall from behind, and the knife slid away into the water.

It took half a dozen men to force them apart. Thorhall shrugged and gave in, but Karlsefni still struggled to be at him, like a mad dog, until he realised that it was his own men he was fighting, and then he stopped, panting, and brushed the sweat out of his eyes. The baby was still screaming, and I was too shocked to move, and then before I could speak, Snorri was saying, 'What is this? What is it?', and Thorhall turned and looked at me, and I thought of the spell I had made, and the dream, and the blessing I had failed to ask, and I remembered that my tunic was undone and I pulled my shawl around me and fled into the house.

It was pitch dark inside, and I stumbled across the hall to the entrance of our room and felt my way to the bed, where I sat shaking, and holding the baby to me, rocking him and trying to comfort him. I didn't know what had happened, but I recognised that look of Thorhall's. It suggested . . . what? Complicity, something shared between us that should not be shared. I remembered how he'd met me coming off the hill. I remembered what Helga had told me about the men saying if there were to be women, they should be for all, and not men's wives. I didn't know what I'd done but I knew I was guilty. I hated the man and had not been able to stop myself dreaming about him. He haunted me, and I was afraid of him.

Karlsefni was angry with me; I knew that from the way he didn't talk to me about what had happened, or tell me how it had been resolved. That night Thorhall was gone, with a few others, and it was Helga who told me they'd gone inland after caribou. Karlsefni sailed for Bjarney the next day. He had to; we were desperately in need of food. I was upset because he hardly spoke to me before he went, and frightened because he was away. Both feelings were quite new to me, and I resented them. I was scared Thorhall would get back first. Indeed he did, but I never saw him, and nor did Snorri. We all expected something to happen, but it never crossed our minds that Thorhall would do what he did.

Agnar, he took my father's ship.

You don't react. Don't you see? Don't you understand what that meant? She was moored in the bay. The weather was calm. We kept no watch at night. Why should we, in that empty land? He came back at night, and he took the ship, and nine men went with him. Thorhall was never heard of again.

A rumour reached us at Glaumbaer years later that they'd been swept off course by the next westerly gale, and blown across the sea to Ireland, where those who'd survived were captured and sold into slavery. It was never confirmed. I don't even know where it came from, or who brought it. As far as I'm concerned, there's been no trace of Thorhall since the day he sneaked out of Vinland, taking my father's ship with God knows what plan in his mind. I think he might have picked up a cargo of some sort in Vinland, and made for Europe. He wouldn't have dared to go back to the Green Land, surely, after doing that, and even in Iceland his crime might have caught up with him.

\*     \*     \*     \*     \*

What do you mean, what had he done? Have you still not understood? Oh you'd have understood all right, if you'd been standing on the shore that morning, looking out to where the ship should have been. Karlsefni came back three days later, far too late to pursue Thorhall, even if we'd known which way he'd gone. He still had his own ship, which could carry up to thirty people, and a cargo. There were forty-five of us, Agnar, and our animals. To carry that number on one ship, we'd have to be sure of a flat calm all the way. A flat calm, in those seas! Now do you understand?

Karlsefni didn't even seem to be angry. It was Snorri this time who blustered with impotent rage. Karlsefni had a temper, as you know, but his anger was never impotent. If Thorhall had been there I think Karlsefni would have killed him, but with the bird flown, his mind turned at once to repairing the damage to the cage. We all crowded into our hall that night to decide what should be done. While the men who'd stayed behind cursed Thorhall and explained at length that his flitting was none of their fault, Karlsefni stared into the fire, saying nothing at all, and his attention seemed to be far away. When he stood up everyone fell silent.

'It's done now,' he said. 'We can all say where we should have been, and what we should have done. But if we'd thought about it, what choice had he? He knew I'd have killed him if I could. In fact I would have done before next winter, given the chance, because I couldn't see any other way for us to go on living here. He's solved that problem for us. Now we have to solve our own.

'We can't all go home without another ship. Then we must build one.' He waited for the mutter of protest to die down, and went on. 'It's no use saying it'll be difficult. Of course it will. This isn't a Norwegian shipyard, I know that. But do we have any choice? We don't, and you know it. Very well. You know what our plans were for the summer. We were going to take two ships south, and get a cargo out of Vinland, and sail home next spring. We can't do that now. But I'll sail south as I planned to do. Thorvald's men said there were tall trees growing in the heart of Vinland, tall enough to carve out the keel of a ship. Don't tell me what the problems are. I know. We can't wait for the wood to season for long enough. Maybe we'll find old wood already fallen. I don't know. We're not shipbuilders, but some of us have seen ships built. We're short of iron; we'll have to get more. It's June now. I can sail at once. I shall sail into Vinland, and find the trees that we need. We have to cut them down and split them. We also have to find food, because we've no supplies to take with us. We won't be back this summer. We'll make a winter camp in Vinland. The rest of you must stay here at Leif's houses and fish and hunt for yourselves. We'll leave you the two small boats. You must get the smithy working and make as much iron as you can. We'll come home as soon as we can the next summer, and in the winter we'll build our ship.'

As soon as he stopped speaking everyone started shouting at once. Some said it was impossible, some said it was the only thing to do. People said two more winters in Vinland would be intolerable. Some said why not sail straight back to Greenland, and send another ship next year to fetch those left at Leif's houses. Others argued that no one in their right mind would agree to be left behind. I knew that Karlsefni wouldn't go without getting what he came for, and I waited to see how he'd handle them. I was right; he argued with them patiently, and of course they had no real alternatives to offer. No one wanted to be left at Leif's houses, wherever the ship went. Suppose, they said, as was all too likely, Karlsefni never came back? They'd be condemned to exile in Vinland as long as life lasted, or, as Karlsefni pointed out to them, until Leif came back again, as he might well do one day. Snorri added that his brother Thorleif still had a ship in Greenland, and would probably set out for Vinland himself if Snorri and Thorbrand didn't come back in a year or two.

The argument went on far into the night, and Karlsefni let them all say what they wished. He knew there was only one conclusion to be reached, but he knew too that it mustn't seem an arbitrary one. In particular, the lesser men who were to be left behind at Leif's houses must feel that the whole plan had their consent, so that they would willingly play their part. Some thought Snorri should stay at Leif's houses too, and take charge of things there, but Karlsefni objected, saying that Snorri knew more about shipbuilding than he did, and he wanted him to help find the right timber. What he did not say was that Snorri was his sworn friend, and if Snorri were to die in Vinland, Karlsefni would see that it was in action and not in a hopeless exile. He was only prepared to take that risk for men he didn't care for. When he tried, Karlsefni could be as wily as Eirik, and there was no trace of anger in him now. I watched him deal with them, apparently ready to consider every point of view that was put before him, and in the end I saw how he got exactly what he wanted.

I was sorry to part from Helga, whose husband's role at Leif's houses was now a vital one. The other women stayed behind too, with their men. If anyone thought I should have remained with them, they never dared say so to Karlsefni, and I heard nothing about it. So that's how it was that I put to sea again on a chilly June morning, with the sun rising over the hill behind us, and a cold half moon sinking into the grey seas ahead.

# EIGHTEEN

# September 15th

The heart of Vinland is old; the seasons have followed one another here since the world was made, but no time has passed; no one has measured the years that have gone by. No one knows the boundaries of this country; its shores stretch on and on, far into the south of the world, and no one has sailed to the end of them. And no one at all has travelled inland to the heart of the country. There is no way in.

For two months and more Karlsefni's ship traces the shores of Vinland, and still the strange land leads them further on, offering no conclusions. They follow Straumfjord far to the west of Leif's houses, and they find hills and rivers and islands, all thickly overgrown with trees, all empty and unnamed. They follow the southern coast of Straumfjord east again, and sail across a landlocked sea where headlands and islands loom unexpectedly out of the haze. When the swell tells them they are back in the open ocean they turn south-west and find another coast, and follow it far into the south until the night is not much shorter than the day. They reach a part of the coast where there are extensive sand dunes, offering some open ground between the forest and the sea. They come to a broad river flowing across the white sand into the sea. When they go ashore for water they find that the river flows out of a tidal lake, a Hop, where a ship could be taken in and moored at high tide. Nowhere could be more suitable for a winter camp, and when the green forest begins to be tinged with red and gold, they retrace their course to Hop.

Their choice is clearly blessed by a kind fate, for at the edge of the forest berries grow in abundance, and among them there are true grapes, blood-kin to the vines that make the wines of Europe. Not only that, but when men follow the river inland, they find caribou trails crossing it, with hoofprints still fresh in the mud, and vanishing into the forest on either side. All that autumn the company feasts at night on fresh meat and raw grapes. They build huge camp fires to keep the mosquitoes away, because there is no shortage of wood here, and the nights stay fine and dry right up until Advent. The cattle graze on the dunes, and although there is no hay they are never short of fodder. After Yule the snow comes, but it does not lie for long, and there is more daylight than has ever been known in winter before. Spring comes early, and while there is still plenty of meat and fish hanging from the rafters of the huts, men are bringing in fresh food again every day. Meanwhile the grape juice ferments in the barrels, and all winter men have been carving new barrels out of Vinland timber, ready for an even larger harvest in the new year.

Now it is summer again, and the sun is higher in the sky than any of the newcomers have ever seen it in their lives before. It beats down on a double curve of white beach divided by grassy dunes. On the side facing the open sea waves curl and break; on the inner side the calm waters of a lagoon lap on wave-ribbed sands. Below the water-line the sand is firm and yellow; above it is white and powdery, scuffed by passing feet. The water in the lagoon is calm and clear as air. From the ship moored off the beach it is possible to look down through green sea, and see the ship's shadow ripple over sand where small crabs scuttle over it.

The forest reaches to the dunes, and where the sea has licked away the sand trees have fallen, their trunks piled up like driftwood above the tideline, their spiky branches barring the way in. But there is a newly-made path along the river, hacked out this last winter through thorn bushes and creepers, among tree trunks as wide as a house, whose canopy seems to touch the sky. The forest is dim and full of noises. Strange birds call, and there are rustlings high above and in the undergrowth. Fish jump, making spreading ripples in the brown river. If a man turns from the dazzling river the forest is green and opaque, like looking into sea water, and if he turns from the forest to the light, it is like coming up from underwater into blinding air. It is always difficult to see properly, and with the trees there is no way to get the lie of the land. Snakes have been seen swimming in the river. Karlsefni finds one lying coiled in the path, and he kills it with his sword. The body is dry and scaly, spotted like the *jewelled hilt of a dagger. Not one of the company has seen a snake before but they all know that these creatures are the enemy of men, and that their bite is deadly. Karlsefni lifts the dead thing with the flat of his sword and throws it into the river.*

*It is impossible to see far into the forest, and impossible to move about without forcing a path with knives and axes. Early in the morning the birds scream and chatter as if in constant warning, and then as the sun rises higher they grow quiet, until by midday the forest sleeps in a strange damp heat that saps men's strength and makes them want to sleep even in the middle of the day. Invisible insects chirp in the grass, and voices sound too loud in the silent heat. The rhythmic thud of iron on wood strikes a disturbing echo far inland. But there is work to be done, and so the afternoon sweats itself away, until the evening comes early and sudden, and the night noises begin.*

*In the dark only the howl of wolves is recognisable. The other calls and shrieks are unknown, and might be made by animals or demons; there is no way to tell. For almost half the time it is as dark as winter, even though it is close to midsummer, and the nights here are hotter than the brightest days at home. It is too hot at night for sleep to come easily, and yet sleep strikes unexpectedly on sunlit afternoons when the light is too precious to waste.*

*The men never say that they are frightened; still less do they admit to the enchantment that the place casts over them. They are tough and active; they have come so far out of the world because they know how to work hard, endure the cold and danger of the sea, and take what they want without pity. But in this place in summer it is impossible to work hard. The air sucks away their strength, and there is a magic in the heat that entwines itself around their purpose and slowly chokes the life out of it. There are afternoons when nothing seems more desirable than to lie in the sun and sleep. They have discovered already that if a man gives in to that the sun has no pity on him, and he will wake up sick and dizzy, with a hammering in his head and a terrible thirst, his skin burning as if it had been in a fire. Nor is there cold or danger to endure, only the dim mystery of the forest that waits behind their camp, full of sweet scents and strange noises. There is nothing to keep guard against, nothing to fight, nothing, therefore, to fear. There is nothing at all to stop them taking what they want, and yet, when the first tall tree cracks under the axe, and the men stand back while it crashes through the undergrowth with a splitting of wood and rending of creepers, they stand aghast at the noise they have caused, while screaming coloured birds fly up into the sudden light. Slowly the forest settles back to calm, and a spear of sunshine points down accusingly through the hole in the high canopy.*

*The camp seems very small, caught between the forest and the sea. They have cleared the scrub from the dunes at the landward end of the spit that divides the lagoon from the sea. It is a hundred yards away from the entrance to the lagoon, through which the tide pours in like a stream into a bucket, and then empties as if the bucket were being tipped out again a few hours later. The sand dunes between the lagoon and the open sea are the only open ground where it is easy to move around. Wild wheat grows among the grasses, just as it does at Leif's houses. The dunes offer no stone or turf for building, so the summer huts are made of split tree trunks, roofed in by sailcloth stretched over leafed branches. The few cattle forage among strange leaves and grasses and seaweed. Perhaps they miss their sweet northern pastures, or perhaps the people only say they do because they sometimes feel homesick themselves.*

We called our camp Hop, because there was a tidal pool where we could moor our ship. The river there had more fish in it than I've ever seen anywhere, so we weren't hungry. As well as trout we caught halibut near the mouth of the lagoon. It was very hot. We built huts for ourselves, and the cattle were set free to graze on the dunes, although we rounded them up at night, because we could hear wolves in the forest. The bull broke his tether shortly after the winter, and disappeared. It was a blow, but not a disaster; we had two calves, and we thought we could keep the cows in milk another year without him serving them again. As soon as we were settled in our camp we started cutting timber. The man in charge of the work was called Gunnar. He'd worked in a shipbuilder's yard in Norway before joining Karlsefni, and Karlsefni had offered him a large reward to join his crew, so he would have an expert man to make repairs in Greenland if they were needed. When Karlsefni married me, and decided to sail on to Vinland, Gunnar's role became even more important, for the ships were our lifeline back to the world. Karlsefni, and Leif before him, had been prepared to build boats at Leif's houses, though neither had thought of building a trading ship there. So Karlsefni had a man to act as stemsmith, and he had the tools.

As soon as we'd moved into our new camp, Gunnar took men into the forest, searching for suitable trees. There was plenty of fallen wood, so with luck they thought they might find some recently fallen trunks that had already seasoned. We weren't sure what all the trees were. Gunnar said many of them were unlike those in Norway, but he cut branches off different ones, and he and Karlsefni examined the wood. The most important thing was that he did find plenty of oak, which was what we needed. They hewed the keel out of one large trunk, and the stem and stern out of another, and then they had to split more trunks into lengths for the planking. They chose a pine trunk for the mast, thin enough to be used whole. The new ship had to be quite a lot smaller than Karlsefni's, so that we could ship the wood and take it back to Leif's houses. After much discussion Gunnar cut the keel to seven metres.

We were able to work outside nearly all winter, and by spring we had a good load of timber piled in lengths to season. We made more barrels too, because there were plenty of grapes in that part of Vinland, and those of us who were not needed to work with the timber were making as much wine as we could. In fact I took over the wine-making, with as many men as could be spared at any particular time to help me. We used to fill the barrels with grapes and crush them with big pestles, and then seal them up with tar and leave them. The important thing is not to let the air get in. But you make wine in your monastery; I don't need to tell you that.

In the summer it was really hot, almost as hot as it is here. The land felt very foreign. Around Leif's houses it was different from Green- land, but still the kind of place that we were used to. The heart of Vinland was another world. I said to Karlsefni, when we were alone at night, that I was sure we were no longer in the world of men, and he admitted he had been thinking the same, except that nowhere had we crossed an ocean so large that he could think it was the waters that surround the world. 'But,' he went on, 'Even if this place isn't part of the world we've known about, it doesn't have to be full of gods or giants or dead men either. It's only land, like the land we left. Maybe the world is just bigger than we knew. You said yourself that Africa is south of us. I think we're in the lands that circle the world. We've not sailed beyond that.'

'It's not heaven or hel,' I agreed, 'But Thorfinn, it's alien. Separate. Alfheim, perhaps. Not part of anything to do with us. Whatever lives in the forest, animals or spirits, we can't even get in without hacking it down as we go. I wonder if we were ever meant to be here.'

He said I was making troubles where there were none, and he knew land when he saw it, and good timber when he found it, and there was no point asking questions if we couldn't answer them. He turned over then, and was soon asleep. Early the next morning the skraelings came, and that put an end to our innocence in Vinland.

I was out on the dunes with Karlsefni and Snorri, looking at the great oak trunk we'd hauled out of the forest. I'd left my Snorri sleeping in his basket. He was over a year old now, and very active. He could walk, but he could crawl even faster, and I seemed to spend all my waking hours keeping him out of danger. But he still slept in the afternoon. On this particular day some of the men were down on the beach, and the rest were still up at the huts. It was still early, and the grass was soaked with dew. The sea was calm, the waves lapping gently on the outer shore.

It was the noise that made me look up. A strange rattling noise that I can't describe, like grouse would sound if there were a whole flock of them, or like stones shaken in a sieve – no, not like either. Too loud, too alien. I jumped round, and looked out to sea.

There were boats. Not like ours. Smaller. Thinner. Later I saw they were made of skins stretched over wooden frames. There were men in them. That's how I knew they were boats, not animals. The men faced us, not rowing, but they had oars they used backwards, without rowlocks. Only they were not men, but black. One of them stood up in each boat, swinging something over his head like a flail. That was the noise. There were nine boats. I thought of my child, and clutched Karlsefni's arm in both hands.

'What's this?' said Karlsefni sharply. 'What does it mean?'

I shook my head, dry-mouthed. He turned to Snorri, putting me away from him. The men below us had stopped work, and stood frozen, staring at the strange boats. 'Skraelings,' said Snorri. 'The wretched folk. Skraelings. Remember Thorvald Eiriksson?' Then Karlsefni shouted an order, and they ran back to the huts for the weapons no one had used since the voyage began. Karlsefni was going after them when Snorri stopped him. 'Wait!'

'No,' said Karlsefni. 'Those are men.'

'I know. But the noise – they may mean to say they come in peace. We're a long way from the place where Thorvald died.'

Karlsefni hesitated. The boats were just offshore. We could see the men clearly. There were six or seven in each boat. We were out-numbered about two to one. Their hair was long and black. Close up their skin was dark brown. The flails rattled like running footsteps breaking ice. Each man held an oar upright, facing the wrong way. I saw no weapons, but I couldn't see any women either.

'Gudrid, go back. Wait in the hut.'

I didn't argue, but retreated ten paces, and stopped. Karlsefni wasn't looking at me, and I had no intention of obeying him; it would be far worse not to see. Our men were coming back to the shore, swords and shields in their hands. Only Karlsefni and Snorri were still unarmed. The first skin boat beached in the breaking waves, and the others drew in beside it.

'Wait!' Our men obediently stood back, their drawn swords in their hands, and their round shields on their arms. Karlsefni touched Snorri on the shoulder, and the two of them went down the dunes, holding their empty hands palms outwards to show they carried nothing.

The brown men stepped through the waves and stood upright on the shore. One man stayed behind with each boat, keeping them afloat. The empty boats bobbed in the breaking waves; they seemed to weigh nothing at all. I watched, ready to run back and hide my son at the first sign of a fight. The newcomers were shorter than our men, and dark as devils. They were half naked, dressed in skins, and their skin was brown as if it were burnt. They had no swords, but some of them had sharpened sticks like short spears. I remembered all the stories I'd ever heard of demons, shapeshifters and half men, creatures out of the fires of hel who creep into the fringes of the world and lurk there, waiting to seize upon mortal men and capture their souls. I crossed myself, and watched my husband walk down the beach to within two yards of the foremost man. For a moment Karlsefni, whose body I knew as well as if it were my own, looked quite foreign to me. I saw him for the first time as tall, and fair, although in comparison to most of our people he was neither, and I saw how he was clothed almost all over in undyed woven wool, wearing leather boots and a knife in a leather sheath at his belt. It flashed across my mind that although his face was tanned and lined, under his clothes his skin was as white and smooth as his son's, and for a moment he appeared to me innocent and vulnerable, facing the embodiment of all our fear.

The skraelings stood still and looked at the two men facing them. They stared round, and saw our company waiting further back, with their naked swords in their right hands and the sheltering dunes behind them. Then one skraeling copied Karlsefni's gesture and spread his hands wide, palms outwards. He stepped forward within two swords' length of Karlsefni and Snorri. I couldn't hear, but I could see that he was speaking. I saw Karlsefni shake his head. The skraeling spoke again, and Karlsefni said something in reply. The brown man gestured with his hands and spoke louder, and that time I heard him. He had a voice like a man, though there was no sense in it. I heard Karlsefni answer: 'I don't understand. Can you speak Icelandic? I don't understand.'

They seemed to give up at the same time. Karlsefni shrugged, and at the same time the other man spread his hands in a similar gesture of hopelessness, and I think everyone was startled by the way they echoed each other, because on both sides I heard men laugh. And then the skraelings seemed to relax, because they came forward, right up to where our men were standing. They didn't try to speak or touch them, but they stared, and muttered, and pointed things out to each other. They couldn't take their eyes off the drawn swords. Our men watched them like wary dogs, and kept their weapons ready. I realised I had my hands twisted together, and my whole body was tense, willing the men to keep control of themselves. It only needed one wrong move, I knew, for the taut thread to snap, and I didn't trust the spinners of it. The fates hunger for battle, and the possession of the dead, but these men were mine, and I prayed to a more merciful God that I should not have to lose them yet. The odd thing was, Agnar, that it was our own men that I was afraid of. It didn't occur to me that the skraelings would change their mood, or suddenly attack. I knew nothing of their nature, but I knew my own people very well, and I knew they couldn't be trusted to keep the peace.

Perhaps the skraelings sensed the same thing, because suddenly one of them spoke, and in a moment they had all retreated to the boats. They were afloat again before we quite realised what was happening. The strange oars were shipped, and the whole fleet rowed quickly away until they reached the headland beyond our lagoon, and disappeared from sight.

It may not sound to you like an alarming incident. No blood was shed; no one was hurt; but that first encounter changed everything, and I don't think any one of us slept so well again after it as we'd done before. Of course we all discussed the strange people interminably, and I think we all knew we hadn't seen the last of them. Snorri wanted us to leave as soon as possible, and abandon all thoughts of a winter camp. If we'd listened to him, his son would have lived, but then no one knows what might have been, and for all we know, an untimely death may save even greater suffering. Only fate sees everything; there is one face of providence that I trust, and one that seems to be arbitrary and capricious. But perhaps when we cease to be mortal, we shall see what the gods see now, and we'll find that the two faces are really one.

Inevitably the skraelings came back. Since the first encounter, we'd kept a watch, and so we saw them as soon as they came into view round the headland. There were so many boats that the sea looked as if it were strewn with sticks of charcoal, and when the skraelings swung their flails the noise was terrifying. Such an alarming approach must, we assumed, mean an attack. Our men ran to arm themselves, then waited at the top of the dunes. We seemed very few compared to the massed boats before us, but it was close to high tide, which meant if it came to a fight we'd be able to rush them from above as they came ashore.

My boy was awake, and I stood at the door of the hut, holding him in my arms. I thought he'd catch my fear, but he seemed quite unaware of it, as he wriggled to get free so he could be off and see what was happening on the beach. I've never felt so vulnerable, knowing he trusted me completely, and yet I couldn't do a thing to protect either of us if our little warband were to be killed. Even if I could escape into the forest, I could never get away from Vinland, so I'd be better dead than free. I couldn't begin to think about being captured. In all the stories I'd heard of foreigners being taken, they'd kill the baby first and rape the woman, and then maybe kill her too and maybe not. That's what our own people did abroad; I didn't know if the half human creatures I saw in front of me would be the same. I had my knife on its cord around my neck. I knew what I ought to do if I could, if the day went against us. I didn't dare to imagine it clearly. I just felt icy inside and not able to think. My hands were cold and sweating, and I hardly seemed to have the strength to keep hold of my boy. I just concentrated on trying to quiet him and not letting him fall. When your worst fears seem to be coming true it's more like a dream than reality. I suppose it's a way of keeping sane to half believe you might wake up and find you're not really in that world at all.

But the skraelings hadn't come to fight. They came ashore just as they'd done before, carrying no weapons. The leaders stood at the foot of the dunes, and spoke to us in their outlandish tongue, making wild gestures, and beckoning our men down. Others were unloading the boats behind them. It was so different to the nightmare: the cold knot inside me unfroze, and only then did I feel my heart thumping and my whole body trembling. I took a deep breath and crept forward to see better. Snorri was quiet now that he could see, watching the scene below him with round-eyed wonder. The skraelings were spreading stuff out on the beach, and pointing emphatically. Furs. They had furs, Agnar. It was so unlike what I expected I found instead of shivering I was trying not to laugh, and I had to swallow hard to stop myself from giggling like an idiot. It was like when Thorstein came home from the hunt and laid all his spoils at my father's feet.

There were deerskins, sealskins, huge brown bearskins, foxskins, wolfskins and some strange pelts I didn't recognise which we were told later in Norway were some kind of cat, but at the time I'd never heard of such an animal. The furs looked so rich and strange and incongruous, piled on the beach in that empty land beyond the end of the world, and I found I wasn't thinking of Thorstein so much as Thorgeir the packman and his son Einar, who had once dazzled my eyes and my judgement with beautifully made objects from far countries. Everything fell into place then, like waking from a horrible dream. Karlsefni, who was after all a merchant, understood at the same moment, for he suddenly sheathed his sword, dropped his shield in the sand, and spread his hands wide in the gesture he'd used to reassure the wild men before. Then he jumped down the dunes, sliding in the loose sand, and stood alone, face to face with the skraeling leader.

Everything happened very quickly after that. Our men were jumping down the dunes, laughing like fools at the unexpected change. I looked down and saw men and skraelings mingling on the sand, black and fair, all talking too loudly and waving their arms, each group trying to force understanding on the uncomprehending other. I began to perceive a pattern sooner than they did, because standing outside I could see it all, and each man down there only knew what was happening to himself. The skraelings, every one of them, were confronting one of our own men, and pointing at his sword, sometimes even reaching out to touch it, apparently quite unaware of its deadly bite. Our men were trying to hold their swords away, protecting the naked weapons with their shields as best they could. I thought at first the wild men were saying the weapons should be put away. In fact one or two men did sheathe their swords, but that wasn't it. The skraelings just grew more excited and pressed in closer. One of them gripped Thorbrand's scabbard, and tried to pull it from his belt. Thorbrand pushed him roughly back. Both sides began to shout and push. Thorbrand whipped out his sword again. I screamed out: 'Thorfinn!', and startled the baby so he jumped in my arms.

Karlsefni swung round. 'Gudrid! Go back! Go back at once!'

'You're not seeing!' I shouted down to him. 'It's the swords! They want your swords!'

He looked about him, and understood at once, now I'd told him. He hesitated, but I could see, and he couldn't, and that was why I could think faster. 'Thorfinn!'

He looked up, and I told him what to do. 'Something else! Offer something else! Quick!' I saw him take that in, but I was faster. We didn't have much, after all, and I could see them, all dressed in skins as if they were wild animals themselves. 'Cloth!'

He was bewildered for a second, but then a moment later he'd sent men hurrying to the huts. All we had was what we'd needed for ourselves: sailcloth, blankets, cloaks, awnings. Our men brought down all they could find and spread it out on the sand. It wouldn't have worked, I don't think, if Karlsefni hadn't had a red cloak which was heaped in among the rest. As soon as the skraelings saw the colour their attention was caught. They seized the woollen cloak and stretched it between them, stroking it and marvelling over it. I don't think they'd ever felt wool in their hands before. They ran their fingers to and fro over the weave, then spread the cloak out again, and seemed to be exclaiming over the colour.

We had hardly any dyed cloth with us, but perhaps that was better: certainly the skraelings treated it like something rare and precious. In the end Karlsefni cut the cloak in strips with his knife and divided it among the leaders. By that time they were working over the rest of the pile, and pulling out material that they fancied. The swords seemed to be forgotten. I think they'd have recollected them sooner if we hadn't produced another novelty. That was our luck; it hadn't occurred to any of us that milk could be unknown to creatures who appeared in human form. Karlsefni sent two men for buttermilk because it was all we had to offer, and when it came he demonstrated how our strange guests might dip the cup in the barrel and drink.

The skraelings stared at the yellow liquid in the barrel and muttered among themselves. They watched Karlsefni drain the cup and fill it, and offer it to their leader, telling them they were all welcome to drink from it. The man took the cup and drank, and exclaimed in surprise. He seemed pleased with the taste, for he went on to drink the lot, dipped the cup again, and passed it on. The skraelings crowded round, and of course there wasn't enough to go round, but the whole business seemed to satisfy them. They behaved with an odd decorum, as if it were some kind of ceremony, and afterwards they seemed much less wary. I wondered if they shared our belief that it's wrong to betray a man after you have offered him food and drink. They seemed to assume that this new drink was worth more than solid goods, and raised no objection when our men went through the furs, taking whatever they liked.

My baby was beginning to grow restless; grown men might bargain with milk as if it were silver coins, but my Snorri had no false values. I carried him back to the hut, and sat in the shelter of the doorway. I began to feed him cold broth with a spoon, while I listened to the clamour of voices from the beach.

What happened next haunts me still. It was nothing dreadful in itself, nothing at all compared to the terror I had felt when the skraelings came back, but of all the things that happened in Vinland, it stays with me as the most unsettling. I shall see her face until I die.

I've been a lonely woman, Agnar: lonely for my own kind, I mean. I've never lacked company: father, husbands, sons, friends, servants; I've never been alone or neglected. Yet in a way I was alone among them all. In most families there's a group of women at the heart of the household. Not in mine. I had no mother, I lost Halldis, and neither of my husbands took me home to a house of women. I've never had a woman for a friend. Other women do, I know. Maybe it's something you have to learn young, but for some reason I've never had the trick of it. I don't know what it is I fail to do.

At Hop I didn't set eyes on another woman for over a year. Or did I? Was it something I dreamed, or hoped for, or imagined, or was it real? It was a hot afternoon. I'd had a bad fright, and I felt limp and tired. I was still used to sleeping in the day, partly because of the heat, and partly because my son used to wake two or three times every night. So in spite of the skraelings still there on the other side of the dunes I felt sleepy, as I quietly gave my son his dinner in the leafy shade of the doorway.

I'll tell you this bit just as I remember it happening, but be warned,

Agnar, I can't swear to the truth of it. All this summer I've tried to describe things to you as they were, though you must realise that if you had anyone else's version it would probably be different from mine. We all have our point of view, but quite apart from that there are some things I can't be too sure about. I can't explain to you what Vinland is, for example – what kind of place, or where it belongs in the scheme of things. In Rome it seems not to exist, or only as a place inside my mind, because I'm the only one here who has ever experienced it. I wish I had someone I could talk to about it. It's hard to make sense of the past when there's no one left who shared it with you. Maybe one day you'll be an old man in Iceland, and you'll think of a long ago summer in Rome that no one lived in but you, and you'll feel the loneliness I feel now; you'll see all this inside your head, but when you try to tell anyone about it you'll hear the words coming out thin and small and distorted, and even as you speak you'll know your story is as useless as a shadow. That's my difficulty now, you see, and this bit I'm about to tell you is the heart of the problem. Or perhaps it's not important at all; maybe after all it was only a dream.

I was sitting in the doorway, as I said, when a shadow fell across me. I looked up and saw a woman standing there. I knew she was a woman, although she didn't wear a dress. She had on a deerskin tunic like the skraelings wore. She was shorter than me, and much darker. Perhaps it was because I was taken by surprise, but although she had all the characteristics of a savage, I saw quite clearly that she was not one. Perhaps it was because she was alone, not in a crowd. I don't know what it was. I found myself looking at her as if she were a person I might know, and just for a moment I wasn't even surprised. I almost seemed to recognise her.

She spoke to me. I didn't understand. She spoke as if she thought I could understand if I wanted. She didn't babble or speak too loud, like the crowd down on the beach, but spoke to me insistently and slowly, so I could tell she was using real words. The only foreign language I'd ever heard in my life then was Latin, and that only read or chanted. But she was speaking to me, and in a hazy way I felt so close to knowing what she was saying, that I realised then for the first time that all languages make sense to someone. I'd realised the skraelings understood each other, of course, but I hadn't thought of their speech as anything but an uncouth babble, just as it had never occurred to me that ours must sound as nonsensical to them. The woman was pointing to me, and she seemed to be asking a question.

I gave her the most likely answer I could think of. 'My name is Gudrid,' I said very clearly. 'What is yours?'

Then I understood she wouldn't know which bit was my name from that, and I repeated 'Gudrid' once or twice more. 'What is your name?' I said again. 'What is your name?'

'Gudrid,' she replied, like an echo.

Just as she spoke there came a clash of metal against metal, then a sudden scream, and the yells of fighting men. My visitor vanished; I never even saw her go. I leapt to my feet, dropping the spoon, and Snorri wailed in protest. I ran to the edge of the dunes, and saw the last of a brief struggle, and the skraelings running to their boats and launching them so fast they looked like basking seals diving back into the sea after being disturbed.

I looked down on the knot of men left on the beach. They stood with drawn swords, apparently too bewildered by the sudden flight of the skraelings to think of pursuing them. The beach around them was piled with furs, and with the woollen cloth that the skraelings had bargained for and not had time to snatch up and take away. There was something else lying down there that was not just a bundle of skins. I looked closer and saw the dark-skinned body, raddled with blood from a great sword wound across the neck. Just for a moment I saw quite clearly what this meant. A man had died because of us, here in Vinland. I hugged my innocent baby to me, and I seemed to hear an echo of the sound which had never been heard in this country before, the clash of sword on sword, and it seemed to me that it was the crash of a door closing on us. I knew for certain then that we were shut out.

# NINETEEN

# September 18th

We should have gone away at once, and if my word had prevailed we would have. I couldn't have cared less if the skraelings thought that we were cowards, or that they were victorious. What could it matter, when their thoughts were completely unknown to us? When I think about it, Agnar, I don't even know what my own child thinks, or my own husband. If you start worrying about other people's thoughts there's no end to it. But you must keep me to the point, my dear. What is it I've got to tell you about? It all seems very remote this morning. I think when this winter's passed I'll go home. Did you hear the wind in the night? It made me realise the wind so seldom blows here, and when there is a breeze in summer it's still stuffy. I'm glad the year has turned. I've never looked forward so much to winter before. This morning, when I saw the first brown leaves blowing across the wet court-yard, and smelt the west wind with the salt still in it, I felt as if I could breathe again. I slept better last night, and I dreamed I was in Iceland.

\*     \*     \*     \*     \*

I'm tired, Agnar, and it was all so long ago. Sometimes it seems like yesterday, so vivid in my mind that I almost believe I could open my eyes and it would all be there again. One of the best things about growing old, you'll find, is remembering things that have been lost for fifty years. It's my childhood that comes back to me most clearly, but I told you about that, didn't I?

*      *      *      *      *

Oh yes, we were talking about Vinland. My son was a baby then. He was born there, you know. Yes, of course, I did tell you about that. He was a healthy baby. I think it was a good place for him. All a small baby wants is its mother, and Snorri had that more than most children. There was no one else to look after him, you see. I wasn't like that with Thorbjorn. Thorbjorn was conceived in Norway and born at Glaum, and though I loved him and looked after him well I wasn't with him all the time. There was a thrall called Inga who looked after him. He loved her. I used to watch them going up to the milking ring together, hand in hand, to see the cows being milked, Thorbjorn in his short tunic, and his brown bare legs and feet. When boys first come out of long clothes I find their little legs very endearing. Thorbjorn used to go off with Inga, and he never made a fuss or used to cry for me. As soon as he was weaned he slept with his elder brother. His security was in Glaum, the house and all the people there, and that was a burden off my shoulders, but all the same, I always felt there was something I gave to Snorri, and he to me, which Thorbjorn never had.

As soon as Snorri could crawl I had to watch him all the time. He was an adventurous baby, always wanting to be off and see what the men were doing, and yet, if he noticed I wasn't there, he'd panic suddenly and scream until they brought him back to me. His father was tolerant about that until he was weaned. Karlsefni could understand how an infant needed milk, but not how a little boy might be frightened without his mother. When the summer came the men used to bathe in the lagoon. It was a thing I'd have loved to do myself, but of course I couldn't, and so it fell to Karlsefni to get Snorri used to the water so that he'd learn to swim. At first Snorri was all eagerness to go, but one day something frightened him. The first I knew about it was when Karlsefni strode into the camp, and dumped a screaming, choking, wet and naked baby on my lap without a word, and stormed off. I wrapped Snorri up and rocked him, and at last he stopped shivering and hiccuping and went to sleep. By the time Karlsefni came back I'd realised there was no point my losing my temper with him, so I just said that the way to make his son fearless was not to frighten him. He didn't answer, and I thought he was too annoyed with us to take it in.

Soon after that we had one of those tremendous thunderstorms that used to happen in Vinland. A few of us were sheltering in our hut, which was wet enough, with the rain dripping through the roof and turning the floor to mud. The boy was standing at the door, holding on to the doorpost, gazing wide-eyed at the torrents of rain. Although it was raining it was still hot. In those Vinland summers I used to just put a shirt on Snorri, so I didn't have to bother with nappies. Anyway, he was standing there looking out, when a jagged fork of lightning shot into the forest, and at the same moment a crack of thunder broke so loud it sounded like the end of the world. I think we all ducked, and Snorri's face crumpled and he turned to run to me, half blinded by the light. I called out and put my arms out to him, but his father was before me. He just took Snorri by the hand and steadied him, and said to me reprovingly, 'He's not frightened; a bit of a storm couldn't frighten him.' One or two of the men surreptitiously made Thor's sign when Karlsefni said that, but Snorri stopped dead, and stared at his father. Then he let go Karlsefni's hand, and went straight back to his place at the door, not looking at me at all. 'The way to make him fearless,' Karlsefni explained to me kindly, 'is not to frighten him.' I didn't say a word, Agnar, I had grown too wise.

Not knowing any other babies, I just took Snorri as he was. He didn't say anything until he was past two – not a word – but he understood us very well, much more than most babies. Perhaps he didn't know what he was supposed to be like, being the only one of his kind in the world, so far as he knew. He listened to us, and in some ways he was precocious, but I don't think it occurred to him that he might talk himself. When he did start, that last winter at Leif's houses, he could very soon say whole sentences. His first word was 'boat', and then 'stone'. 'Mother' and 'father' came later. When I look back now, I think how much I was hampered by having him with me all the time. I didn't notice it then, it was just the way life was, but when I think about it I hardly travelled a mile from our camp in Vinland. Everything I did seemed to happen in slow motion. He'd play on the shore for hours, happy with stones and shells and bits of wood, but if I took my eyes off him for a moment he was quite apt to run headlong into the sea. So I stayed and watched him. I wonder now what I thought about all those hours. I can't remember. When we finally put to sea we put a harness on him, and tethered him. He liked best to stand by the helmsman at the steerboard, and help steer the boat, especially when his father was there. In rough weather it was hard to keep him quiet down in the body of the ship; he was never ill at sea.

*     *     *     *     *

Oh yes, the skraelings. We should have gone, Agnar, after we killed one of them. I didn't see it happen. Karlsefni said that some of the skraelings had wandered over to the pile of timber. When Snorri saw they were touching the tools stacked there, he ran after them. But before he could get there one of the skraelings had seized an axe and was examining the blade. Thorbrand tried to get the axe away from him, but the skraeling swung it out of reach. Someone came at him with a sword, and the skraeling beat away the weapon with the axe. Then as he swung it again, another of our men grabbed it from behind, and when the skraeling turned on him, he felled him with one stroke. When the skraelings saw the rest of our company coming down on to them with drawn swords they fled, as I saw myself, when I came running to see what the noise was about.

We knew we wouldn't have seen the last of them. Not only had we killed one of them, but they'd left behind all their furs and the goods they'd traded them for. I thought, and Snorri thought, we should leave at once, and so did some of the others. Karlsefni would not go. We still had to cut the tree trunks into manageable lengths so we could stow them aboard, and he absolutely refused to leave behind any of the timber we needed for the boat. I said we could get more elsewhere, but I couldn't deny the fact that what we had was already partly seasoned. He was determined we'd finish the job, and as he said, a delay now might mean another year in Vinland. The time had come when no one wanted that. I think we were all beginning to think longingly of our own homes.

The men who supported Karlsefni, and they were in the majority, were quite ready for a battle with the skraelings. They were, after all, freemen, trained to fight, and they'd had no chance to use their weapons since the day they'd left Iceland. Quarrelling among themselves was on the whole denied to them, as even the fiercest of them had to see that we needed the whole crew to stay alive and amicable if everyone was to get back to Leif's houses. Our people are not afraid of dying in battle, as you know, Agnar, but I think they were afraid of being left behind, alive or dead, to be alone for ever in the lands outside the world. If they died in battle, of course, they would not be alone, for some of their companions would go with them on their last journey, and their ghosts need not wander, but would be taken at once to the place prepared for them at the feast which lasts until the end of the world. Even in Vinland death in battle is the one insurance against eternal loneliness, I suppose. But I'm a woman, and I had my son to think of, so the fates had nothing to offer me, and I urged Karlsefni to get out while we could.

Instead of doing any such thing we built a stockade around our camp, and kept watch day and night. Even with that extra task, we worked feverishly with the timber. For three weeks nothing happened. Our work was nearly finished, and I began to hope that we might after all leave before the skraelings came back.

The attack came at sunrise. They must have crept along the shore while it was dark, because they came along the beaches by land, from both sides at once. Our guards were watching the sea, not the forest, and so the skraelings would have surprised us completely. It was the bull that saved us. We'd never caught him again once he'd got ashore. He'd appear from time to time and graze among the cows, but if any man attempted to approach him he'd toss his horns and charge. Once he'd frightened off pursuit he'd lumber off into the forest. We'd let him be; we had enough to do without keeping him under restraint to no purpose, and the cattle had been able to forage for themselves all winter. In the end it was his waywardness that saved us. He was on the dunes with the rest of the cattle, and somehow the approaching skraelings had him cornered between the camp and the sea. We were roused by his bellowing, and saw the skraelings, less than a hundred yards away, at the same moment as we saw the bull charge.

I don't know what kind of monster they thought this was, but they broke ranks and fled. The bull got one of them though. We saw him toss the man on his horns and trample over him, then charge away into the forest.

Soon we heard the same rattling noises that had heralded the skraelings' arrival before, and we saw another band of them running towards us from the opposite direction. And that was all I did see, because a hail of stones came crashing in over our stockade, and I had to take the baby into our hut. That was worse; I could hear, but I couldn't see anything but the backs of the bowmen who remained in the stockade, shooting at the skraelings as they approached. But the noise outside was frightful: the shouting of war-cries, the screaming of wounded men, thuds and trampling, and sometimes huge blows on the stockade wall that shook the timbers and made the whole thing shake. I wanted to act but there was nothing I could do. Snorri didn't cry, but he clung to me like a limpet, He didn't hide his face though, as a scared child usually does, but kept his head up, his eyes so wide open it seemed as if he were listening with them.

Something crashed against the stockade; there was a splintering of timber and a wild rhythmic yelling. I jumped to my feet and unsheathed my knife. I don't know what I could have done, with a baby clinging round my neck, but I stood at the door, with the knife poised in my hand. I wasn't scared; everything was too unreal for that. I felt a strange cold calm inside me and I would have done anything, if I'd had to.

There was no clash of weapons, it's funny how I noticed that. No metal on metal, just thuds and thumps and screams. I remember one voice that kept on screaming, just outside the wall, and the noise going through my head, and me wishing it would stop. At last it did stop, and afterwards I saw the skraeling, pinned through his stomach to the wooden wall, and not able to wrest the sword away. He was dead by the time the fight was over.

It felt like a long time, but when the quiet came it was still only just after dawn. The noise was gone, and I heard voices speaking Icelandic, and someone opened the gate.

The skraelings had gone, all but five dead, who lay in their blood between the stockade and the beach. There was one body that was not a skraeling, a bundle of woven cloth that did not move. Karlsefni turned the man over. His clothes were soaked in blood but his face was clean and white. When Karlsefni moved him his head rolled horribly on the broken neck. I could see very clearly who it was: Snorri's son Thorbrand. Snorri walked over quite slowly, and stood looking down at the body. Karlsefni, crouched beside it, didn't move. No one spoke. Then Snorri stooped and picked up his son as if he were a child and not a grown man, and walked away, carrying the body in his arms. We watched him kick open the door of his hut and shove his way inside with his difficult burden. No one went to help him. We saw the door shut on us, and slowly Karlsefni stood up. The sand round his feet was red with Thorbrand's blood.

*After a battle the fates move slowly across the field. They take the souls of the dead and carry them away to Valhalla, where all men who die in battle feast until Ragnarok, the last battle of all, which is the end of the world. In battle a man need not face death alone; he need not fear that he will be forgotten and cease to exist in the minds of men.*

*But in this battle it seems that the end of the world is already here. The enemy are not warriors but strange half men who are perhaps not subject to fate, and who have no place in the eternal halls. Their ghosts, if they have any, have faded away to some alien place. Their bodies lie in a heap on the shores of the world out of which they came, but there is no sign of their souls.*

*A ghost hovers over Karlsefni's camp at Hop. It watches men bringing down timber and barrels of wine to the shores of the lagoon. It watches a ship being prepared for sea, with supplies of water and dried meat, enough for a long voyage. It watches blankets and pots and weapons being carried down from the huts and piled on the shore. It sees a few cattle rounded up and led down to the beach. It sees the ship brought close in at high tide, and the cargo carefully stowed aboard.*

It returns to one of the huts whose door has remained shut while all this is happening. It looks down and sees the body of a young man covered by a brown cloak. It sees how the young man's sword, with the blood cleaned from it, lies beside him, and how his shield has been placed by his left arm. It sees the young man's father sitting silently beside the body, while hour follows hour. It sees the grief that no living being will ever be allowed to see. The walls of the hut are thin, and the father of the young man neither moves nor makes a sound. Only the ghost witnesses the helplessness of a father who could do nothing to save his son.

The ghost turns away and sees men digging a grave at the edge of the forest. It sees a man choose a stone and scratch the mark of a cross on it. It sees two men carry the stone across the dunes and lay it beside the open grave. It sees Karlsefni go to the door of the hut and call out his friend's name. It sees the door of the hut open at last, and it watches while the body wrapped in the brown cloak is carried to its grave. It sees everyone in the camp gathered around the grave, where the body of the son is laid at the feet of his father. It sees the body lowered into the soil of this land where no man of his people has ever lain before. It sees earth sprinkled, and the sign of a cross made over it.

The ghost waits until the last of the cargo is stowed into the ship. It watches while men, and one woman with her small son, climb aboard. It sees the ship loosed from its mooring, and, as the tide begins to stream out of the lagoon, the wooden ship goes with it, out into the open sea. It sees the square, brown sail hoisted. The ship turns sunwise, borne by the river current, until the wind fills the sails, and gradually she makes headway, and ploughs a white furrow out to sea.

The ghost looks down on the grave, which is covered by the stone with the cross scratched on it, and it knows that no living man will ever come there again in the knowledge of its presence. It looks down at the abandoned huts that have been built upon the sand, and knows that no one will ever return to live there in the time that used to be it. Its people have left nothing behind them that anyone will ever find again. There is nothing left but a ghost, and it will be nothing too, when no one is left who is able to remember.

# TWENTY

# *September 19th*

Wait, I'm not ready yet. I'm still looking at it. My dear, I thought you'd have forgotten all about it long ago. They really don't mind you bringing it here today? Such a precious thing, and you told them it was only so an old woman who never learned to read could have a look at it. They must be kind men, in spite of the strange lives they lead. Do you mind if I turn the pages? Is that really all right? I won't damage it, will I? Look, Agnar, it has faces in it. And see the patterns. It's like metalwork. Karlsefni loved metalwork. He loved patterns like these. Look at the pictures. Look, Agnar, that's a man, those are arms and legs, and a body all twined up with the pattern. Oh, it's a letter, is it? How do you mean? A sound? I'm not sure that I understand. But that's a bird. Red and yellow and blue. Karlsefni loved bright colours. I'd never seen so much colour in my life as when we got to Norway. At the king's court everyone had dyed clothes, and jewels, and the king's rooms seemed to me then to be crammed with beautiful things: wall hangings, carved chests and chairs and tables, cups and dishes of engraved gold. People wore bracelets and necklaces and brooches of precious stones set in worked silver, or even gold. There seemed to be every colour in the world there, colours like these. And yet, Agnar, compared to Rome it was all nothing. Until I came here I had no idea what could be made by men. I went to the cathedral in the Lateran, and it was all the colours of heaven; arches soaring high above my head, stone transformed into gold like the wings of angels. For the glory of God, like this book in front of me.

See, there's a green. And purple, or is it dark blue? I can't tell, my eyes are old. But look at the strange beast, Agnar, look at its long twisted body and its claws, look at the patterns coming out of its jaws. And look, there's another one there: that's its body going right round the edge of the page. Look, it has the faces of men in its angles. Is all painting made like metalwork, Agnar? When we got to Norway, Karlsefni gave me a mirror like this – I'm not being blasphemous, I hope. It was a secular thing, but the patterns on the frame were very like this. It was real gold, Agnar, very extravagant of him, but the beast carved round the frame was just the same, like Jormungand, with his jaws trying to swallow his tail, and beautiful patterns chased all over him, and birds and small beasts hiding in the folds of his body, like the squirrels in Yggdrasil running up and down. And where the black letters are on this page there was real Venetian glass and I could see my face in it, as clearly as I see the writing here. I'd never seen my own face before, Agnar. Some people think it's wrong. No woman, or man either, should contemplate their own beauty. But isn't all beauty for the glory of God? Karlsefni said how beautiful I was, again and again, when we got to Norway. He gave me dyed cloth and a gold necklace and rings of twisted gold with rubies in them to hang from my ears, and the first night I wore them he kept looking at me across the king's table as if he'd never seen me before. Then when we did go to bed he made love to me as if it were the first time he'd ever known me. It was like beginning all over again, Agnar, and I'm sure, though I can't prove it, that that's when Thorbjorn was conceived.

But I shouldn't be thinking of sexual passion in the presence of a holy book. Look now, Agnar, this page is all black writing, but even here there's a man's face, look, and his body twined around the red bit. What do you mean, the letter? Explain. Oh, but wait, there are more faces. In between the pattern, see, the more you look the more you see them. They're the faces of men, aren't they, Agnar? Who are they? What are they doing? Explain it to me.


\*　　\*　　\*　　\*　　\*

In the writing? It's all in the black letters? Can you see it? Very well, read me a bit. What are you doing? Why are you turning the pages so fast? Stop that writing and answer me!

*    *    *    *    *

How do you mean, suitable? Isn't it all the word of God? How can any part not be suitable?

*    *    *    *    *

Suitable for me. I like that. Like a present, and you choose it. Very well, I'm listening.

*    *    *    *    *

Of course, I hadn't thought of that. How clever you are, my dear. Can you really turn it into Icelandic as you go along? Are you sure that isn't blasphemous?

*    *    *    *    *

That's true. Well, maybe I'm turning into you and you're turning into me. And I'm the one who's always said we can't be overheard here. Come on boy, put that pen down. Don't keep on writing when I've nothing to say. I thought you were going to read to me.

*    *    *    *    *

Oh my dear one, I don't know what to say to you. How did you understand that it was so? Out of the whirlwind, yes, out of the north, in terrible majesty. Oh yes, it was like that. Agnar, I never knew it was written in that book that the world was not made for us. Read it to me again, how the stars sang in the morning, and we were not there.

*    *    *    *    *

He's right, Agnar, he's right. The springs of the sea are beyond us, and the gates of death are not opened to us. What did your cardinal think that I could possibly tell you? I know nothing, Agnar, nothing. I declare to you freely I don't know it all, nor even the smallest part of it. Read to me again about the rain and the ice, the wilderness outside the world that was neither born nor begotten, nor even thought of by the minds of men.

\*     \*     \*     \*     \*

This world that we have made for ourselves is very small, Agnar. Sometimes we seem to be prisoners in it, and when we die perhaps the doors will open again and set us free. Maybe that's the only thing I've learned. However much you learn, however far you explore, you have no way of seeing beyond where you are. And yet the book is very beautiful to look at, and to touch. Even the leathery smell of it is good. How can we make beautiful things, Agnar, when we know so little? No one ever explained it to me so clearly before, but I think now that your God in the book is greater than the fates because he does much more than spin out the threads of human lives. But that kind of greatness makes me afraid. What are we, in the face of it? The boundaries of the world become so large, and so very cold. Will anyone be waiting for us when we die? Will the meaning of our suffering be hidden from us even then? If there is any mercy, which is what the book is meant to be about, I thought, surely then we'll be allowed to understand? What do you think, Agnar?

\*     \*     \*     \*     \*

Well of course, you have to say that, don't you? But a promise like that doesn't seem to me to come from the same place as what you've just been reading. It's too small, too specific. And yet everything in there is the word of God, isn't it? I know you're a theologian, Agnar, but it's quite enough for me to understand that I can't understand, which is what I knew already.

Now, I would like to look at the other pictures, please, and then we'll get on with the work. You realise we've nearly finished, don't you? It's going to be hard to part, my dear. I've grown very fond of you. I suppose I should be glad there're only a few pages left to go, and our job is nearly done, but I'm going to miss you very much. That's odd really, when I think how I've resented sitting here through all the summer days when I might have been getting on with my own pilgrimage, which is after all what I came here for. But at this moment, you, writing away there, seem even more important to me than my children. I love them most, of course, but now they're far away, in another part of my life. Just now it's you and me that matter, and the words on the page. I find myself wishing – though I know it couldn't be sustained – that life could always be that simple.

\*　　\*　　\*　　\*　　\*

It's kind of you to say that but, I hope one day you'll find a more fulfilling kind of happiness. I think you may. Now, enough of all this talk. Let me tell you how we built our ship.

We brought the new keel home in Karlsefni's ship, laid over our own keel, and the other wood stacked and lashed down around it. It made the voyage very uncomfortable, as it was so difficult to move about with all that timber. They discussed towing some of it, but we'd come a long way south, and it would have been like having an unwieldy sea anchor all the way home, and the ship would have been very difficult to steer even in the best conditions. As well as the keel, we had the stem and stern posts, an unwieldy divided trunk which Gunnar wanted for the keelson, a pine trunk for the mast, and split oaks for the planking. Tucked in around that, we had barrels of wine, the furs the skraelings brought, and our cattle and possessions. We were lower in the water than on any other voyage I ever made, with the sea barely six inches below the gunwale amidships. We knew we might have to jettison some of the cargo if the weather turned on us, but as it was we had a straightforward voyage north again, and reached Leif's houses soon after Lammas, with everything intact.

The first job was to enlarge the boathouse at the top of the beach. As we'd be working through the winter, the whole job, after the first month or so, had to be done under cover. Once the keel and the stem and stern were hewn into their final shape, and fastened together, I, ignorant as I was, began for the first time to believe in the whole project. We had an outline, and my imagination could supply the rest. But of course it takes more than imagination to build a ship.

All the half trunks we'd brought home had to be split in half again, and then again, as many times as necessary to get the planks thin enough. Meanwhile Gunnar was hewing out the keelson from the forked trunk he'd chosen. There were ropes to be made too, which had to be done out of sealhide, as we had no hemp. We did have quite a lot of spare rigging with us; both some of our own and some left by Leif's expedition. The most crucial thing was that Karlsefni's ship had carried a spare sail. If we hadn't had that, the whole project would have been impossible, because we had no more wool. In fact shortage of wool turned out to be our biggest problem. We'd killed all the sheep in that first terrible winter, and although, because there were women on the expedition, we'd brought two looms to Leif's houses, they'd hardly been used since we arrived. It was a kind fate, in a way, that prevented the skraelings taking away the cloth we'd bartered, because we had to unpick a lot of it to get thread enough for caulking. Then the loose wool had to be soaked in grease made from fat and birchbark. Working with the wool would have been a wretched task, only the women did it together, and I was glad to be among them again. They were kind to Snorri too, and he was happy playing indoors in winter when we were all there. There was one horrible moment when he swallowed a spindle whorl, but Helga held him upside down by his ankles and banged him on the back, and the stone fell out of his mouth. She saved his life by doing that. It's strange to think a spindle whorl brought him closer to death than a skraeling warband.

The real frustration was the smithy. Have you any idea how many iron nails you need to hammer out for a ship, Agnar? They'd been working bog iron at Leif's houses while we were away, but whether it was the furnace, or the fuel, or the Vinland bog iron, that wasn't right, I don't know. Helga's husband was a good smith, and he made good nails, but we never had enough iron. No man was going to give up his sword to make nails, but we had to use the ponies' bits, and shield bosses, and even an axe head, just to get the metal we needed for the ship.

I'm no shipbuilder, Agnar, but I can tell you that there's never been a winter, and a spring too, when I worked so hard. There was a period when it just seemed to be chaos. As I say, you have an outline, you imagine a ship, and it seems quite possible. But then you try to bring all the pieces together, and there's a long time when there seems to be far too much of everything, and you can't believe it will ever all come together. It's like working with too many threads in your hand at once, and your mind can't make any order out of them. You just have to look at one bit at a time, and stop imagining the whole, or you'd be too discouraged to go on. You'd just be seeing all the time how much there is to be done. The whole is too much to remember, and so you do a little of one thread, and then it reminds you of something else, and after that you can't make sense of the first bit without the next, only you can't do the next until you've finished the first: so you get the rope for a block, for example, but you don't know the thickness you need because the block isn't made, and you can't carve the block until you're sure of the thickness of the rope. It all gets so complicated you can't think of anything else, and you dream about it at night, and you think you'll manage as long as nothing else happens, and as soon as you think that there's another disaster, another tree trunk that won't split along the grain, another length of rope that isn't long enough; and it wasn't even my job, Agnar, except that we were all caught up in it. Sometimes there were arguments, even blows, but only about the ship. No one had time that winter for quarrelling about anything else.

When I think about those people now, Agnar, I feel a bond with them I share with no one else. I didn't like all of them, I have difficulty remembering their faces, and I wouldn't even try to remember all their names. A few were thralls, most were free-men, and two – Karlsefni and Snorri – later became chieftains in their own country. At Leif's houses I naturally spent time with the other four women, but in a way I'd shared more with the men who'd been on the voyage south. Nineteen mortals from this world have been into the depths of Vinland, eighteen of us came back. Nearly all of those men must be dead now. I don't know what happened to most of them. Some stayed in Greenland, fewer went home to Iceland, and our own crew sailed with us from Greenland to Norway, and all but two came back with us to Iceland, and half a dozen settled in the valley of Glaumbaer. I suppose they all told their story to someone. Some of them have been back to Vinland, bringing desperately needed timber home to Greenland. Oh yes, those voyages still go on. I don't know how far south they go these days. They never make winter camps, I'm told, because of the skraelings. They quickly fell the timber they need and go. The only voyage we heard about in detail was the dreadful expedition made by Freydis. She made Vinland into a place of hel, a land of murder and betrayal. I wouldn't want to face the ghosts she left behind her.

And yet, Agnar, even now, when I think about those people, I miss them. When I was there it never seemed like home, but we made something there worth having. Literally, you could say – after all, we managed to build a ship.

Anyway, by the time the pack ice melted, we had the rudder in place, and the mast stepped, and the planking laid inside the ship. We launched her on a fine spring day, and when she slid into the sea she lay neatly, low in the water, looking surprisingly small after all the effort that had gone into her. I stood with my son and watched them hoist the sail, and slowly slip out to sea. We walked along the shore, following them, until we stood on the sandy spit that guarded our bay from the north, and watched the new craft gradually grow smaller, and then disappear behind the offshore islands. It was only when I watched her out at sea, riding the waves as if that's what she'd been born to do, that I really believed in her. As soon as she was in the sea she was something more than the thing we'd made. She was a ship, and a ship can go anywhere; it can take men wherever they choose, out of one world, if they like, and into another. Somehow I hadn't thought of us, right until that moment, as real shipbuilders. We had the expertise: Gunnar had that, and of course all men know enough about ships to be of use. We had the persistence: after all, our lives depended on doing the job properly. But as well as those two things you need something else – luck. And the fates were kind to us. Don't get me wrong, Agnar, you can't rely on them if you don't work for yourself as well. But all the work you do will come to nothing if they don't smile on you. They may never favour you, all your life long, but if you're one of the lucky ones, sometimes you'll seize a chance, and find them with you all the way.

Our ship stood her sea trials well. Karlsefni and Gunnar came home smiling, and the rest of the crew were drunk on success even before the cask of wine was broached. It was Pentecost, and we had the best feast we ever sat down to in Vinland. Then we made our last preparations, and on Ascension Day we barred the doors of Leif's houses, took our cattle on to the already loaded ships, and sailed home with the richest cargo anyone ever brought out of the wilderness that lies beyond the world.

# TWENTY-ONE

# *September 23rd*

There's one other thing I should tell you about Vinland. We were home at Glaum, at about this time of year, or perhaps a little later. It was very stormy, and as we sat at the hearth we could hear the west wind howling round the house. I can't remember now exactly who was there: we often had visitors in the autumn; between harvest and winter is a good time for people to get away from home. It was beginning to get dark, and the boys had just come in. That year was the last summer they were both at home, and they were always riding off together. Sometimes they'd be back the same night, sometimes they'd disappear for weeks. I used to worry about Thorbjorn getting into fights, and if he did pick a quarrel, and get killed, Snorri would be bound to avenge him. I was never at ease when they were away. I used to try not to watch for the horses coming back, but I did. I couldn't help it. Once they really leave, you can't go on worrying; you'd only destroy yourself. In fact Snorri sailed for Norway the following spring, and I only had news of him once in three years, and that was six months after he'd last seen the man who brought it. I prayed for him every day, but I didn't feel anxious, as I did when he was a young man roaming about with his friends in Iceland. By the time Snorri came home from Norway, Thorbjorn had already gone.

Thorbjorn went to Mikligard when he was still only seventeen, and joined the Varangian guard. It was more than ten years before he came home again, and when he first walked in, just for a moment he seemed a complete stranger. Then I saw it was Thorbjorn, turned into this foreigner with brown skin and bleached hair and unfamiliar clothes. He had a ruthless air about him, a suggestion of pent energy that I found disquieting, threatening even, although he was my own son. He'd been a truculent, sturdy boy, no taller than his father but very strong, a hard worker at home but always much too ready to pick a fight. The man who came back was less obviously aggressive, but Agnar, I'd have been afraid to be his enemy. Being his mother, however, it soon became clear to me that I'd never be allowed to lack anything he thought I wanted, for as long as I lived. He brought us home a chest full of treasure from the East, silks and jewels in strangely worked settings, and a sinister curved sword for his brother that looked as if it would snap in two, only it was forged to be as tough and supple as a whiplash, and everyone who saw it marvelled over it. This was just at the time when Karlsefni was beginning to be ill, and I was very anxious about him. I remember vividly how he sat there at the table with Thorbjorn, studying the strange metalwork, and asking Thorbjorn question after question about the countries he'd been in, the way things were made there, how men resolved their quarrels, about the seas and the tides and all the strange gods that the infidel believed in. Karlsefni didn't leave home again after that winter. The following June he was in too much pain even to ride to the Thing, which he hadn't missed once since the year we came to Glaum. But he never lost his curiosity, Agnar. When he couldn't travel himself, he made do with asking endless questions of everyone who did. He was a good listener, Karlsefni, a good reader of men.

But you must make me keep to the point. At the time I'm speaking of, Thorbjorn was only fifteen, and he'd never been further than Thingvellur. He and Snorri were very close just before Snorri went away. Snorri had always tolerated Thorbjorn, and, I suspect, quite often kept him out of trouble – Snorri was never a jealous boy – but four years makes a lot of difference between children. Thorbjorn grew up very quickly though, and once that happened they nearly always went about together. They've been parted for years at a stretch since then, but when they're together, it's always as if the time between had made no difference at all. I'm glad I've been able to give my sons the thing I never had myself – one another, I mean. Until I had my boys, I was always envious of brothers and sisters, I always wanted to be two against the world, not one. Since Thorbjorn was born I've not felt like that, because it was a precious gift that I was able to give to them.

You must stop me talking about my sons, Agnar, or I'll never get to the point. I miss them, you know. I miss them and my daughters-in-law and my grandchildren, and I want to see my great-grandchild. I think I'm ready to go home.

\*     \*     \*     \*     \*

Yes, good boy, you keep me to the point. Very well, we were in the hall at Glaum: me, Karlsefni, our two sons, both with damp clothes and flushed faces after galloping home through wind and rain, our guests sitting with us close to the fire, and the house thralls clearing away the last of the meal. The dusk was drawing in outside, and the wind was rising to a storm.

We didn't hear anyone coming because of the wind, but a thrall came running in to say a group of horsemen had been sighted on the road which leads west out of the Glaum valley. The men hurried outside, and I pulled a cloak round my shoulders and followed. As the strangers reined in at our door and Karlsefni greeted them, I suddenly saw in my mind another picture: my father at the door of Laugarbrekka, and a group of horsemen in wet cloaks riding up to us out of the gale. I smelt the steaming horses, and I seemed to hear the sea roaring over the skerry to the south, and feel the salt spray coming in on the wind and stinging my cheeks. I was aware of myself as very small, a little girl clutching the doorpost, staring wide-eyed at the storm and the sea and the armed men appearing so suddenly out of the dusk. I don't know if it was a real memory, but it was so vivid that for one moment I was overwhelmed by it. Then it vanished, and I stepped forward, once again the mistress of Glaumbaer, to welcome our unexpected guests.

It was a man called Gudleif, whom Karlsefni knew. Like Karlsefni, he'd made a great reputation for himself as a seagoing trader. We wondered to see him so far north of his own home in Borgafjord at the beginning of winter, but he said there was a matter he needed to discuss with Karlsefni. As soon as he and his men had eaten and drunk, he told us his story.

*The hall at Glaum is filled with shadows. The fire glows along the length of the hearth, and half a dozen oil lamps cast little pools of light from brackets in the wall. The people shift on their benches, and settle down to hear Gudleif's story. As soon as he has well begun they are motionless, their attention palpable. Karlsefni sits in his carved chair, his chin in his hand, his face a little in shadow so it's not possible to see what he is looking at. On his left hand his son Snorri gazes at Gudleif as if he were listening with his eyes. He looks shocked, like a man being unexpectedly told his own dreams, or some tale that he had forgotten that he knew. Beside him, Thorbjorn watches Gudleif appraisingly. The only time he looks like his mother is when he frowns; there is the same vertical line between his eyebrows, which will one day be permanently etched. On Karlsefni's right hand Gudrid sits leaning on her elbow, with her hand covering her mouth. Her eyes give away nothing, except that she never takes them for one moment from Gudleif's face.*

*Gudleif sits on the bench on the opposite side of the hearth. As he speaks he knows his own power. He can make these people see pictures in their minds. He can take them on a journey far from their own hearth and show them another country. He has brought the image of it back with him from the ends of the earth, and it is in his gift to pass it on. These people can never go there; the way is closed. The place where he went is only an idea now, but when he looks at their faces he knows he has carried them away, and his words are all that is needed to make the story real.*

The previous summer Gudleif had left Norway for Dublin on a trading voyage, his plan being to sail home to Iceland from there. It was already well into the autumn when he finished his business in Ireland and set out for home. He was less than a day's sail west of Ireland when he ran into an easterly, which veered north and by nightfall had turned to a full gale. There was nothing he could do but run before it into the open ocean, and for days there was little visibility, and no sign of land. At last the wind began to abate; it was close to the equinox, which made it very difficult to guess how far south they were, but the air was warm and when Karlsefni asked him, Gudleif said there had been no ice. They did see land at last, due west. It was nothing like Iceland or Greenland; there was just a long line of low-lying hills with no mountains. When they came close they saw the hills were covered with forest that was still green as if it were summer.

It wasn't anywhere they recognised, but they were exhausted, and they needed water, so they closed the coast and sailed along it until they found a sheltered bay with a beach of white sand, where they moored and went ashore. While they were filling their water casks at the stream, they heard a sound, and when they looked round, they saw strange brown people running along the beach from both sides. Gudleif and his men had put down their weapons so they could manoeuvre the full barrels, and in any case there were so many skraelings that when Gudleif's men did try to fight with their bare hands they were quickly overpowered. The skraelings seized them all and carried them into the forest.

They didn't go far. There was a good path, though narrow, so they travelled quickly through the dim light of the trees, and then came out, blinking, into a sunny clearing, where they found themselves in the strangest encampment any man ever saw. There were several small fires burning outside, and grouped around them there were round tents made of skins sewn together, stretched over wooden frames. As soon as the skraelings came in with their prisoners a group of children came running, and pushed their way right up to the Norse men, not showing any fear at all, but chattering in a strange language, and even trying to touch the strangers. There were women there too, who came away from the fires to stand and stare, and although they kept their distance, no one tried to call the children to order.

Gudleif and his men were brought into the middle of the camp, and hobbled together with strips of hide; their hands were tied behind their backs. No one tried to speak to them, but it was clear that some kind of argument was going on among the skraelings. Gudleif could only suppose that the debate was whether to kill them or to make them slaves. It occurred to him that they were obviously too dangerous to use as slaves unless they were made harmless, and when he thought about how that could be done he knew it would be better to die, even if they had to do the job themselves. But the argument died away, and nothing was done. Everyone seemed to be waiting. It was hot in the middle of the clearing, and the prisoners grew more and more thirsty. Sometimes they spoke to each other about the chances of escape, but at present far too many people were watching. So they sat still, while their skraeling guards watched over them.

At last a new group of men came into the camp. One seemed to be some kind of chieftain, because their captors bowed before him and spoke to him with deference. Gudleif hardly noticed him. He was looking at the man beside him. An old man, with white hair. A man more than a head taller than any skraeling in the camp. A man tanned by the sun, but still paler-skinned than a skraeling could possibly be. A man dressed in a deerskin tunic and leggings just like the skraelings, but with a tattered woven cloak worn over one shoulder, leaving his sword arm free, although he had no weapon. Gudleif watched as the skraelings conferred, never taking his eyes off the strange man. The group moved closer, and Gudleif saw that though the man's cloak was torn and full of holes the ring brooch that fastened it was bronze, and carved on it was an elongated beast, its mouth swallowing its tail. The chieftain, with the strange man beside him, stood looking down on the prisoners. Gudleif looked into the eyes of the stranger, and saw that they were a clear pale blue.

'Well, well.' The man looked them over, and shook his head. It didn't occur to Gudleif to be surprised that he spoke to them in Icelandic. 'So where've you landed from?'

Gudleif stood up, and the skraelings made no attempt to stop him. 'Who are you?'

'Just what I was about to ask you, my friend.'

'I'm Gudleif, Gudlaug's son, from Iceland.'

'From which part of Iceland?'

'Borgafjord.'

'Where in Borgafjord?'

'From Reykholt. You know it?'

'Oh yes, I know Reykholt. Did you have an uncle, or a great-uncle perhaps, called Thorfinn?'

'You know my family?'

'I think we must have a talk.' The stranger turned to the skraeling chieftain beside him, and began to speak rapidly in the skraeling tongue. Gudleif looked from one to the other, trying to follow the discussion. He could make nothing of it, but eventually the Icelander turned back to him, and said, 'If your bonds are released, will you guarantee that you and your men will behave peacefully while you are here?'

Of course Gudleif promised at once, as this seemed a far more hopeful turn of events. But the man interrupted him. 'That's not all. You'll have to stay here tonight, as it's almost dark. But I want you to promise to leave as soon as it gets light, and furthermore, you must swear never to try to come to this place again, and never to tell anyone else where it is.'

'I couldn't if I tried,' said Gudleif, 'since we don't know where we are ourselves.'

'All the better. Swear to me you'll sail east again until you reach lands you know, and never try to discover again where this place is. There must be no sailing directions, you understand?'

'I understand what you say. But why not?'

'This isn't your world. There'll be worse trouble if you don't keep out of it. If I hadn't been here they'd have killed you. If you, or anyone else, comes back, I won't be here any longer, and then there'll be no mercy.'

'You won't be here? You'll come back with us now, I hope?'

But the man was speaking to the skraeling chief again. Then he said, 'Gudleif, will you swear?'

Gudleif spoke to his men, and they willingly agreed to the terms offered. Then he made a formal oath, and when he had spoken, the Icelander repeated what Gudleif had said in the skraeling language. After that all the men had their bonds cut. They were still rubbing their wrists and ankles when water was brought to them, and they drank eagerly.

'Now, you Icelanders,' said the stranger. 'We'll bring you food tonight and you can sleep where you are. Do you swear to stay where you are and cause no trouble, while I speak to Gudleif privately?'

One of the men said he'd sleep where he was, but he'd rather not shit there, and it was agreed the crew could go one at a time as far as the edge of the forest if they needed to. Then the Icelander took Gudleif into his tent. Presently a skraeling woman appeared with freshly cooked meat, which she served to the Icelander, and then to Gudleif, before going away again and fastening the flap of the tent behind her. The two men ate, and then they talked on through the night, while the moon rose and set again outside, and at last the brief darkness gave way to dawn.

The Icelander was full of questions about all the leading people in the Borgafjord area, and then he went on to ask about Breidavik and Snaefelsnes. He asked about Snorri the Priest, and about the outcome of the feuds in the Snaefel area. Eventually he began inquiring about the farm at Frodriver, and Thurid who had been married to Thorir the farmer there, and about her son Kjartan. Gudleif told him about the death of Thorir. He didn't know Thurid, but he was able to describe Kjartan very well, because he'd met him at the Thing only three years earlier, and had been very impressed by him. Everyone spoke well, he told the Icelander, of the way Kjartan had handled the ghosts that haunted Frodriver after his father's death, although he'd been scarcely more than a boy at the time. He had an authority that everyone respected, both the living and the dead. It seemed to him that the Icelander couldn't hear enough about Kjartan, whom everyone called Thorir's son, and Gudleif did his best to tell him everything he could.

At last Gudleif broached the subject that had been in his mind since the Icelander had first spoken to him. 'And what of yourself, sir?' he asked. 'I won't ask about this long exile of yours, if you don't want to tell me how it happened. But you'll come back to Iceland with us now, won't you?'

There was a pause before the Icelander shook his head, but Gudleif was sure that he had already made up his mind. 'No,' he said. 'I won't go back. The time is long past for that. I don't want to end up as a living ghost in my own country. No, Gudleif, I'm a dead man now, and it's better if I stay that way. But there is something I'd like you to do.'

Of course Gudleif said he'd do anything that he could. The Icelander turned back the skins that covered the bedplace in the tent, and brought out a good Norwegian-made sword. Then with some difficulty he twisted off the gold ring that he wore on the third finger of his right hand. 'Take these,' he said, 'And give the sword to Kjartan of Frodriver, and the ring to his mother Thurid.'

'And what shall I tell them about the man who sent them the gifts?'

'Tell them he loves Thurid of Frodriver better than her brother Snorri the Priest at Helgafell. And tell them you swore that no one would ever try to come to look for me. They wouldn't find me if they got here. This is a large country, with few harbours, and it's a mistake to think that meetings are possible beyond the mortal world.'

That was really all that Gudleif had to tell. He and his crew set sail the next day, and even though it was so late in the year, they managed to sail east until they reached the coast of Ireland. They wintered in Dublin, then went home the following summer. Gudleif travelled to Frodriver and handed over the gifts as soon as he could. He told Thurid and Kjartan he wanted to talk to Karlsefni, not in order to break his oath, but to ask questions about Karlsefni's voyage in order to satisfy some questions in his own mind.

I was touched, Agnar, that even in the midst of such strange events, Thurid sent messages to me. She told Gudleif to say that she'd not forgotten the child that Halldis used to bring to Frodriver, and she could tell even when I was quite little that I was going to be beautiful. She said she was an old woman now, but she'd be glad to see me again if it were possible. We knew Kjartan, of course, because we met him occasionally at the Thing, but I remembered, as I had not done since the day it happened, the first time I ever saw one man kill another, and how a little boy had run with shining eyes to dip his axe in the dead man's blood. But most of all I was thinking of Bjorn of Breidavik, who used to come to visit us at Arnarstapi. I could see him in my mind most vividly of all. A strong, fierce man in a Norwegian cloak, who used to sit drinking at our hearth, but who could still be bothered to talk to someone else's little girl, and carve toys out of wood for her, when her own father didn't care whether she existed or not.

I was thinking of all this, while the murmur of conversation broke out again around me. Men talk of Vinland during the winter at every hearth in Iceland, but who bothers to go there now? Only Greenlanders desperate for timber. It was just a dream, I suppose, that it should ever amount to anything else, but men like to have their dreams.

Snorri had been very quiet all evening. It was Thorbjorn who kept asking questions, in that truculent way he had, as if he wasn't prepared to believe anybody's answers. In the end Gudleif turned to my elder son, and said to him, 'And what about you, Snorri? Do you have any ambitions to go travelling?'

Snorri was never a great talker. He told Gudleif briefly that he was going to Norway in the spring with his father's ship.

'Oh yes, Karlsefni keeps up his interests there, I know. So you're off on your father's business, as a good son should be?'

'Yes.' My son might be inarticulate, but he had a dogged regard for the truth, and would make sure he told the whole of it, unoriginal though it might be. 'But it's on my own account as well,' Snorri explained to Gudleif. 'I've heard enough stories. I want to see the world myself.'

Well, he did see the world, Agnar, for what it's worth. And so have I, and so have you. I'm old and I'm tired, and sometimes I think that the more we see, the less we know. Yes, I'm tired, and it's late: the shadows have crept almost the whole way across the wall there. Another day, Agnar. It will all keep for another day.

# POSTSCRIPTUM

# December 22nd, 1051, at Rome

I, Agnar Asleifsson, finished the task today which was set me by His Holiness Cardinal Hildebrand. This morning I wrote an official report of the work I have done over the past six months: three months of interviews with the woman from Iceland, and three months making a Latin transcription of those interviews, and writing out a fair copy for the Cardinal. What will he do with it? Read it, presumably, since he commissioned the work in the first place. I have a feeling, however, that the moment of need has passed. That controversy over Adelbert's treatise, what has come of it now? Adelbert is dead, conveniently enough, of Roman fever. There is a notorious ague in this city that comes in off the marshes and strikes men down, particularly those who are not accustomed to it. It is a city of sudden death, and the noxious air seems to have become much more virulent since Pope Leo came back to Rome in '49.

The divisions of June are forgotten in the new alliances of December. This is the spiritual heart of the world. This is the place where the boundary between the temporal and eternal is closed; this is the city of St Peter, and here our salvation is always before us, the word made flesh. I have believed this always; I was told of it in a far-off, outlandish country, and since then I have been slowly drawn towards Rome, the centre of my world, on a pilgrimage that has taken my whole life.

I miss her more than I can say. In the autumn she was still frail after her long illness, and that was why I wrote to the sisters at Viterbo. I thought the hot springs might benefit her; she had often told me how

239

healing such springs could be in her own country. The message came just as we were finishing for the day. It was the 23rd September; I know that because it's the last date in the manuscript. I could see how the prospect delighted her. She craved clean cold air, she said, and mountains. Rome was soft and wet and feverish, and it made her tired. 'Agnar,' she said to me, 'you thought of this. You're like a son to me. There's nothing I'd like better. I can go at once, can't I? In the hills, you say? Hot mud springs, and clear air, and perhaps snow when the winter comes? I can go tomorrow, can't I? I've finished the story, really. Of course, I would have gone on as long as you liked, but I've told you everything of significance that I have to say. How will I go? Can you escort us?'

At first I thought that was impossible, but at her request I did ask permission, and was granted leave to see her as far as the lake Bracciano. I would have hired a litter for her, but she insisted on riding. 'I've ridden since I was two,' she said. 'What kind of fine southern lady do you think I am? I want to see where we're going.'

The change in her was remarkable. I hadn't the heart to say we'd stopped the narrative right in the middle of a scene, and when I thought about it later, I thought perhaps we hadn't. After all, what else did I expect her to tell me? Did I want some kind of answer? I'd forgotten even what the question was, until I turned back to the letter I'd had from Hildebrand. I'd read that letter before I met Gudrid, but from the moment that she began to speak I'd never referred to it, and barely even thought of it again. Death, Judgment, Hell and Heaven. Did Hildebrand expect her to come up with something definitive? Of course not. Did I realise it was just a ploy, ammunition to be used by one faction against another? Hildebrand intended to discredit Adelbert, but Adelbert is dead, and already almost forgotten. I was frustrated that our work came to so sudden an end. I had somehow thought she had more to tell me.

But I couldn't be angry with her, as we rode out of Rome through a sickly drizzle, that faded away when we got away from the river, and turned into sun when we were barely past the Vatican hill. She rode easily, as if she'd been born to it, and you only knew how stiff her body was when she had to be lifted up to mount and dismount. All the time we were on the road she looked about her with eyes that had suddenly become bright again, and quite mischievous. She wore no veil, and naturally that attracted attention from passers-by. Men thought she'd be young, you see, from the way she rode alone, and that made them turn their heads, and when they saw she was old, they shrugged and sometimes spat, but usually they went on without a word. Sometimes they shouted after her, and I blushed, but if she knew what kind of things they were saying she gave no sign of it. They meant nothing to her, but she was interested in everything else: in the vineyards, the orchards, the grazing cattle, the hills ahead, and the sea away to the west. She asked me the kind of questions a farmer would ask, about growing seasons, and breeds and crops, but I couldn't answer her at all. I left my father's farm when I was ten years old, and I'd talked very little with peasants in any of the countries that I'd been in since. But we travelled together in great harmony. When the day grew hot we stopped at a tavern to eat, then sat over our wine until the shadows began to lengthen, and then we rode on again through the white dust, until our clothes were coated with it, and we could feel dust in our hair, and gritty dust between our teeth, and dust sore around our eyes. Then the sun sank in glorious clouds of red out to the west where the sea was, and we talked about Hati the wolf who chases the sun across the sky every day, and about the Bifrost, the rainbow that links our world to the gods', and many other tales that I remembered from my earliest days, from before the time when Rome was even the shadow of a name to me.

We parted on the shores of Bracciano. She didn't weep when we said goodbye. I watched the little party of men and horses until they were just a dark patch moving along the white road. It was I that shed tears then, which I certainly hadn't expected to do. Then, reluctantly, I turned my horse south again, and set my face to Rome.

'If I don't see you before, we'll meet in Iceland.' Why did she say that? Does she know? Was it a figure of speech, or simply a blind wish? She looked so fragile, surrounded by her escort. Will she see Iceland again? Will I? Suddenly my world is full of questions, in a way that it hasn't been since I read the forbidden works of the Infidel, out of the locked cabinet in the library at Reims. But the questions I ask now are different from that. Now, I seem to see myself at the centre of them. Is that a sin? I don't know where I stand any more, and I miss her. That was three months ago. I have made the transcript into something suitable for the Cardinal, who I suspect no longer wants it. No doubt it will be catalogued and filed in the library at the Lateran, and perhaps it will sit on a shelf there and gather dust until the end of time. I am left with my original manuscript. It is shamefully untidy, but she talked so much, and I had to write so fast. I still have a pain in my right arm from it, from the wrist to the elbow. For some weeks after she left I kept my arm in a sling, except, of course, when I was working. The Infirmarian says now I must rest it properly, if I wish to have full use of it again, and I am forbidden to write until the end of Lent. So that puts paid to my translation of Gregory for the time being. I ought to feel more frustrated than I do. As it is, I feel almost glad that I shall have some time to think.

Last night I had a dream. I was in a place I did not recognise. I think I was searching for something. There was a compulsion, anyway. I am not sure that I can describe it.

*The beach is white sand, and the land lies colourless under a white moon. The darkness under the trees huddles thick as cloth. The sea shines like melted silver. The forest makes no sound, as if there were nothing in it, no life there at all. The little boat leaves deep cuts in the surface of the sea, V-shaped like a flight of geese in an autumn sky. The man sees them stretching behind, and knows that his mark is made so far, and can never be melted away. The boat touches the sand without a sound, and he steps ashore. The sand feels cool under his feet. At the top of the beach wild wheat scratches his legs, and the vines tangle themselves around his ankles. There is no path. There has never been a path. Trees stand in his way. He tries to push through but the forest is closed against him. He takes the knife from his belt and cuts into the tree before him. If once his mark is made, his hold is certain. The bark of the tree is soft as moss, and resinous. He forces the knife in. His arm aches with the effort. The knife touches hard wood, and he pushes it in with all his might, and carves the necessary letters. The pain in his arm is like fire. The letters are vanishing into the bark as the tree absorbs them. There is no sound. He tries to write, but the letters disappear under his hand, and he cannot see to hold the quill. The moon is round and white as a drop of melted wax, but there is no light in the forest, and no way in.*

I woke up feeling that I had trespassed, or even violated something. I have lived with her story for a long time now, and I begin to fear that it is taking over my own. I thought about burning the original script. Certainly I'm not proud of the penmanship, and I don't particularly want anyone to see it. I like things to be neat, and I pride myself on my fair copying. This was not exactly a copy, of course, but then a casual reader might not realise that.

I won't burn it. Life is long, and I don't know what I shall want to refer to again by the time I reach the end of it. I shall put it in a safe place. I keep thinking of her certainty that we would meet in Iceland. I would like to think it were true. If you write down a person's story, there is a way in which it becomes yours. That's a dangerous statement; I seem to be talking of a kind of possession, but it isn't that, or if it is, I possess her as much as she me. She lived it, but I wrote it down. Doesn't that make it in some sense mine?

Her two sons are alive and in Iceland. I am not her child. Next spring she'll go back to her family and forget me. She is a woman, after all, and so her own people must be more to her than a chance-met stranger. But that's wrong. I know more of her than anyone else, more of her now than her own sons do. One thing I should have learned by now is that she doesn't forget. Anything that's part of being alive she'll remember, and she won't care if it's the correct thing to do or not. She sees things her own way, and I think she has taught me something about how to do that too. I have grown to love her. It seems dangerous to admit that, almost a heresy. But isn't it a greater heresy even to imagine that an attachment to a mortal woman could come close to being heretical? Rome feels very foreign to me today. Did Peter feel that too, when he came here? Was this the end of the world to him, or its centre? Both, I suppose, just as it is for me. Perhaps when he knew he must die here he began to think about the place where he was born. The land he came from is beyond Chistendom now, the country of the Infidel. But for him it was home. There are times now when I begin to think I should like to go home myself.